# KING
## OF
# GREED

## ANA HUANG

PIATKUS

PIATKUS

First published in 2023 by Bloom Books,
An imprint of Sourcebooks
First published in Great Britain in 2023 by Piatkus

1 3 5 7 9 10 8 6 4 2

A CIP catalogue record for this book
is available from the British Library.

ISBN 978-0-349-43635-7

Printed and bound in Great Britain by Clays Ltd, Elcograf S.p.A.

Papers used by Piatkus are from well-managed forests and
other responsible sources.

Piatkus
An imprint of
Little, Brown Book Group
Carmelite House
50 Victoria Embankment
London EC4Y 0DZ

An Hachette UK Company

www.hachette.co.uk

www.littlebrown.co.uk

**Ana Huang** is a *New York Times, USA Tod...* and #1 Amazon bestselling author. She writes new ... porary romance with deliciously alpha heroes, strong ... plenty of steam, angst, and swoon sprinkled in.

A self-professed travel enthusiast, she loves incorporating beautiful destinations into her stories and will never say no to a good chai latte.

When she's not reading or writing, Ana is busy daydreaming, and scouring Yelp for her next favorite restaurant.

# Also by Ana Huang

## KINGS OF SIN SERIES
A series of interconnected standalones
*King of Wrath*
*King of Pride*
*King of Greed*

## TWISTED SERIES
A series of interconnected standalones
*Twisted Love*
*Twisted Games*
*Twisted Hate*
*Twisted Lies*

## IF LOVE SERIES
*If We Ever Meet Again* (Duet Book 1)
*If the Sun Never Sets* (Duet Book 2)
*If Love Had a Price* (Standalone)
*If We Were Perfect* (Standalone)

*To knowing your worth and never settling*
*for less than you deserve.*

# *Playlist*

◄◄  ►  ►►

*Million Dollar Man*
**Lana Del Rey**

*Cold*
**Maroon 5 feat. Future**

*Same Old Love*
**Selena Gomez**

*Love Me Harder*
**Ariana Grande & The Weekend**

*Unappreciated*
**Cherish**

*Just Give Me a Reason*
**Pink feat. Nate Ruess**

*Dancing with a Stranger*
**Sam Smith & Normani**

*Without You*
**Mariah Carey**

*Love Don't Cost a Thing*
**Jennifer Lopez**

*We Belong Together*
**Mariah Carey**

*Revival*
**Selena Gomez**

*Two Minds*
**Nero**

*Lose You to Love Me*
**Selena Gomez**

*Amor I Love You*
**Marisa Monte**

# KING

## OF

# GREED

# CHAPTER 1

## Alessandra

ONCE UPON A TIME, I'D LOVED MY HUSBAND.

His beauty, his ambition, his intelligence. The wildflowers he'd plucked for me on his way home from a graveyard shift, and the gentle kisses he'd trailed over my shoulder when I stubbornly refused to heed my alarm clock.

But *once upon a time* was a long time ago, and now, as I watched him walk through the door for the first time in weeks, all I felt was a deep, dull ache in the places where love once resided.

"You're home early," I said, even though it was near midnight. "How was work?"

"Fine." Dominic shrugged out of his coat, revealing an immaculate gray suit and crisp white shirt. Both custom-made, both costing upward of four figures. Only the best for Dominic Davenport, the so-called King of Wall Street. "Work was work."

He gave me a perfunctory kiss on the lips. A familiar whiff of citrus and sandalwood brushed my senses and made my heart squeeze. He'd worn the same cologne since I gifted it to him a decade ago during our first trip to Brazil. I used to find the loyalty

1

romantic, but the new cynic in me whispered it was only because he couldn't be bothered to find a new scent.

Dominic didn't care about anything that didn't make him money.

He flicked his eyes over the lipstick-smudged wine glasses and remnants of Chinese takeout on the coffee table. Our housekeeper was on vacation, and I'd been in the middle of cleaning up when Dominic came home.

"Did you have friends over?" he asked, sounding only marginally interested.

"Just the girls." My friends and I had celebrated a financial milestone for my small pressed flower business, which was nearing its two-year anniversary, but I didn't bother sharing the accomplishment with my husband. "We were supposed to go out to dinner, but we stayed in at the last minute instead."

"Sounds nice." Dominic had already moved on to his phone. He had a strict no-email policy, so he was probably checking the Asian stock markets.

A knot formed in my throat.

He was still as breathtakingly handsome as the first time I saw him in our college library. Dark blond hair, navy eyes, a sculpted face set in a semi-permanent pensive expression. It wasn't a face that smiled easily, but I liked that about him. There was no fakeness; if he smiled, he meant it.

When was the last time either of us had smiled at the other the way we used to?

When was the last time he touched me? Not for sex, but for casual affection.

The knot pulled tighter, restricting the flow of oxygen. I swallowed past it and forced my lips to curve upward. "Speaking of dinner, don't forget our trip this weekend. We have a Friday night reservation in DC."

"I won't." He tapped something on his screen.

"Dom." My voice firmed. "It's important."

I'd put up with dozens of missed dates, canceled trips, and broken promises over the years, but our ten-year wedding anniversary was one of a kind. It was unmissable.

Dominic finally glanced up. "I won't forget. I promise." Something flickered in his eyes. "Ten years already. It's hard to believe."

"Yes." My cheeks might crack from the force of my smile. "It is." I hesitated, then added, "Are you hungry? I can heat up some food and you can tell me about your day."

He had a bad habit of forgetting to eat when he was working. Knowing him, he hadn't touched anything except coffee since lunch. I used to visit his office and make sure he ate when he was starting out, but those visits stopped after Davenport Capital took off and he became too busy.

"No, I have some client things to take care of. I'll grab something later." He was back on his phone, his brow furrowed in a deep frown.

"But..." *I thought you were done with work for the day. Isn't that why you're home?*

I bit back my question. There was no use asking things I already knew the answer to.

Dominic was never done with work. It was the world's most demanding mistress.

"Don't wait up for me. I'll be in my office for a while." His lips grazed my cheek on his way past me. "Good night."

He was already gone by the time I responded. "Good night."

The words echoed in our palatial, empty living room. It was the first night I'd been awake to see Dominic come home in weeks, and our conversation had ended before it really began.

I blinked back an embarrassing sting of tears. So what if

my husband felt like a stranger? *I* felt like a stranger to myself sometimes when I looked in the mirror.

At the end of the day, I was married to one of the richest men on Wall Street, I lived in a beautiful house most people would kill for, and I owned a small but thriving business doing what I loved. I had no good reason to cry.

*Get it together.*

I took a deep breath, straightened my shoulders, and plucked the empty takeout boxes off the coffee table. By the time I finished cleaning up, the pressure behind my eyes had disappeared like it'd never been there at all.

# CHAPTER 2

*Dominic*

THERE WAS AN OLD ADAGE THAT BAD THINGS CAME IN
threes, and if I weren't so scornful of superstitions, I might've
believed it after this shit show of a day.

First, a ridiculous tech malfunction reset our email and calendar systems that morning, and we'd spent hours getting everything
back in order.

Then, one of my top traders quit because he was "burned
out" and "found his true calling" as a fucking yoga teacher, of all
things.

Now, an hour before U.S. markets closed, news leaked that
a company we had a large position in was being investigated by
the Securities and Exchange Commission. Stocks were in free
fall, which meant the value of our position was declining by the
minute, and my plans to leave early had disintegrated faster than
tissue paper in a washing machine. As the CEO of a major financial conglomerate, I didn't have the luxury of delegating crisis
management.

"Talk to me." Brisk strides took me from my office to the
emergency staff meeting three doors down in thirty seconds. My

muscles coiled so tight, it was a miracle they didn't cramp. I'd lost millions in minutes, and I didn't have time to beat around the bush.

"Rumor has it the SEC is going hard on this one." Caroline, my chief of staff, matched my pace with ease. "The new chairman wants to make a splashy first impression. What better way to do that than to go head-to-head with one of the biggest banks in the country?"

For fuck's sake. It was always the newbies that crashed their way through their first year like a bull in a china shop. I had a good relationship with the old chairman, but the new one was a goddamn thorn in my side, and he'd only been there for three months.

I checked my watch as I pushed open the door to the executive conference room. A quarter past three. I was supposed to fly out to DC with Alessandra at six. If I kept the meeting short and drove straight to the airport instead of stopping at home first like I'd originally planned, I could still make it.

*Dammit.* Why did the chairman have to upend things on my wedding anniversary, of all days?

I took my seat at the head of the table and reached for my lighter. It was instinct at this point; I didn't even have to think about it. "Give me the numbers."

Thoughts of DC and upcoming flights melted away as I flicked the lighter on and off while my team debated the pros and cons of dumping our position in the bank versus weathering the storm. There was no room for personal concerns in times of emergencies, and the solid, comforting weight of silver focused my thoughts on the task at hand instead of the insidious whispers crowding my brain.

They were always there, filling my head with doubts like how I was one bad decision away from losing everything. How I was and always would be the butt of every joke, the foster kid whose own biological mother abandoned him and who flunked sixth grade twice.

The "problem student," my teachers lamented.

The "idiot," my classmates jeered.

The "slacker," my guidance counselor sighed.

The voices were loudest in times of crisis. I reigned over a multi-billion-dollar empire, but I walked through the halls every day with the prospect of a crash hanging over me.

*On. Off. On. Off.* The increased speed of my flicks matched my escalating heartbeats.

"Sir." Caroline's voice cut through the buzzing in my ears. "What's your verdict?"

I blinked away the unwanted memories lurking at the corners of my consciousness. The room came back into focus, revealing my team's anxious, expectant expressions.

Someone had pulled up a presentation sometime in the past minute, even though I'd repeatedly said I hated slide decks. The right side was filled with a comforting mix of charts and numbers, but the left contained several lengthy bullet points.

The sentences swam before me. They didn't look right; I was sure my brain had added some words while erasing others. The back of my neck heated while my heartbeats thundered with such fury, it felt like they were trying to punch through my chest and knock the words off the screen in one fell swoop.

"What did I say about presentation format?" I could barely hear myself over the noise. It grew louder every second, and only my painful grip on the lighter prevented me from unraveling. "No. Bullet points."

I bit out the words, and the room fell deathly silent.

"I-I'm sorry, sir." The analyst presenting the slides paled to the point of translucence. "My assistant—"

"I don't give a damn about your assistant." I was being an

asshole, but I didn't have time to feel bad about it. Not when my stomach was turning and a migraine was already crawling its way behind my temple.

*On. Off. On. Off.*

I turned my head and focused on the charts instead. The switch in focus, combined with the clicks of the lighter, calmed me enough to think clearly again.

*SEC. Tumbling stocks. What to do with our position.*

I couldn't fully shake the sense that one day, I would fuck up so royally that I'd destroy everything I had, but that day wouldn't be today.

I knew what to do, and as I laid out my strategy for holding on to our position, I pushed every other voice out of my head— including the one telling me that I was forgetting something damn important.

# CHAPTER 3

## Alessandra

HE WASN'T COMING.

I sat in the living room, my skin ice cold as I watched the minutes tick by. It was past eight. We were supposed to leave for DC two hours ago, but I hadn't seen or heard from Dominic since he left for work that morning. My calls had gone to voicemail, and I refused to check in with his office like some random acquaintance begging for a minute of the great Dominic Davenport's time.

I was his wife, dammit. I shouldn't have to chase him down or guess his whereabouts. Then again, it didn't take a genius to figure out what he was doing right now.

*Working.* Always working. Even on our ten-year anniversary. Even after I'd stressed how important this trip was.

I finally had a good reason to cry, but no tears came. I just felt…numb. A part of me had expected him to forget or postpone, and wasn't that the saddest part?

"Mrs. Davenport!" Our housekeeper, Camila, entered the room, her arms laden with freshly laundered linen. She'd returned from her vacation last night and had spent the day tidying up the penthouse. "I thought you already left."

"No." My voice sounded strange and hollow. "I don't think I'll be going anywhere this weekend after all."

"Why…" She trailed off, her eagle eyes taking in the luggage next to the couch and my white-knuckled grip on my knees. Her round, matronly face softened with a mix of sympathy and pity. "Ah. In that case, I'll make dinner for you. Moqueca. Your favorite, hmm?"

Ironically, the fish stew was what my old childhood house-keeper made me when I was heartbroken over a boy. I wasn't hungry, but I didn't have the energy to argue.

"Thanks, Camila."

While she bustled off to the kitchen, I tried to sort through the chaos swirling through my brain.

*Cancel all our reservations or wait? Is he simply late or is he not going on the trip at all? Do I even* want *to go on this trip now, even if he does?*

Dominic and I were supposed to spend the weekend in DC, where we'd met and gotten married. I had it all planned out—dinner at our first-date restaurant, a suite at a cozy boutique hotel, no phones or work allowed. It was supposed to be a trip for *us*. As our relationship frayed further every day, I'd hoped it would bring us closer again. Make us fall in love the way we had a lifetime ago.

But I realized that was impossible because neither of us was the same person we used to be. Dominic wasn't the boy who gave himself a hundred paper cuts making origami versions of my favorite flowers for my birthday, and I wasn't the girl who floated through life with stars and dreams in her eyes.

*"I don't have the money to buy you all the flowers you deserve yet," he said, sounding so solemn and formal I couldn't help but smile at the contrast between his tone and the jar of colorful paper flowers in his hands. "So I made them instead."*

*My breath caught in my throat. "Dom…"*

*There must've been hundreds of flowers in there. I didn't want to think about how long it took him to make them.*

*"Happy birthday,* amor.*" His mouth lingered on mine in a long, sweet kiss. "One day, I'll buy you a thousand real roses. I promise."*

He'd kept that promise, but he'd broken a thousand more since.

A salty trickle finally snaked its way down my cheek and shocked me out of my frozen stupor.

I stood, my breaths shallowing with each step as I walked quickly to the nearest bathroom. Camila and the staff were too busy to notice my silent breakdown, but I couldn't bear the thought of crying alone in the living room, surrounded by luggage that would go nowhere and hopes that'd been shattered too many times to mend properly.

*So, so stupid.*

What made me think tonight would be different? Our anniversary probably meant as much to Dominic as a random Friday night dinner.

Dull pain sharpened into knives as I locked the bathroom door behind me. My reflection stared back from the mirror. Brown hair, blue eyes, tanned skin. I looked the same as I always did, but I hardly recognized myself. It was like seeing a stranger wear my face.

Where was the girl who'd pushed back against her mother's modeling dreams for her and insisted on going to college instead? Who'd lived life with unapologetic joy and unbridled optimism, and who'd once dumped a boy for forgetting her birthday? That girl would've never sat around waiting for a man. She'd had goals and dreams, but somewhere along the way, they'd fallen by the wayside, consumed by the gravity of her husband's ambition.

If I pleased him, if I organized the right dinners with the right people, if I made the right connections, I would be useful to him.

Years of helping him accomplish his dreams meant I hadn't lived—I'd served a purpose.

Alessandra Ferreira was gone, replaced by Alessandra Davenport. Wife, hostess, socialite. Someone defined only by her marriage to *the* Dominic Davenport. Everything I did for the past decade had been for him, and he didn't even care enough to call and tell me he'd be late for our fucking ten-year anniversary.

The dam burst.

A solitary tear turned into two, then three, then a whole flood as I sank to the floor and cried. Every heartbreak, every disappointment, every piece of sadness and resentment I'd harbored poured out in a river of grief edged with anger. I'd bottled up so much over the years that I was afraid I'd drown beneath the waves of my own emotions.

Cold, hard tile dug into the backs of my thighs. For the first time in forever, I allowed myself to *feel*, and with that came blinding clarity.

I couldn't do this anymore.

I couldn't spend the rest of my days going through the motions and pretending to be happy. I had to take back control of my life—even if it meant destroying the one I currently had.

I was hollow and brittle, a million shattered pieces that hurt too much to pick up.

My sobs eventually slowed then subsided altogether, and before I could second-guess myself, I pushed off the floor and stepped back into the hall. The temperature-controlled penthouse maintained a perfect seventy-three degrees year-round, but tiny shivers wracked my body as I grabbed what I needed from the bedroom. The rest of my essentials were already packed and waiting in the living room.

I didn't allow myself to think. If I did, I would chicken out, and I couldn't afford to at this stage.

A familiar sparkle caught my eye when I pulled my suitcase handle up. I stared at my wedding ring, a fresh ache tearing through my chest as it blinked up at me in a seeming plea to reconsider.

I faltered for a split second before I set my jaw, slid the ring off my finger, and placed it next to my and Dominic's wedding picture on the mantel.

Then I finally did what I should've done a long time ago.

I left.

# CHAPTER 4

*Dominic*

"ÁLE!" MY VOICE ECHOED THROUGH THE PENTHOUSE. "I'm home."

Silence.

My brows dipped. Alessandra usually stayed in the living room until it was time for bed, and it was too early for her to go to sleep. My emergency work meeting had segued into a second emergency meeting after several investors called, panicking about the falling stocks. Still, it was only half past eight. She should be here unless she'd gone out with her friends again.

I tossed my coat on the bronze tree by the door and loosened my tie, trying to ignore the niggling sense that something was wrong. It was hard to think properly during my work-fueled adrenaline crash.

I'd nearly had a heart attack the first time Alessandra went clubbing with Vivian and didn't tell me. I came home early, didn't see her, and pictured the worst. I'd called every damn person in my phone book until she finally called me back and reassured me she was okay.

I reached for my cell only to remember it'd died that afternoon. I hadn't had time to charge it amidst all the chaos.

*Dammit.*

"Ále!" I called out again. "Where are you, *amor*?"

Still no answer.

I crossed the living room and took the stairs to the second floor. Forty million dollars bought quite a few perks in Manhattan, including a private elevator entrance, twelve thousand square feet spread over two floors, and sweeping views that encompassed the Hudson River to the south, the George Washington bridge to the north, and New Jersey to the west.

I barely noticed any of it. We wouldn't live here forever; I already had my eye on a bigger, even more expensive penthouse that was currently under development by the Archer Group. It didn't matter that I spent only a fraction of my time at home. Real estate was a symbol, and if it wasn't the best, I didn't want it.

I opened the doors to the master suite. I expected to see Alessandra curled up in bed or reading in the sitting area, but they were as empty as the living room.

My eyes landed on the suitcase by the closet. It was the one I usually took for short trips. Why—

My blood turned to ice.

*DC. Anniversary. Six p.m.* No wonder I'd been walking around with an impending sense of dread all evening. I'd forgotten our goddamned wedding anniversary.

"*Fuck.*" I pulled out my phone only to remember it was dead.

A fresh litany of curses spilled out as I yanked open various drawers, searching for a charger while our conversation from Wednesday night replayed in my head.

*Dom. It's important.*

*I won't forget. I promise.*

Thick, slimy dread gnawed at my stomach. I'd missed dates before. I wasn't proud of it, but last-minute emergencies were the nature of my work, and Alessandra always seemed to take it in stride. I had a sinking feeling this time was different, and not only because it was our anniversary.

I finally found a charger and plugged my phone in. After what seemed like an eternity, it gained enough charge to blink on.

Six missed calls from Alessandra, all received between five and eight p.m. Nothing since then.

I tried calling her back, but it went straight to voicemail. I bit back another curse and pivoted to the second-best option: her friends. I didn't have their numbers, but luckily, I knew someone who did.

"It's Dominic," I said brusquely when Dante picked up my call. "Is Vivian there? I need to talk to her."

"Good evening to you too," he drawled. Dante Russo was a friend, a longtime client, and the CEO of the world's largest luxury conglomerate. Most importantly, he was married to Vivian, whom Alessandra had gotten quite close to over the past year. If anyone knew where my wife was, she did. "Tell me why, exactly, you need to talk to Vivian this late on a Friday night?"

A hint of suspicion leaked into his voice. He was fiercely protective of his wife, which was ironic considering he hadn't wanted to marry her at all when they initially got engaged.

"It's about Alessandra." I didn't supply any further details. My marriage was none of his damn business.

A short pause greeted my answer. "Hold on."

"Hello?" Vivian's elegant, dulcet tones floated over the line two seconds later.

"Is Alessandra with you?" I skipped the niceties and cut straight to the chase. I didn't care if she thought I was rude; I only cared about finding my wife. It was late, she was upset, and New York was filled with unsavory people. She could be lost or hurt right now.

My gut twisted into knots.

"No," Vivian said after way too long. "Why?"

"She's not at home, and it's not like her to be out this late." I skipped over the wedding anniversary part. Once again, our marriage was no one else's business except ours.

"Maybe she's with Isabella or Sloane."

*Isabella and Sloane.* Alessandra's other friends. I didn't know them as well as Vivian, but it didn't matter. I'd talk to the goddamn cat lady who was always falling asleep in our lobby if she had an inkling of where Alessandra was.

Unfortunately, Isabella and Sloane were also clueless to Alessandra's whereabouts, and my calls after I hung up with them went to voicemail again.

*Dammit, Ále. Where are you?*

I headed downstairs again and nearly crashed into Camila.

"Mr. Davenport!" Her eyes widened. I'd forgotten she was back from vacation. "Welcome—"

"Where is she?"

"Who?"

"Alessandra." The name came out through gritted teeth. I sounded like a damn broken record, but Camila must've been here when she left.

"Ah. Mrs. Davenport was quite upset about the missed flight." The housekeeper's pursed lips told me exactly what she thought about my tardiness. "I made her favorite soup to cheer her up, but when I came back from the kitchen, she was already gone."

"You didn't hear her leave." My voice was flat. Cold.

"No." Camila's eyes darted left and right.

I liked the woman well enough. She was competent, discreet, and one of Alessandra's favorite staff members, but if she was hiding something from me and Alessandra got hurt as a result…

I went deathly still. "I'm asking you one last time," I said quietly. Blood roared in my ears, nearly drowning out my words. "*Where is my wife?*"

A tremble betrayed Camila's nerves. "I really don't know, sir. Like I said, I came out and she was gone. But when I was looking for her…" She pulled something from her pocket. "I found this on the mantel."

A familiar diamond glittered in her palm. Alessandra's wedding ring.

A sick, sour feeling spread through my stomach.

"I was going to put it in your room," Camila said. "But considering—"

"When?"

"About half an hour ago."

The answer hadn't fully left her mouth before I grabbed the ring and brushed past her toward the elevator, my pulse pounding with a mix of dread, panic, and something else I couldn't quite name.

*Half an hour.* It was nine and Alessandra's last call to me had been at eight, which meant Camila had found the ring not too long after she left. She couldn't have gone too far.

My hand closed around the diamond. She wouldn't have taken it off unless—

*No.* She was pissed, as she had a right to be, but I'd find her, explain, and everything would go back to normal. Alessandra was the most understanding person I knew; she'd forgive me.

The diamond dug a painful groove in my palm.

*Everything will be fine.* It had to be. I couldn't imagine any other alternative.

# CHAPTER 5

## Alessandra

INSTEAD OF GOING TO ONE OF MY FRIENDS' HOUSES, I checked into a hotel and paid for the week with cash. I didn't want Dominic tracing my whereabouts via my credit card. Luckily, I had my own money from Floria Designs and the foresight to stash an emergency bundle at home when the business took off. It was enough to cover the hotel and hold me over while I figured out what to do.

Was leaving without a word the coward's way out? Probably. But I needed time alone to think, which was why I didn't update my friends immediately either.

I'd turned my phone off after leaving the penthouse, and I left it off while I unpacked, showered, and tried not to think about the past few hours or the sharp ache in my chest.

*"Dom!" I laughed when Dominic stepped into the shower and wrapped his arms around my waist from behind. "You're supposed to be ordering room service."*

*"I did order room service." His mouth trailed over my shoulder and up my neck. Despite the steam clouding the bathroom, goose bumps of pleasure pebbled my skin. "But I decided I want dessert first."*

*"What if I don't agree?" I teased. "Maybe I want to follow the normal order of things. Not all of us can be rule breakers."*

*"In that case…" Dominic's mouth reached the corner of my lips. One hand palmed my breast while the other dipped leisurely between my legs. Pleasure spiraled in my stomach, and I couldn't hold back a soft sigh. "I'll just have to find a way to convince you, won't I?"*

I closed my eyes, letting the hot water wash away my tears. We were miles and years away from our first weekend getaway as a couple, but I could almost feel the phantom strength of his embrace. We'd had sex twice in the shower; by the time we came out, our room service meal had been cold, but we hadn't even cared. We'd devoured the food like it'd been freshly made.

I stayed in the shower longer than I should've, but the water, heat, and emotions of the night conspired to pull me under. The moment my head hit the pillow, I was out.

When I woke up the next morning and finally turned on my phone, I had dozens of missed texts, calls, and voicemails from my friends and Dominic. He must've reached out to them after he came home and found me missing.

I sent a quick message to the group chat assuring my friends I was okay and that I would tell them everything later before taking a deep breath and opening Dominic's voicemails.

My heart instantly squeezed at the sound of his voice, which grew increasingly panicked with each message.

**Dominic:** Where are you?

**Dominic:** Ále, this isn't funny.

**Dominic:** I'm sorry I missed our flight. A work emergency came up and I had to deal with it. We can still make the rest of the trip.

**Dominic:** Dammit, Alessandra. I understand if you're mad, but at least let me know you're okay. I don't—fuck.

A string of curses blended with the unmistakable patter of rain against concrete in the background. The message's timestamp read 3:29 a.m. What the hell was he doing out so late?

*Looking for you.*

I squashed the thought as quickly as it popped up, partly because I didn't believe the new Dominic would do something like that and partly because it hurt too much to think he *would*.

His last message was two hours ago at 6:23 a.m.

**Dominic:** Call me back. Please.

The squeeze in my chest became unbearable. I wasn't ready to face him, but sleep had cleared last night's emotional fog, and the desperation in his voice eroded my earlier vow to avoid him until I had a plan. It was better to see him and rip the Band-Aid off, so to speak, than let the uncertainty fester.

"Violet Hotel." I didn't give him a chance to speak when he picked up. "Lower East Side."

I ended the call, my stomach a mess of nerves. I hadn't eaten dinner last night, but the thought of food made my stomach revolt further. Nevertheless, I forced down some trail mix from the minibar. I'd need the energy. If there was one thing Dominic was good at, it was persuading people to do what he wanted.

I was already second-guessing my choices. In the bright light of day, my ring finger felt impossibly bare and my decision to leave seemed impossibly rash. Should I have waited and talked to Dominic before walking out? What if—

Someone knocked at the door.

My stomach pitched again. I suddenly regretted telling him where I was, but it was too late.

*It's like pulling off a Band-Aid. Just get it over with.*

Still, no amount of internal pep talk could've prepared me for the sight awaiting me when I opened the door.

"Oh my God." A gasp escaped before I could hold it in.

Dominic looked like hell. Disheveled hair, rumpled shirt, purple smudges of exhaustion beneath his eyes. His clothes were plastered to his body, and his usually pristine shoes looked like they'd gone through a Tough Mudder obstacle course.

"What—" I didn't get a chance to finish my question before he grabbed my arms and swept his eyes over me.

"You're okay." Relief softened the rough edge of voice. He sounded like he was either recovering from a horrible cold or he'd been shouting all night.

"I'm fine." *Physically.* "Why are you all wet?"

He was dripping water all over the floor. Nevertheless, I pulled him inside and shut the door behind us. It was a low-key hotel, but I didn't want to risk people seeing or overhearing us. Manhattan was a small island, and Manhattan society was smaller still.

"I got caught in the rain." Dominic's eyes swept over the room and stopped on my open suitcase. "And it's hard to see puddles at four in the morning."

"Why the hell were you wandering around Manhattan at four in the morning?"

His disbelieving eyes snapped back to mine. "I come home from work to find my wife gone and her wedding ring in our damn housekeeper's pocket. She's not answering my calls, and none of her friends know where she is. I thought you—" He took a deep breath and released it in one long, controlled exhale. "I went to your usual places until I realized they were all, of course, closed that late at night. So I had my security team sweeping the city while I checked your favorite neighborhoods. Just in case. I didn't know…"

My breath stuck at the mental image of Dominic wandering the streets in the rain looking for me. It was so incongruous with the cold, disinterested man I'd become used to that it almost sounded like he was spinning a fairy tale instead of telling the truth.

But the evidence was there, and it sent a fresh, crippling wave of pain through my chest.

If only he cared that much all the time. If only it didn't take me leaving to unbury a piece of the person I'd fallen in love with.

"When did you get home?" I asked quietly.

Dull red tinged his cheekbones. "Eight thirty."

Two and a half hours after our scheduled departure time. I wondered whether he'd forgotten about our anniversary or whether he remembered but ignored it anyway. I couldn't decide which was worse, but it didn't matter. The end result was the same.

"I didn't mean to miss the flight," Dominic said. "There was a work emergency. Ask Caroline. The SEC—"

"That's the thing." My earlier concern melted away, replaced with a familiar exhaustion. Not the type that followed a sleepless night, but the type built over years of hearing the same excuse. "There's *always* a work emergency. If it's not the SEC, it's the stock market. If it's not the stock market, it's some corporate scandal. No matter what it is, it always comes first. Before me. Before *us*."

Dominic's jaw tightened. "I can't ignore those things," he said. "People depend on me. *Billions* of dollars ride on my decisions. My employees and investors—"

"What about me? Do I not count as people?"

"Of course you do." He sounded baffled.

"And when I was depending on you to show up like you promised?" Emotion clogged my throat. "Was that less important than a multibillion-dollar corporation that'll probably be just fine if you took *one* weekend off?"

Tense silence mushroomed and nearly choked us until he spoke again.

"Do you remember our senior year of college?" Dominic's gaze burned into mine. "We barely saw each other outside of school because I had to work three jobs just to cover basic living expenses. We ate fucking instant ramen on our dates because I couldn't afford to take you out to nice restaurants. It was miserable, and I promised myself that if I ever made it out, I would never be in that situation again. *We* wouldn't be in that situation again. And we haven't."

He gestured between us. "Look at us. We have everything we've ever dreamed of, but the only way to *keep* it is to do my job. The penthouse, the clothes, the jewelry. All of it goes away if—"

"What good is any of that if I never *see* you?" My frustration bubbled over to its tipping point. "I don't *care* about the fancy penthouse or clothes or jet. I would rather have a husband. A real one, not one just in name."

Maybe I didn't understand because I came from a well-off family and therefore could never fully empathize with the obstacles Dominic had to overcome to get to where he was. Maybe I was too out of the loop to understand the stakes of the Wall Street game. But I knew myself, and I knew that I'd been a thousand times happier eating ramen with him in his dorm room than I'd ever been attending some fancy gala draped in jewels and a fake smile.

Dominic's eyes darkened. "It's not that simple. I don't have a rich family to fall back on if things go to shit, Ále," he said harshly. "*Everything* is on me."

"Maybe, but you're Dominic Davenport. You're a *billionaire*! You can afford a weekend off. Hell, you could retire this minute and still have enough money to live in luxury for the rest of your life!"

He didn't get it. I could tell by the stubborn look in his eyes.

The fight bled out of me, and my exhaustion returned tenfold. My voice dropped to a whisper. "It was our ten-year anniversary."

Dominic's throat flexed with a hard swallow. "We can leave

now," he said. "We have almost two full days left. We can still celebrate our anniversary like we'd intended."

No matter how much I tried to explain, he didn't get *why* I was upset. It wasn't about physical, tangible things like flights and dinner reservations. It was about a fundamental disconnect in our values and what we deemed important for a good relationship. I believed in quality time and conversation; he believed money could fix everything.

He'd always been ambitious, but I used to think he would hit a point when he'd be content with what he had. I realized now that point didn't exist. He would never have enough. The more he acquired—money, status, power—the more he wanted at the expense of everything else.

I shook my head slowly. "No."

I hadn't known what my plan was when I woke up that morning, but it was now crystal clear.

Even if it killed me, even if the easiest thing was to fall into his arms and sink into the memory of what we used to be, I had to go through with it. I was already a shell of myself. If I didn't get out while I could, I'd dissolve into dust, nothing more than a collection of lost time and unrealized dreams.

The stubborn gleam in Dominic's eyes faded, replaced with confusion. "Then come home with me. We'll talk it out."

I shook my head again, trying to breathe through the needles stabbing at my heart. "I'm not coming back."

He stilled. Confusion melted into realization, then disbelief. "Ále—"

"I want a divorce."

# CHAPTER 6

*Dominic*

I WANT A DIVORCE.

The words swirled around us like a cloud of poisonous fumes. Theoretically, I understood what they meant, but I couldn't comprehend them.

Divorce meant breaking up. Breaking up meant separating. And separating was simply impossible. It was something that happened to other people, not to us.

Her wedding ring burned a hole in my pocket.

"*I can't believe I married someone who likes mint chocolate chip,*" I said as Alessandra hoovered down a bowl of her favorite ice cream. "*You know you're basically eating toothpaste, right?*"

"*Delicious toothpaste.*" *Her mischievous smile hit me right in the gut. We'd been married exactly one week, two days, and twelve hours, and I still couldn't believe she was mine. "You knew about my taste in dessert before our wedding, so you can't complain now. I'm afraid you're stuck with me and my mint chocolate forever.*"

*Forever.*

*The concept seemed laughable a year ago. Nothing lasted*

*forever. People, places, relationships...everything had an expiration date.*

*But for the first time in my life, I allowed myself to believe someone when they said they would stay.*

*My hand found hers and laced our fingers together. "Promise?"*

*Her face softened. We were technically supposed to be watching the latest action blockbuster, but the explosions were mere background noise at this point. "I promise."*

A door slammed in the hallway, and the memory fizzled as quickly as it arose.

The buzzing in my ears returned. "You don't mean that."

Alessandra simply stared at me, her eyes bright with unshed tears but her face set with quiet determination.

Christ, why was my tie so damned tight? I couldn't breathe properly.

I reached up to loosen it, but my fingers found nothing except damp cotton. No tie, only a vise around my neck and a fist strangling my lungs.

"You never told me." I dropped my arm, wondering where the hell we went wrong. "You never said a thing about any of this until now."

Had I missed more dates than I should've these past few years? Yes. Did Alessandra and I talk as much as we used to? No. But that was the nature of building an empire, and I thought we understood each other. We'd been together for so long; we didn't need to constantly reassure each other of our relationship.

"I should've." Alessandra looked away. "That was my fault. I kept it all to myself when I should've told you how I was feeling. It's not just about one trip or dinner. It's not even about a dozen trips and dinners. It's about what missing them represents." Her eyes met mine again, and my heart twisted at the hurt I saw in them. Had I really been so blind I'd missed how unhappy she'd been all this time? "You've made it clear, time and again, that I'm not a priority."

"That's not true."

"Isn't it?" She gave me a sad smile. "Do you know what I asked myself every night when you were staying late at the office again? I wondered, if there was an emergency at work and at home at the same time, who you would choose. Me or your investors?"

The buzzing intensified. "You know I would choose you."

"That's the thing. I don't." A tear slipped down her cheek. "Because you haven't chosen me. Not in a very, very long time."

Silence fell between us, punctuated by my rapid breaths and the deafening ticks of the clock in the corner. Any response I might've had was crushed beneath the weight of her tears.

Poverty. Failure. Sabotage. I'd endured plenty over the years and survived, but seeing Alessandra cry was the one thing that could bring me to my knees. Every damn time.

"I've made so many excuses for you, both to my friends and to myself, but I can't do it anymore." Her voice dropped to a whisper. "We've been holding on to something that doesn't exist anymore, and we need to let go. We'll both be happier."

Every syllable chipped away at the composure I'd spent a decade constructing. An army of emotions stormed through me—anger, shame, and a fierce desperation that I hadn't felt since I was a teenager fighting to get out of my godforsaken hometown.

I wasn't supposed to feel any of those things anymore, dammit. I was a goddamn CEO, not a helpless boy with no family and no money to his name. But when faced with the prospect of losing Alessandra...

Panic seized my chest. "You honestly think we'll be happier if we divorce? That I'll be happier without you? This is *us*." The word ripped from my throat, raw and loaded with emotion. "*Você e eu. Para sempre.*" You and me. Forever.

Alessandra's quiet sob ripped at my heart. I reached for her, and when she shrank back, the rip turned into a full-blown chasm.

"Don't make this any harder than it has to be." The words were barely audible. "Please."

My hand dropped to my side as the fist squeezed tighter around my lungs. I didn't know how we got here, but I damn well wasn't walking away without a fight.

"I fucked up yesterday," I said. "And I've fucked up many more times before that. But I'm still your husband, and you're still my wife."

She closed her eyes, her tears now a quiet, steady stream running down her face. "Dom…"

"We'll work this out." The thought of living without her was incomprehensible, like asking a heart to stop beating or the stars to give up the night. "I promise."

We had to.

Maybe I haven't expressed it as much as I should have, but Alessandra was an indelible part of me. She had been since the moment I laid eyes on her eleven years ago, though I hadn't known it at the time.

Without her, there was no me.

# CHAPTER 7

*Dominic*

*Eleven Years Ago*

"I DON'T NEED A BABYSITTER."

"She's not a babysitter," Professor Ehrlich said patiently. "She's a tutor. One of our best, in fact. She's worked with multiple students with dyslexia—"

"I don't need a tutor either." The thought of some know-it-all condescending to me every week made me want to crawl out of my skin. I'd made it this far on my own, hadn't I?

I didn't have any tutors growing up and my teachers had been mediocre at best, destructive at worst. Yet here I was, sitting in a top economist's office at the prestigious Thayer University, less than a year away from receiving my double economics and business degree. I could practically taste the money and freedom already.

Professor Ehrlich sighed. He was used to my stubbornness, but something in his tone had my gut tightening with unease.

"You do need one," he said, his voice gentle. "English literature and composition is a core requirement. You already failed it once, and it's only offered in the fall. If you fail it again this semester, you won't graduate."

My pulse spiked, but I kept my expression neutral. "I won't fail. I've learned from my mistakes."

I didn't understand why I had to take English in the first place. I was going into finance, not goddamn publishing. I was acing my economics classes, and that was what really mattered.

"Perhaps, but I'd rather not risk it." Professor Ehrlich sighed again. "You have a brilliant mind, Dominic. I've never met anyone with such a natural gift for numbers, and I've been teaching for decades. But talent will only get you so far. A Thayer degree opens doors, but to get it, you need to play by the rules. You want to make it big on Wall Street? You have to graduate first, and you can't do that if you insist on choosing your pride over your future."

My knuckles turned white around the armrests.

Maybe it was the fear of losing when I was so close to the finish line, or maybe it was because Professor Ehrlich was the only teacher who'd ever given a damn about me.

Whatever it was, it forced me to swallow my knee-jerk distaste over his suggestion and relent, at least partly, through gritted teeth.

"Fine. I'll meet with her once," I said. "But if I don't like her, I'm not meeting with her again."

———

The following Monday, I showed up at Thayer's main library, ready to get the meeting over with. It was nearly empty this early in the semester, so it shouldn't take long to find my tutor among the stacks.

Professor Ehrlich had given us each other's contact information, and she'd left me a voicemail that morning confirming our appointment.

*I'll be on the second floor wearing a yellow dress. See you soon.*

She didn't sound as chirpy as I'd feared. In fact, her voice was oddly soothing. Rich and creamy, with a gentle calm that wouldn't be out of place in a yoga studio or a therapist's office.

Still, I was predisposed to not like her. Professor Ehrlich aside, I didn't have the best record with anyone in a teaching position.

My eyes landed on a flash of color near the window.

Yellow dress. Coffee and a familiar blue English comp textbook. That had to be Alessandra.

She had her head bent over something on the table, and she didn't look up even when I pulled out the chair opposite hers. *Typical.* I'd tried working with a handful of tutors in high school and quickly ditched them when it became clear they were more interested in checking their messages and texting.

I opened my mouth, but my irritation died in my throat when Alessandra finally lifted her head and our eyes met.

Her voice was made for radio, but her face was made for the goddamned silver screen. Full lips, high cheekbones, skin that glowed like liquid silk in the sunlight. Chestnut hair spilled in thick, silky waves over her tanned shoulders, and her blue-gray eyes sparkled with warmth as she stood and held out her hand.

Thayer was filled with beautiful girls, but there was beautiful, and there was her.

"You must be Dominic," she said. Somehow, she sounded even better in person. "I'm Alessandra, but my friends call me Ále."

I finally found my voice. "Hello, Alessandra." I placed extra emphasis on her full name. We weren't friends. We just met, and my reaction to her was purely physical. It didn't mean anything.

"Nice to meet you." If she was put off by my pointed use of her full name, she didn't show it.

"Since this is our first meeting and the semester hasn't fully kicked off yet, I didn't prepare any study materials," she said after we settled into our seats. "You're heartbroken, I'm sure."

"Inconsolable."

Alessandra's quick grin sent an equally quick frisson of warmth through my veins. I shifted, half wishing I'd never showed up and half wishing I'd never have to leave.

"I thought we'd discuss expectations and get to know each other a bit during today's session," she said. "Even though this is a formal tutoring partnership, it helps if we like each other."

One of *those* types. I should've figured. "As long as you don't ask me to braid your hair," I said. "Neither of us would be happy."

Her laugh almost brought a smile to my lips.

Almost.

"No hair braiding, I promise, but I can't guarantee I won't show up with cookies every now and then. They're wonderfully unhealthy and, if things get down to the wire, they work quite well as bribes." Another grin, another frisson of warmth. "Don't ask me how I know."

For the next hour, we discussed our schedules for the semester, Professor Ruth's irrational love of juxtaposition, and random shit like our favorite music artists and colors. Alessandra also dug deep into my learning habits—what type of environment I preferred; whether I learned best through sound, visuals, or hands-on activities; even what time of day I usually got the most tired.

I'd never paid attention to half those things before and balked at answering, but for someone who resembled a grown-up Disney princess, she was like a damn pit bull with a bone.

I eventually relented and answered after some thought.

Learning environment: big table, natural light, some background noise as opposed to total silence.

Learning medium: visuals.

Time of day when I usually wanted to take a nap: early afternoon.

"Perfect. This was very helpful," she said at the end of our hour. "I think we'll get along just fine. Anyone who's a fan of Garage Sushi is friend material."

Our mutual interest in the local indie band had been a pleasant surprise, though I hardly considered it a solid basis for a friendship.

"Does the same time next week work for you?" she asked. "I don't have class on Mondays, so I'm flexible."

"No. My SAT tutoring gig starts next week." Rich people spent ridiculous amounts of money to get their kids into the Ivy League, and the cash I raked in from my math lessons went a long way in covering my expenses.

"What about in the morning?"

"Work."

"Night?"

"Work."

Her brows rose. "So you work, tutor, then go back to work?"

"Two different jobs," I said stiffly. "Cafe in the morning, Frankie's at night." I'd stacked all my classes on Tuesdays and Thursdays so I could work the other days. Between the coffee shop, diner, tutoring, and occasional lawn-mowing gig on the weekend, I earned just enough to sort of fit in at Thayer.

I didn't actually care about ingratiating myself with my classmates, most of whom came from wealthy prep school backgrounds I could never relate to, but the biggest benefit of attending a school like Thayer was the networking. In order for people to take me seriously, I needed to look the part, and looking the part was damn expensive.

Alessandra's face softened. She was the type of student who belonged without trying. She didn't mention what her parents did, but I could tell just by looking at her that she came from money.

"What time do you get off work?" she asked. "We can meet then. Based on our schedules, Mondays are the—"

"I don't get off work until eleven." I challenged her with a cool stare. "I'm guessing that's too late for you." I left out the part about how I usually studied after work. I didn't know why, but I focused better when I was tired.

I liked Alessandra more than I thought I would, but I wasn't convinced about this whole tutoring thing. The last thing I needed was her to bail on me in the middle of the semester because I wasn't progressing fast enough for her.

"Good thing I'm a night owl," she said, meeting my stare with a serene one of her own. "See you next Monday."

---

I didn't believe for a second Alessandra would give up her Monday night—or any night—to tutor me. She probably had a date or party to attend, which was just fine. If we couldn't make a time work, then we couldn't make a time work. Despite Professor Ehrlich's reservations, I was confident I could pass English on my own. I had to. Not graduating was not an alternative.

I wiped down a table at Frankie's, trying to ignore an unwanted pang of jealousy at the thought of Alessandra on a date. I had no claim on her, nor did I want any. I'd hooked up with a few girls at Thayer but never bothered dating any. I was busy enough without dealing with the drama of romantic entanglements.

"Whoa." Lincoln let out a low whistle from the booth where he was scarfing down a burger and fries instead of closing up shop. He was the owner's nephew and one of the laziest fucking human beings I'd ever encountered. "Who is *that*?"

I glanced up, already annoyed that someone was walking in five minutes before closing time, but for the second time in a week, my annoyance died a quick death.

Brown hair. Blue eyes. An armful of books and a half-teasing, half-challenging smile as she took in my shock.

*Alessandra*. Here. In Frankie's. At eleven fucking o'clock on a Monday night.

What the *hell* was she doing here?

"We're closed," I said, even though we weren't supposed to turn away customers until the absolute last minute and it wasn't my place to turn them away in the first place.

Lincoln stopped drooling long enough to glare at me. "Dude," he hissed. "What are you *doing*?"

"I'm not here for the food," Alessandra said calmly. "We have a tutoring session, remember? I'm here to give you a ride." She sat at a counter stool. "Don't mind me. I'll wait until you're done."

"That's your tutor? Damn, I should've stayed in school." Lincoln resumed ogling her in a way that made me want to rip his eyes out of their sockets.

"I'm tired." I stepped in front of him, blocking his view. It was either that or earn myself an arrest for assaulting my boss's nephew. "We'll schedule our session for another day."

"Perfect," she said, ignoring Lincoln's indignant protest. "You focus better when you're tired, right?"

How—*Professor Ehrlich*. I was going to kill him.

I could tell by the look on Alessandra's face that she wasn't going to budge, so I didn't argue further. I'd learned how to pick my battles a long time ago.

Eventually, Lincoln tired of leering at her—either that, or he was put off by my death stare—and left me to close up shop.

"Don't you have other things to do?" I asked when Alessandra and I finally settled into a booth. "It's almost midnight."

"Like I said, I'm a night owl." She gave me a mischievous smile. "And I heard the milkshakes here are really good."

I snorted, reining in the small laugh that'd almost escaped. "What happened to not being here for the food?"

"Technically true, but I'll never turn down a shake if someone offers me one."

"Right." She had to have an ulterior motive for showing up. People didn't go above and beyond like this out of the goodness of their hearts.

Alessandra must've picked up on my lingering suspicion because her teasing expression sobered.

"Look, I know you don't trust me yet, and I don't blame you, but I want to make one thing clear," she said. "I'm your tutor, not your mother or a drill sergeant. I promise I will do my very best to help you pass English, but this is a partnership. You need to work with me, and if you really don't want to—if you feel like I'm wasting your time and you would rather never see me again—then you need to say so now. I don't give up on my students, but I'm also not going to force them to do something they don't want to do. So tell me. Are you in or are you out?"

Surprise flitted through me, followed by begrudging respect and something infinitely more uncomfortable. It formed a knot in my throat and blocked my knee-jerk defensive response.

No one had ever called me out quite so calmly and effectively before. No one had cared enough.

"In," I finally said with no small amount of reluctance.

Maybe this was an act and she'd walk away after her initial enthusiasm waned. She wouldn't be the first one. But something in my gut told me she'd stay, and that scared me more than anything else.

Alessandra's shoulders relaxed. "Good." Her smile returned, a warm beam of sunshine beneath the fluorescent glare of the overhead lights. "Then let's get started, shall we?"

Over the next two hours, I understood why Professor Ehrlich sang her praises so highly. She was a damn good tutor. She was patient, encouraging, and empathetic without being condescending. She also came more prepared than a Girl Scout with a bag full of highlighters for color coding, L-shaped cards to frame sections of the textbook and help focus my attention, and a recorder so I could replay our audio lesson at my leisure.

The most damning thing was, it *worked*. At least, it worked better than my usual methods of gritting my teeth and persevering through brute determination.

The only downside was how distracting Alessandra herself was. If she talked for too long, I got lost in her voice instead of her words, and every time she moved, a faint whiff of her perfume drifted across the table, clouding my thoughts.

*Christ.* I was a grown man, not a hormonal teenager with a crush. *Get it together.*

I reached for the blue highlighter at the same time she did. Our fingers brushed, and an electric current jolted up my arm.

I yanked my hand away like I'd been burned. Pink colored Alessandra's cheeks as tension coated the expanse of our booth.

"It's getting late. We should head out." My voice sounded cold to my own ears even as my heart slammed against my ribcage with alarming force. "I have class tomorrow morning."

"Right." Alessandra gathered her materials back into her bag, her face still glowing with a hint of color. "Me too."

Neither of us spoke during the drive back to campus, but my brain couldn't stop replaying what happened in the diner.

The softness of her skin. The hitch in her breath. The tiny, almost imperceptible stutter of my heart during the millisecond our hands grazed, followed by the unexpected shock to my system.

I blamed it on sheer exhaustion. I'd never reacted so viscerally to such a small touch, but the body did strange things under duress. That was the only explanation.

Alessandra pulled up in front of my dorm. We stared up at the imposing brick building, and another awkward beat passed before I broke the silence.

"Thank you." The sentiment came out stiffer than intended. I wasn't used to thanking people; they rarely did anything that warranted genuine appreciation. "For the ride and for coming out to Frankie's. You didn't have to do that."

"You're welcome." Alessandra's earlier mischief returned. "It was worth it for the vinyl booths and fluorescent lights alone. I hear they're really flattering for my skin."

"They are." I wasn't joking. She might be the only person on the planet who could still look like a supermodel in a shitty, poorly lit diner.

A smile curved her mouth. "Same time next week?"

I hesitated. This was it. My absolute last chance to walk away before she did.

*You want to make it big on Wall Street? You can't do that if you insist on choosing your pride over your future.*

*I don't give up on my students, but I'm also not going to force them to do something they don't want to do. So tell me. Are you in or are you out?*

I blew out a breath. *Fuck.*

"Sure," I said, ignoring my twinge of anticipation at the thought of seeing her again. *I hope I don't regret this.* "Same time next week."

# CHAPTER 8

## *Alessandra*

"I HAVE TO RUN TO A MEETING, BUT MAKE YOURSELF AT home," Sloane said. "Just remember the house rules. No smoking, no shoes on the carpet, and no feeding The Fish outside of the prescribed hours and amounts, which are taped to the table next to his bowl. Any questions?"

"No. All sounds good." I mustered a small smile. "Thanks again for letting me stay here while I figure things out. I promise I'll be out of your hair soon."

Out of all my friends—of which there were only three or four total, but that was an issue for another day—Sloane was the least warm and fuzzy. However, both Vivian and Isabella lived with their significant others, and despite her general lack of visible emotion, Sloane always went to bat for her friends.

I was tired of living in a hotel, and she hadn't hesitated when I'd asked if I could stay with her while I went apartment hunting. And she'd greeted my arrival with a mug of coffee, a stiff hug, and a Karambit knife wrapped with a bow—for basic defense or offense, depending on how pissed I was at Dominic, she explained.

"Don't worry about it." Sloane's face softened the tiniest smidge. "We'll get drinks later. You and I can bitch about men while Viv and Isa pretend they're not in sickeningly sweet relationships."

My laugh came out rusty but genuine. "It's a plan."

It'd been a week since I told Dominic I wanted a divorce. None of my friends seemed surprised by my decision to leave him, which said all there was to say about how other people perceived our relationship.

My phone lit up with an incoming call.

*Dominic.* Again. He'd been calling nonstop over the past week, and every time his name popped up, it was a fresh stab in my chest. Still, I couldn't bring myself to block him yet, so I let his calls roll to voicemail. I haven't listened to any of them since the first one; it hurt too much.

"What do you mean *he's in Mykonos*?" Sloane's quiet fury chilled the air as she left for her meeting. As a high-powered publicist who ran her own boutique public relations firm, she was always putting out fires for her clients. "That is unacceptable. He *knows* he should be here for the meeting…"

Her voice faded, followed by the slam of the front door. Dominic's call also ended, and I breathed a sigh of relief only to tense again when another incoming call rolled right into his missed one.

*Pearson, Hodder, and Blum.*

Waves of anxiety buffeted my stomach. I wasn't sure what was worse—hearing from my husband or from my divorce attorney.

"Alessandra, this is Cole Pearson." The deep voice settled some of my nerves. Cole was one of the top divorce attorneys in the country. He cost an arm and a leg, but he was the only one who stood a chance against Dominic's fleet of high-powered lawyers.

"Hi." I put him on speaker while I unpacked my suitcase.

I needed something to do with my hands or I'd dissolve into an even bigger mess. "How did it go?"

The waves intensified as I waited for his answer.

I'd filed for divorce a few days ago and, in true Cole fashion, he'd expedited the process so he could serve Dominic the papers today. I wanted to get the divorce over with quickly before I lost my nerve or he somehow convinced me to go back.

Most days, I was sure I was doing the right thing, but there were other days when I woke up in an empty bed and missed him so much, it hurt to breathe. I haven't been happy for a while, but I couldn't forget eleven years together just like that.

"We served him the papers," Cole said. "As expected, he refused to sign."

I closed my eyes. Knowing Dominic, he would drag this out for as long as possible. He had the money and power to tie us up in the courts for years, and the thought of sitting in limbo for that long made me nauseous.

"Luckily, we have provisions for that." Cole didn't sound too worried, which made me feel slightly better. "We'll push the divorce through one way or another, but I want you to be prepared. This is Dominic Davenport. It could get ugly."

"Even though we don't have children and I don't want any of his assets?" The penthouse, the cars, the jet. Dominic could have it all. I just wanted out.

"The problem isn't the assets, Mrs. Davenport," Cole said. "It's you. He doesn't want to let *you* go, and unless you can convince him otherwise, it's going to be a long fight."

---

"I'm so sorry, but Mr. Davenport is in meetings all day." Dominic's assistant, Martha, sounded only marginally apologetic. "However, I can take a message and have him—"

"It's an emergency." My fingers tightened around my bag strap. "I'd like to speak to my *husband* directly." I emphasized the second to last word. It didn't matter that he would be my ex-husband soon if I had my way; as long as we were married, I had certain perks, which *should* include seeing him without his assistant treating me like I was a vagrant who'd wandered in off the street.

Her eyes swept over me, probably taking in my lack of visible injuries and physical distress. "I understand, but I'm afraid he's booked back-to-back. Like I said, I'm happy to take a message and have him call you back at his earliest convenience." She ripped a Post-It note off the pad on her desk. "Is this related to a social event or some sort of home issue?"

My skin flushed. Normally, I wasn't a violent person, but I was hungry, tired, and irritated after my call with Cole. It took every ounce of willpower not to grab Martha's coffee and toss it in her smug, condescending face.

"Neither." I dropped my polite tone. "If Dominic is currently in a meeting, I can wait. I assume he has to eat lunch at some point, correct?"

Martha pursed her lips. "He has a lunch meeting at Le Bernardin. Mrs. Davenport, please, I must insist you—"

"What's going on?" A cold voice interrupted her mid-sentence.

We both froze for a split second before our heads swiveled toward the now-open door to Dominic's office. The sun backlit his frame, and the width of his shoulders filled the doorway, making him look even more imposing than usual.

My throat dried, and the leather bag strap dug into my palm before I forcibly relaxed my grip.

"Mr. Davenport!" Martha jumped up from her chair. "Your call ended early. I was just telling Mrs. Davenport that you—"

"Repeat that." Dominic stepped into the main office. The

shadows peeled away from his form, revealing chiseled cheek-bones, stormy eyes, and a frown that could deter Satan himself.

He wasn't looking at me. Instead, he pinned his attention on Martha, who shrank beneath his ire. "I said I was telling Mrs. Davenport that—"

"*Mrs.* Davenport." The words were lethal in their quiet-ness. "As in my wife. If she wants to see me, she sees me. Don't ever prevent her from doing so again or the only part of a New York office you'll see is the outside when I throw you out. Understand?"

Martha's face paled to the point of resembling chalk. "Yes, sir. I understand."

Vindication battled with sympathy for dominance. In the end, the latter won out.

"That was harsh," I said quietly as I followed Dominic into his office. He still hadn't looked at me.

"Not as harsh as she deserved." Instead of sitting, he leaned back against his desk, the picture of cool confidence, but when his eyes finally met mine, the exhaustion in them tugged at my heart-strings in a way that had me biting back my concern.

*It doesn't matter. It's not your job to make sure he's getting enough rest.*

Dominic's gaze swept over my face, lingering on my eyes and mouth. "You're not getting enough sleep."

My skin heated. "Thanks a lot." I guess he wasn't the only one who looked tired.

I tucked a strand of hair behind my ear with a self-conscious hand. I *hadn't* been getting enough sleep. I'd thrown myself into researching how to open a physical store for Floria Designs, which was a longtime dream, and when I wasn't working, I was agoniz-ing over the divorce. Anxiety and overwork weren't exactly a winning beauty combo.

"You know what I mean." He brushed a thumb over my cheek with agonizing tenderness. "Sleep or not, you're always beautiful."

My chest clenched. If only he was this attentive when our relationship wasn't on the brink of ruin.

I usually got a small brush of his lips or brief, blissful moments of our bodies connecting in the middle of the night, but he hadn't touched me like this—casual, familiar, *intimate*—in ages.

I should move away and put some much-needed distance between us, but I couldn't help leaning into him. *One minute. That's all I need.*

"I'm not the only one who hasn't been sleeping." His dark circles and sallow complexion gave him away, but still, he was so beautiful it hurt.

"It's difficult to sleep when your wife refuses to pick up your calls," he said quietly.

A painful lump blocked the flow of oxygen to my lungs. *Don't let him get to you.*

I forced myself to step back and ignore the flash of hurt in his eyes. "I'm not here to discuss our sleep habits," I said, purposely skipping past the second part of his statement.

Dominic's confident mask snapped back into place, erasing any hint of vulnerability, but his gaze burned into mine with unsettling intimacy.

"Then why are you here, *amor*?" The velvety nickname caressed my skin and sent an involuntary wave of nostalgia crashing over me.

*"I can't believe you speak Portuguese." I shook my head, still in disbelief over how he'd conversed with my family over dinner in their native language. "When the hell did you learn to speak Portuguese?"*

*"I've been attending lessons at the Foreign Languages Institute every Wednesday night." A tiny grin tugged at his lips as he rinsed*

*the last plate and placed it on the rack. We'd offered to do the dishes since my brother had prepared the food and my mother had disappeared immediately after dessert with her latest boy toy.*

*"Close your mouth,* amor, *or a fly will get in."*

*"You told me you were working Wednesday nights," I accused.*

*"I was. I was working on learning Portuguese." Dominic shrugged, a hint of color rising on his cheekbones. "This is my first time meeting your family. I figured it would be a nice thing to do."*

*An ache unfurled behind my ribcage. "You didn't have to do that. They would've loved you regardless."*

*Learning foreign languages didn't come easily for him, but the fact that he'd done it anyway because he wanted to make a good impression on my family...*

*The ache deepened. God, I adored this man.*

*"Maybe, but I wanted to." Dominic's face softened. "Faria qualquer coisa por você."*

The weight of the memory nearly crushed me before I sucked in a painful breath and shoved it aside.

That was then. This was now. *Focus on the now.* "Cole told me you refused to sign the papers."

My answer doused the room in ice.

The warmth vanished from his expression, and Dominic's jaw flexed as he straightened to his full six feet, three inches. "On a first-name basis with your lawyer already, I see."

He might as well have slapped me in the face.

Anger flared hot and sudden at his implication. "Don't even *think* about playing the jealous husband card. Not when you didn't care *who* I spoke to or hung out with before I dented your ego—"

"You think this is what this is about? My ego?" His eyes flashed. "Dammit, Ále, it's been a week. One week, and you already have that asshole lawyer serving me divorce papers. We haven't even tried to fix things yet. There's marriage counseling—"

"We tried that once, remember?" I fired back. It'd been a few years ago, when I'd been so frustrated by his long hours, I'd talked him into going to couples' therapy. "You didn't show up because of a—surprise, surprise—work emergency."

He probably didn't even remember. I hadn't asked him to go again because the only thing more humbling than exposing our relationship woes to a stranger was having your husband skip the appointment altogether. The memory of the counselor's pitying gaze stung to this day.

Dominic's mouth snapped shut. His throat worked with a hard swallow, and silence thundered in the wake of my response.

"You have two weeks to sign the papers, Dominic," I said. "Or this will turn into a war, and we both know that'll hurt your bottom line more than it does mine." He had a multibillion-dollar company to run; I didn't.

I didn't want to get into a legal fight with him, but if that was what it took, that was what I'd do. I needed to take control of my life again, and I couldn't do that without closing this chapter with Dominic.

*No matter how much it hurts.*

# CHAPTER 9

*Dominic*

I STOPPED SLEEPING IN THE PENTHOUSE. I TRIED, BUT even with a full staff and the best entertainment money could buy keeping me company, it felt unbearably empty without Alessandra. Everything reminded me of her—the dresses in the closet, the white lilies lining the hall, the lingering floral scent of her shampoo in our bed.

Instead, I took up residence in my office, where I already had a sleeping area set up for the all-nighters I occasionally had to pull.

My phone buzzed with an incoming call. As always, my heart tripped over hope it was Alessandra before disappointment set in.

*Unknown number.* It was the fourth such call today. I didn't know how they found my private cell number, which was unlisted and only available to a small group of vetted contacts, but it was getting damn annoying. I'd picked up the first time and heard nothing but silence.

If it weren't for Alessandra, I'd get a new number tomorrow and be done with it.

It'd been two weeks since she showed up at the office and demanded I sign the papers. Her fucker of a lawyer kept hounding me, and no matter what I did, she refused to see me. Gifts. Calls. I'd even booked a damn session at Manhattan's top marriage counselor, which she hadn't shown up to.

I rubbed a hand over my face and tried to focus on the screen. I was still dealing with the SEC investigation into DBG Bank, which was picking up steam and throwing our office into chaos. Something about it bugged me, though I couldn't quite pinpoint why.

Finally, after thirty minutes of fruitless effort, I gave up and called it a night. Since it was only ten and I couldn't stand the thought of sleeping in the silent office this early, I grabbed my jacket off the back of my chair and headed to the one place that had any hope of making me forget about Alessandra, if only for a little while.

---

The New York branch of the Valhalla Club sat on a heavily guarded estate on the Upper East Side. That much private land was unheard of in Manhattan these days, but the club was founded over a century ago, when there'd been more leeway for a group of extremely wealthy, extremely connected families to claim dominion over a vast swath of real estate.

Valhalla hadn't changed in that it remained an exclusive society for the world's richest and most powerful, but its reach had expanded past its New York flagship and into every major city across the globe, including London, Shanghai, Tokyo, Cape Town, and São Paulo.

I wouldn't have had a snowball's chance in hell of becoming a member had it not been for Dante Russo, a descendant of one of Valhalla's founding fathers.

"You look like hell," Dante said as I approached the bar where he sat with Kai Young, CEO of the Young media empire.

"Great to see you too, Russo." I took the seat on Dante's other side and ordered a bourbon.

Dante had been one of my first investors. He ran the Russo Group, the world's largest luxury goods conglomerate, and a combination of luck, timing, and sheer perseverance had wrestled him away from his investment guy to my fledgling company. Where Dante went, the rest of high society eventually followed, including Kai, who'd also become a good friend over the years.

I knew I was the odd one out in the trio. Both Kai and Dante came from money so old, it belonged in a museum, whereas my billions were brand new, but at the end of the day, money was money. Not even the pedigree snobs at Valhalla dared snub me openly when I controlled the fate of their investments.

"He's right," Kai said mildly. "You look like you haven't slept in weeks."

*Because I haven't.*

"Keep it up and you'll scare away your investors," Dante added. "Your face was ugly enough without adding the dark circles and scowl to the mix."

I snorted. "Look who's talking." He'd gotten in so many fights, his nose was permanently fucked up, though that hadn't stopped women from throwing themselves at him before he got married.

"Vivian likes my face just fine."

"She's your wife. She's obligated to pretend." *Like how Alessandra pretended she was happy when she wasn't.* A sharp pang grabbed hold of my heart and twisted.

I tossed back my drink, trying to lose myself in the burn of alcohol while Dante and Kai exchanged glances. I hadn't told them what happened with Alessandra, but she was good friends with Vivian and Isabella, Kai's girlfriend. I assumed they'd filled their partners in on what happened.

"Speaking of wives, how are things with Ále?" Kai asked, his tone so placid, he might as well be talking about the weather.

"Fine," I said curtly.

"Heard she served you divorce papers at work." Unlike Kai, Dante possessed the tact of a socially inept bull.

My shoulders tensed. "That was a misunderstanding."

"No one hires Cole fucking Pearson for a misunderstanding." A touch of sympathy crossed Dante's face. "Tell me you're not brushing this off. If you divorce, your assets—"

"I know what happens to my assets." The logical part of me said I should care more; I didn't. "We're not getting divorced." I reached for my lighter, but for once, the familiar flicks of the flint wheel couldn't calm the storm raging inside me. "We'll work it out. Go to counseling, take a nice long trip somewhere."

I'd forgotten about the time she asked for couples' therapy until she brought it up at my office. It'd been three years ago, and I'd been swamped with a huge acquisition at the time. She'd only asked once, so I'd figured it was an impulsive request rather than the sign of a long-standing issue. When we were dating, Alessandra never hesitated to tell me when she had a problem.

We just needed to reconnect, that was all. We could recreate our honeymoon in Jamaica or spend two weeks traveling through Japan. I couldn't realistically take more time than that off work, but two weeks would be enough, right? Once Alessandra and I spent time alone together, we'd be fine. That'd been her reason for going to marriage counseling in the first place.

Dante and Kai remained silent.

"What?" Irritation crept into my veins. I was already on edge from exhaustion, stress, and a strange ache that seemed to follow me everywhere. I didn't need my friends' silent judgment too.

"I don't think a vacation or counseling is going to solve your problems," Dante said.

"Why the hell not?"

He gave me an incredulous look. "You missed your *ten-year wedding anniversary*. I forgot about a dinner party *once* and Vivian wouldn't talk to me for days. If I missed an anniversary..." He grimaced. "Let's not go there."

"What Dante is trying to say is, a few weeks at a luxury resort won't make up for years of suppressed feelings," Kai cut in, diplomatic as always. "Clearly, Alessandra has been...discontent for a while. The anniversary was the straw that broke the camel's back, so to speak. You can't buy your way out of it."

I stared at them.

"Oh, for fuck's sake," Dante said. "Let's stop beating around the bush. *You're* the problem, Dom. Even someone who's met you both once can tell you barely paid attention to Alessandra when she was around. How many times have you stayed at the event while she went home because she didn't feel well? How many dinners did you take with clients instead of with her?" He shook his head. "Your obsession with work is good for my portfolio, so I'm not complaining about that. But you can't be surprised Alessandra's fed up."

"There's no short-term fix for something like this," Kai said, his tone a touch gentler than Dante's. "It requires an entire lifestyle and mindset shift."

"You sound like a fitness coach commercial." *On. Off.* I flicked my lighter with unsteady hands.

Despite my blithe reply, my mind whirled with chaos. Dante made the same points Alessandra had, but whereas hers had cut with precision, his punched me right in the gut.

It was one thing for the other person to point out the flaws in a relationship. It was another for a third party to do so with unerring accuracy, especially when I'd thought everything had been fine. Not great, but not horrible. Obviously, I'd been wrong.

*On. Off.* The tiny flame blurred as snippets from the past few years streamed past my mind's eye.

When had our marriage devolved to the state it was now? Alessandra and I used to eat dinner together every night. We had an unmissable date night every Friday, and we never went to bed without telling each other about our days. Then I started Davenport Capital and things changed, slowly but surely.

*"I'm sorry,* amor, *but the investor is only in town tonight,"* I said. *"He heads one of the biggest insurance companies in the country. If I can get him onboard…"*

*"It's okay. I get it." Alessandra gave me a soft, reassuring kiss. "You'll just have to make it up to me later."*

*Guilt loosened its grip on my muscles. "I will. I promise."*

*It was my first time missing our sacred Friday date night. I hated letting her down, but I needed investors and snagging Wollensky would be a huge coup.*

*One of these days, the whole world would know the name Dominic Davenport, and with recognition came status, money, power—everything I'd ever dreamed of. Once that happened, I could make it up to Alessandra a thousand times over.*

*"If you miss next week's date, though, we'll have a problem," she teased, chasing away images of private jets and black Amex cards. "I practically had to pledge my firstborn to get a reservation at Le Fleur."*

*I laughed. "I'm sure our firstborn will understand." I curled an arm around her waist and pulled her closer for another kiss. "Thank you for understanding," I murmured. "This is just one time. It won't happen again."*

Except it had. *Just one time* turned into two, then three, until we entered a new normal. I'd assumed she was okay with it because she rarely expressed otherwise except for that one time with the counseling. But the way she got quieter and quieter over the years, the way she left events early when she wasn't hosting them and utter lack of surprise when I canceled plans...

Waves of realization crashed over me, stunning me into near immobility. *Fuck*.

"Like I said, lifestyle and mindset shift." Kai read my expression like a book. He lifted his glass to his lips and arched an eyebrow. "The question is, are you willing to do it?"

# CHAPTER 10

# *Alessandra*

FATE SMACKED ME IN THE FACE WITH A GIANT RED SIGN. RETAIL SPACE FOR LEASE.

The sign was plastered over the window of a tiny storefront in NoMad, tucked between a cafe and a nail salon.

I'd passed plenty of *for lease* signs on my way back from another day of unsuccessful apartment hunting, but for some reason, this one screamed at me. Maybe it was the quiet street, the giant windows, and the exposed brick walls I spied inside. Or maybe it was my frustration over the standstill in divorce proceedings and desire to *do* something. To find a piece of myself that didn't revolve around my marriage.

Whatever it was, it compelled me to call the number on the sign and leave a voicemail requesting more information.

Dominic could stall all he wanted, but I wasn't putting my life on hold for him anymore. Cole could deal with the divorce while I started building a new life—one where I had control over my own finances and future.

"I'm free any day," I said after I left the requisite contact information. *Does that make me sound too desperate?* Normal people didn't sit around all day waiting for a phone call, right? "Any day between nine and five," I added hastily. *Much better.* "I look forward to hearing from you soon. Thank you."

I hung up, my palms clammy.

*This was it.* My first step toward independence. Well, besides moving out, which didn't fully count because I didn't have my own place yet and most of my belongings were still at the penthouse. I couldn't bring myself to return to Hudson Yards and pack up yet.

The early October air cooled some of my nerves as I cut across the street toward Sloane's apartment. I'd started Floria Designs two years ago on a whim, and it'd blossomed into a small yet thriving business. It wasn't raking in millions or anything, but it earned a solid profit and I enjoyed the work. However, now that I was stepping out on my own, it was time to take it to the next level.

I wanted to take control and create my own future; I didn't want to be someone who put herself last.

My phone rang when I entered the lobby of Sloane's building. My heart skipped a beat, but instead of the Realtor calling me back, the name was a familiar one.

"You never call, you never text. It's like I don't exist anymore," Marcelo said when I picked up. His teasing tone brought a smile to my lips. "What happened to sibling loyalty?"

"I'm not the one setting impossible culinary standards for the rich and famous," I said. "How can anyone eat another steak after they've tasted yours?"

"Ah, flattery. It'll work on me every time." My brother laughed. He was two years my junior and already one of the most celebrated chefs in São Paulo's dining scene. We chatted for a few minutes about work and his need for a vacation before he asked, "When are you visiting again? I haven't seen you and Dom in ages."

My smile faded. I hadn't told my family about my separation yet. One, it was hard enough to track down my mother on a regular day. Two, I only saw them once or twice a year. They had no idea I was unhappy in my marriage, and I couldn't summon the energy to detail the reasons behind the separation yet.

"Ále?" Marcelo prompted when I remained silent. "You okay?"

"Yes, I—" My response abruptly cut off when the elevator doors slid open.

*Oh, you've got to be kidding.*

"I have to call you back," I said, not taking my eyes off the spectacle waiting for me outside the apartment. "I'm fine, but something…something came up."

Correction: a hundred somethings, judging by the number of bouquets littering the hallway. Pink roses for affection, white lilies for forgiveness, golden trumps for strength and triumph over obstacles. I tried to ignore the meaning behind each bouquet as I focused on the garden that had exploded inside the building. It didn't take a rocket scientist to figure out who they were from.

*I'm going to* kill *Dominic.*

"Hi. Alessandra Davenport?" The delivery boy handed me a pen and clipboard. "Can you sign, please? We have more downstairs but, well, we can't fit them all in the hall."

I didn't touch the pen. "How did you get up here?"

Sloane was in Europe dealing with Xavier Castillo, one of her most difficult clients, and building security wouldn't let any deliveries in without informing the recipient first.

The delivery boy shrugged. "A…" He checked his phone. "Mr. Dominic Davenport called and arranged it. He said he knows the building owner?"

I was going to have a *serious* talk with the head of security after this.

"Thank you, but I don't want the flowers," I said. "Can you

please bring them back to the store? I don't want them to go to waste."

Panic filled the boy's face. He exchanged glances with the other employees from the flower shop, all of whom wore similar stricken expressions.

"Our boss said we *have* to make this delivery. He's going to check for your signature when we get back."

I suppressed a groan.

The boy couldn't be more than eighteen or nineteen. He was probably doing this as a side gig, and it wasn't his fault Dominic was so…so *insufferable*. If he thought inundating me with flowers was going to make me back down from the divorce, he didn't know me at all.

*And isn't that the problem to begin with?*

"How about this?" I took the clipboard. "I'll sign, but you take the flowers to the nearest hospital instead. Your boss doesn't have to know I didn't keep them."

It took some cajoling, but the boy eventually relented and agreed to my plan. On his way out, however, he handed me the note that accompanied the flowers and left before I could protest.

I entered the apartment, my eyes locked on Dominic's messy, familiar scrawl.

*I'm sorry I missed our anniversary dinner and so many more dinners before that. Flowers alone won't make up for it, but give me a chance to make amends in person and I will. A thousandfold.*

His handwriting became near illegible toward the end, but I understood him. I always did.

A tiny drop of wetness smudged the ink. My heart threatened

to smash free from my chest as Dominic's words dragged me back in time.

*One day, I'll buy you a thousand real roses. I promise.*

*I won't forget. I promise.*

*We'll work this out. I promise.*

So many promises. He'd only kept a fraction of them, but I fell for them every time.

*Not this time.*

I ignored the ache in my chest as I set my jaw, crumpled the note, and tossed it in the trash. After a quick shower, I flung open my closet doors and searched for an appropriate *fuck you* outfit.

I'd stayed home too many nights waiting for Dominic when I should've been out living life, and it was time to make up for lost time.

Starting with tonight.

---

"You're beautiful."

I turned my head, examining the speaker through the buzz of three gin and tonics and one apple martini. He looked like he was in his mid-twenties. Floppy hair, designer suit, and the preppy, clean-cut look of a fresh Ivy League grad turned investment banker.

Dominic would chew him up and spit him out for breakfast.

*Stop thinking about Dominic.*

"Thank you," I said with a small smile. His pickup line wasn't groundbreaking, but it was better than previous compliments on my "great tits" and offers to show me a "night I'd never forget."

"I'm Drew." He held out his hand.

"Alessandra."

I wasn't interested in him romantically or sexually. I was still married, and despite my frustration over Dominic's stonewalling, I wasn't a cheater. But Drew seemed nice enough, and I was getting tired of drinking by myself. The whole point of going out was to meet new people.

*Baby steps.*

"So, Drew, what do you do?" I defaulted to basic small talk. As expected, my new barmate launched into an energetic spiel about the bank he worked for while I sipped my drink and tried to remember how to be a normal, single person on the dating scene again. I wasn't single *yet*, but I should start practicing, right?

Luckily, Drew possessed the enthusiasm of a newborn pup and carried the conversation on his own. Every now and then, he remembered to ask me a question about myself, and he scooted closer with every answer until his knee touched mine.

"That's great," he said after I gave him a brief overview of what I did for Floria Designs. "So, uh, are you free this weekend? I have tickets to the Yankees game. Box seats." A hint of braggadocio entered his tone.

*No, thanks.* I'd never understood the fascination with baseball. I couldn't even *see* the ball half the time.

I opened my mouth, but an icy voice sliced between us before I could respond.

"She's not." A hand rested on my lower back, followed by the brush of a soft wool suit and the scent of a familiar cologne. "My *wife* and I have plans."

My entire body stiffened while Drew scrambled off his stool, his face red and his eyes starstruck. "Mr. Davenport! Wow, I am a huge fan. I'm Drew Ledgeholm. We learned about you in my finance class…"

I stifled a groan. Of *course* he recognized Dominic on sight. Everyone loved a rags-to-riches story, and Dominic was basically a legend to every bright-eyed Wall Street newcomer.

He seemed less than impressed by Drew's fanboying. In fact, he looked like he was ready to tear the other man into pieces with his bare hands.

Drew must've realized it too because his voice eventually petered out. I pinpointed the moment Dominic's revelation about me being his wife sank in. His face paled, and panic crept into his expression as his eyes darted between us.

"She's your wife? I didn't know…I mean, she's not wearing…"

Three pairs of eyes honed in on my bare ring finger. Dominic's expression darkened, and the temperature dropped another dozen degrees.

"Now you do." If his voice had been cold before, it was positively arctic now. "I believe you have somewhere else to be. Don't you, Drew?" The calm acknowledgment of his name came off more menacing than any direct thread could.

Drew didn't bother answering. He fled, leaving me with one pissed-off husband and the embers of anger glowing in my stomach.

I shrugged off Dominic's hand and spun to face him. "Seriously? What is wrong with you? You scared that poor boy half to death!"

"That *poor boy* was hitting on *my* wife." Dominic's eyes blazed. "What did you expect me to do? Pat him on the back?"

"He didn't know I was married." I shook my head. "What are you doing here anyway? Don't tell me you're stalking me." I wouldn't put it past him. He would go to any length to win.

A touch of visible amusement cooled his anger. "The bar is down the street from my office, *amor*. I had a client meeting here."

"Oh." *Right*. I'd picked the bar out of a list of "best happy hour spots in the city" and completely forgot it was so close to Dominic's workplace.

His expression softened. "Ask me again on another day, and my answer might be different. I would stalk you if it meant you'd talk to me again."

"How romantic."

"I'm past romantic, Alessandra. I'm desperate."

I ruthlessly tamped down the sympathy unfurling behind my ribs. So what if he sounded miserable? He brought it on himself.

Still, I diverted my attention to the exit sign above his shoulder so I didn't have to meet his eyes.

I should leave. Every second I spent in his company was another opportunity for him to break down my walls, and I didn't fully trust myself with him yet, especially not when I had so many drinks in my system.

"Did you get my flowers?" Dominic didn't try to touch me again, but his gaze might as well have been a caress. It lingered on my face, tracing the lines of my jaw and cheekbones before kissing my mouth with its warmth.

"Yes." I notched my chin up even as my skin tingled with awareness. *I shouldn't have had that martini.* Alcohol always lowered my inhibitions, which was *not* a good thing when Dominic was in the vicinity. "I donated them to the nearest children's hospital."

If he was upset about me donating thousands of dollars' worth of florals, he didn't show it. "I'm sure they appreciated it."

A smile ghosted his mouth when I sighed, and I caught the tiniest glimpse of the man he used to be—the one who carried me uphill in the pouring rain because my heel broke, who kissed me good night every night no matter how late he came home, and who attempted to bake one of the elaborate cakes I'd saved on Pinterest for my birthday. His cake had come out decidedly un-Pinterest-like, but I'd loved it anyway. It was the thought that counted.

A stab of sentimentality drained the fight out of me. I sighed again, already exhausted from keeping myself together in his presence.

"Sign the papers, Dom."

## CHAPTER 11

*Dominic*

I DIDN'T BELIEVE IN FATE AS A GENERAL RULE, BUT AS WITH all rules, there were exceptions. I've only had two: the day I met Alessandra in Thayer's library and today.

Of all the bars and all the nights in the world, we were both here tonight. If that wasn't a message from the universe, nothing was.

"If you don't, I'll get half of everything. We never signed a prenup," Alessandra reminded me. The draft from a passing server blew wisps of hair into her eye. "We…" Her sentence trailed off when I brushed the strands back. My hand lingered next to her cheek, savoring her warmth.

"Do you want to be rid of me that desperately?" I murmured.

In any other situation, I would've balked at the thought of losing half my fortune, but all I could think about was how badly I wanted to kiss her. A real kiss, not like the perfunctory ones I usually gave her when I came home because I'd been too tired from work.

The regret of a thousand missed opportunities trickled through my veins.

Alessandra's face softened for a split second before hardening. "I served the papers, didn't I?"

I might've believed her had it not been for the tiny hitch in her voice, but her response still had its intended effect. It slashed through my composure, drawing blood and pain with one viciously clean slice.

Alessandra wasn't the type who enjoyed hurting people, and her defensiveness was a testament to how much I'd hurt *her*. Out of everything, that knowledge cut the deepest.

I'd thought I'd been doing the right thing by providing for us, but our definitions on what that looked like had clearly diverged over the years.

*There's no short-term fix for something like this.*

Kai's words echoed in my head, underpinned by a familiar sweet, warm croon as the music segued into a new song.

My breaths stilled at the same time as Alessandra's. The sign outside the bar had proclaimed tonight Latin night, but what were the chances they would play *this* exact song at *this* exact moment?

Like I said, I didn't believe in fate…except when it came to us.

"Dance with me." I lowered my hand and held it out. She didn't take it. I'd expected the refusal, but it stung nonetheless. "What would tonight look like if things were different?" I asked quietly. "If we were the people we used to be?"

A visible swallow betrayed Alessandra's emotions. "Don't."

"Indulge me." My voice softened further. "For old time's sake."

The music swirled around us, carrying us away from the bar and into the past.

---

*"Come on, dance with me." Alessandra laughed at my grimace. "Just once. I promise you won't combust into flames."*

"Debatable." Nevertheless, I took her outstretched hand. I hated making a fool of myself, but I'd never been able to deny her anything. "I don't know how to dance to this."

It was our last night in Brazil. Her mother and brother were out, leaving us alone for the evening. A breeze filtered through the open windows, carrying with it the scent of summer, and a woman's exquisite voice crooned from the old record player spinning in the corner.

"Don't worry. It's not like the samba I tried to teach you yesterday." Alessandra pulled me to the center of the living room. "Just put your hands here like this..." She placed my hands on her hips. "Hold me like this..." She pressed her cheek against my chest, her breath catching when I stroked her gently through the thin cotton of her dress. "And sway," she finished with a whisper.

I tucked my chin against the top of her head and closed my eyes as we swayed to the music. I ignored the small velvet box burning a hole in my pocket; for now, I was happy just holding her.

We'd come a long way since our first meeting nine months ago, and I silently thanked whatever higher power was out there for putting me in her path—even if they'd had to drag me there kicking and screaming.

"My mom used to play this song whenever she had a new boyfriend." Alessandra lifted her head. "I heard it a lot."

I believed it. Whereas Alessandra was easygoing and down to earth, her ex-supermodel mother lived in a world of her own. She'd arrived at dinner yesterday wearing a feather minidress, diamond necklace, and her rock star boyfriend's mouth glued to her neck.

"Who's the singer?" I asked.

"Marisa Monte." Her smile was so soft and warm I felt it deep in my bones. "It's called 'Amor I Love You.'"

Present-day Alessandra wasn't smiling, but the sheen in her eyes gave me an inkling of hope. As long as she felt something, we were salvageable, because what I feared wasn't her hate; it was her indifference.

"If things were different, we would've shown up together," she said. "We would order drinks, tell each other about our days, and complain about the rush hour traffic. We'd make up life stories about the people around us and argue about whether it was too early to put up Christmas decorations. We would be a normal couple, and we would…" Her voice caught. "We would be happy."

The brokenness of the last word cleaved my heart in half. The picture she painted was a tribute to simpler times, and while I never wanted to be the powerless, penniless boy I'd been when we'd first met again, I *did* want to be the man she fell in love with.

I wanted her to smile at me the way she used to.

I wanted her by my side, happy and laughing and whole.

I wanted *us* back, even if it meant stripping away parts of the person I'd worked so hard to build.

"One dance." I hadn't begged anyone for anything in a long time, but I was begging now. "Please."

The song ended. The moment of nostalgia dissipated, but I barely noticed as I waited for Alessandra's response.

She stared at my outstretched hand. My heart slammed against my ribcage, and just when I thought she would walk away and take the damn organ with her, she slipped her palm into mine.

Relief crushed the air from my throat.

I drew her closer, careful not to move too fast lest I spooked her.

One dance. One song. One chance.

"Do you remember the first time we went to a bar together?" I asked. "I passed English comp, and we celebrated with shots at the Crypt."

Alessandra shook her head. "How could I forget? You almost got arrested."

We hadn't lasted more than five minutes inside before some drunken asshole hit on her. He'd refused to leave us alone, and his advances had grown increasingly aggressive until I punched him, he punched me back, and the altercation escalated into a brawl that brought the cops onto the scene.

"It would've been worth it," I said. "I hope his nose was never the same."

Her reluctant laugh sent tendrils of warmth spiraling through my chest. I hadn't realized how much I'd missed the sound. Even before she left, she hadn't laughed much. Not in the way she used to.

Alessandra gradually relaxed as I drew more memories into the present—our first date, our graduation, our first trip together to New York. Our future was uncertain, but once upon a time, we'd been good together. We could get back to that place. We just needed time.

The song ended, and she moved to pull away before my arm tightened around her.

"Not yet," I said, the words ragged. I wasn't ready to let her go, but I didn't know how to make her stay.

Alessandra's mouth trembled, then firmed. "One dance. Remember?"

"Yes." I dipped my head, wishing I had the power to turn back time. "But I have a final request. A kiss. Just one."

She closed her eyes. "Dom…"

"For old time's sake," I repeated, the words mere tatters in the tiny space between us.

The uneven rhythm of her breaths matched mine. She didn't respond, but she also didn't leave, which I interpreted as tacit agreement.

My mouth hovered over hers, giving her one last chance to pull away. When she didn't, I closed the remaining distance and brushed her lips with the lightest of kisses. It was so soft, it counted more as a graze than a kiss, but it detonated every emotion I'd tried so hard to bury. Pain, longing, regret, love. No one could make me feel as much or as deeply as Alessandra did, and any control I might've had left snapped at her nearly inaudible sigh of pleasure.

I deepened the kiss, my mouth molding to hers with an ease that came from years of practice. My hand slid in her hair; hers gripped my shoulders. I explored her mouth with deep, sweeping strokes, drunk off the taste of apples and gin and *her*. After two weeks apart, kissing her felt like coming home.

Desire ramped up with every passing second. It curled around us in thick ribbons, drawing my skin taut and serrating her breaths, but I had enough presence of mind left to remember we were in public.

Somehow, I maneuvered us into a nearby hall where the staff restroom was surprisingly unlocked. It was nice as far as restrooms went, but I barely noticed the gold detailing or the marble floors. I was too focused on Alessandra—her flushed cheeks, her parted lips, the way she shivered when I set her on the counter and rucked her skirt up around her waist.

Neither of us spoke lest we shatter the delicate spell keeping our problems at bay.

Our problems would still be there tomorrow, but tonight? Tonight was for us.

I kissed her again. Harder this time, desperate to drink in as much of her as possible. No matter how long we'd been together, or how bad I'd been at expressing myself in recent years, I couldn't get enough of her. I never would.

I curled one hand around the back of her neck while the other traced the lacy edge of her underwear. Her stiffness from earlier in the night had melted away, and when I stopped at the sensitive juncture between her thigh and heat, she let out a noise of protest.

"Shh." I kissed my way down her neck, stopping at the places that drove her wild. The spot behind her ear, the hollow of her throat, the curve of her neck and shoulder. "Patience."

I knew Alessandra's body like I knew the back of my hand, and every deliberate detour elicited moans that escalated into a full-blown cry when I finally slid her underwear aside and rubbed my thumb over her clit.

I bit back a groan. She was already so damn wet for me.

Heat raced down my spine as I worked her with leisurely strokes, circling and teasing until she was dripping all over my hand. She bucked against me, her face etched with frustration and lust.

"Dom." A breathless plea fell from her lips. "*Please.*"

I hardened to the point of pain. God, nothing in the world ever sounded as sweet as the sound of my name on her lips.

Another cry tore from her throat when I finally thrust two fingers inside her. She was so wet, she took them easily, and her hips jerked again when I buried them to the knuckles.

"Oh God." Her nails dug painful grooves in my shoulders. "I can't…that's…*fuck…*"

Her words splintered as I finger fucked her into a sobbing, incoherent mess. Her moans and the slick sounds of my fingers pumping in and out of her filled the bathroom, drowning out my harsh breaths.

I almost lost it at the sight of her stretched so beautifully around me, but I forced myself under control. I'd focused on myself for too long. This was about her, and I wanted to enjoy every second, even if it was at my own expense.

I kept my eyes on Alessandra as I slammed my fingers back in and curled them so they hit her most sensitive spot.

She fell apart instantly. Head back, skin flushed, cries hoarse as she spasmed around my fingers. I kept the heel of my hand pressed against her clit while she rode out the waves of her orgasm, and I didn't withdraw until the last of her shudders subsided.

I pressed my forehead against hers, my chest aching with a fierce mix of lust and longing. Our breaths mingled, and despite the erection pressing painfully against my zipper, my arousal took a back seat to the unbearable intimacy of the moment. Still, despite my best efforts, I couldn't prevent post-sex clarity from creeping between us.

I wanted Alessandra back in our bed, our house, our *life*. I'd been missing a vital piece of myself since she walked out, and it was incredible to think I'd somehow taken her for granted when I needed her more than I needed to breathe.

"Come home." My raw plea whispered over her mouth.

Alessandra closed her eyes, her expression torn. She might've relented. I felt the softening of her shoulders, detected a telltale change in the rhythm of her breaths, but before she could respond, a shrill ring ripped through the air.

*Fuck.* I pulled back and ended the incoming call. It was from that fucking unknown number again, but when I glanced up less than five seconds later, I could tell I'd already lost her.

Panic dug vicious claws into my gut. "Ále—"

"I can't." Her anguished response landed with sickening finality. *I can't.*

I spent my life dealing with lengthy contracts and complex calculations, but it was funny how two simple words could devastate me with the brutal efficacy of a nuclear bomb.

The next beat stretched painfully between us before she pushed me away and slid off the counter. I didn't say anything when she fixed her clothes, and I didn't stop her when she left without meeting my eyes.

*I can't.* What was there to say after that?

It was only when the door clicked shut behind her that my numbness shattered.

"Dammit!" I slammed my fist against the counter. Pain exploded, both from the impact of flesh against marble and from her departure.

I'd pushed her too far, too fast, and now I risked her throwing her guard up even more. All for a kiss and several stolen minutes alone.

*Was it worth it?* a voice whispered.

*Yes.* The answer came without thought.

She was always worth it.

I'd take any moment with her, no matter how quick or fleeting, because I didn't know how many we had left.

I closed my eyes, my head pounding with each heartbeat. I hadn't felt this uncertain since I was a teenager on the fringes of a shithole town, and I hated it. I'd poured a lot of time and money into stamping out any potential loss of control, but it took only one response from Alessandra to unravel my efforts.

I waited until the sharpest spikes of my migraine passed before I straightened. By the time I exited the bathroom, I'd ruthlessly forced my outward composure back into place, but I was so lost in my thoughts, I didn't notice the shadow waiting for me until it peeled off the wall and stepped into the light.

I almost stepped around him before his face came into focus.

A fist of shock punched through my turmoil over Alessandra. *No. It can't be.*

Knife-blade cheekbones slashed through the dark, and jet-black hair matched the color of his T-shirt, pants, and boots. He'd changed plenty over the years—smooth skin had given way to dark stubble; teenage lankiness had morphed into solid muscle.

But those eyes were the same. The distinctive green orbs glittered, cold and amused, beneath the hallway's dim lighting.

The noise and music from the bar became indiscernible as blood thundered in my ears.

Any hope I'd had of him being an uncanny doppelgänger vanished when a mocking smile stretched across his face.

"Hello, brother."

# CHAPTER 12

*Alessandra*

I WOULD NEVER DRINK GIN AND TONICS OR APPLE martinis again. They were fine and well when it was nighttime and I was high off the buzz, but in the bright light of morning, my recent exploits with Dominic brought a deep flush to my skin.

I couldn't believe I'd let him kiss me. I couldn't believe I'd kissed him *back* and followed him into a bar bathroom, of all places, where I'd orgasmed so hard my toes curled just thinking about it.

I groaned, banging my forehead lightly against the cabinet while I waited for the coffee to brew. Thank God Sloane was still in Europe, or she'd instantly know something was up. That woman had a bloodhound's nose for sniffing out secrets.

*What would tonight look like if things were different?*

*A kiss. Just one.*

*Shh. Patience.*

My skin heated at the memory of Dominic's mouth and hands. Kissing, caressing, exploring. Bringing me expertly over the edge as only he could do. For all our problems over the years, physical attraction had never been one of them. Even at our lowest point, the sex had always been good.

"At least you didn't go home with him," I muttered.

I'd almost caved. Alcohol and sex had already done a number on my judgment, and his uncharacteristic vulnerability would've been the final straw.

*Thank God for that call.* Obviously, the universe had been looking out for me because I refused to be someone who ran back to her partner after a few pretty words and a nice—okay, a spectacular—orgasm.

Last night had been a fluke. It was never going to happen again, especially not after the divorce went through—and it *would* go through.

The coffee finished brewing. I poured myself a cup and ignored the singsong voice in my head that said I could blame the alcohol all I wanted, but there was a part of me that had *wanted* to go home with him.

It was the middle of the workweek. I had orders to complete, bills to pay, and a business to run. What I *didn't* have was time to agonize over my bad decisions.

I ate a quick breakfast and poured myself a second cup of coffee before hunkering down at my desk.

No Dominic. No divorce. Just work.

Luckily, I had plenty of emails and meetings to keep me busy through the morning. I'd hired two assistants to manage logistics and customer service last year, and I'd just finished a video call with them when my cell rang.

"Hello?" I picked up without checking the caller ID first, too distracted by a new order requesting I create a pressed flowers collage shaped like the customer's wife's vagina. The sad part was, it wasn't the strangest request I'd ever gotten.

"Hi, I'm looking for Alessandra Ferreira," a deep male voice rumbled over the line.

All thoughts of floral vaginas flew out of my head.

I straightened, my heart picking up speed. I'd only used my maiden name once recently. "Speaking."

"This is Aiden Clarke returning your message from yesterday. You were interested in learning more about the storefront in NoMad."

"Yes." The word squeaked out at an embarrassing pitch. I cleared my throat and tried again. "I mean yes, I am."

Honestly, I'd forgotten about the storefront until his call. It'd seemed like a good idea yesterday, but I knew *nothing* about opening a physical store. Then again, I hadn't known anything about operating an online business until I did it, so there was something to be said for taking the jump.

Dreams were worth chasing.

After a brief screening, Aiden offered a tour and meeting for later that day. I accepted without hesitation. No risk, no reward, right?

I sped through the rest of my work and arrived at the storefront after lunch, overcaffeinated and breathless after nearly getting mowed down by a speeding cab.

My eyes searched the sidewalk for a shiny suit and professionally whitened smile—the hallmarks of a New York Realtor—but I only saw a man who could double as a lumberjack in his flannel shirt and jeans.

"Alessandra? I'm Aiden," he said. "Glad you could make it, and sorry again about the last-minute meeting. I have a business trip tomorrow and don't quite know when I'll be back."

"No problem." I tried to hide my surprise. He was younger and better-looking than I'd expected. Late thirties at most, with dark brown hair and a neatly trimmed beard. Combined with his casual outfit and friendly demeanor, he looked like he should be buying everyone a round of beer at the nearest pub instead of managing prime real estate. "Thanks for getting back to me so quickly."

"Not a problem. I'm a bit compulsive about returning calls." His eyes crinkled with a grin. "According to my best friend, it's why I'm still single. I can't stick to the *wait three days until you call* rule."

I laughed. "It's a stupid rule anyway."

I did wonder briefly if he was hitting on me by bringing up his relationship status so early, but I brushed the sentiment aside. We'd just met, and I wasn't narcissistic enough to think every man who saw me was interested in me.

Aiden didn't give off any flirty vibes again during our tour, so I chalked up his quip to mere friendliness.

The walk-through was quick given how small the space was. In addition to the main floor, there was a bathroom and another room that could serve as an office and/or a supply closet. Aiden was honest about the parts of the interior that needed work, which I appreciated, and he listened attentively when I explained what I wanted to do with my business.

"How much is the rent?" I asked at the end of the tour. I probably should've confirmed that at the beginning, but I'd been too enamored by the exposed brick walls and natural light to think about the details.

When Aiden quoted me the price, I flinched. I *definitely* should've asked about the price first. There was no way I could afford it with my shop's current profits, and I didn't want to complicate the divorce by using my and Dominic's joint bank account.

"I'll be honest. I own several properties in the city, but this one is my favorite." Aiden rapped his knuckles against the wall. "It's a fixer-upper, but it has charm."

I would've chalked his words up to Realtor talk if I didn't agree. "You own it personally?"

"Yep. My father bought a couple of places for cheap back in the day, and I added to it. We rent out to about a dozen businesses across the city." Another flash of a smile. City landlords were rarely *nice,* and I couldn't wrap my head around the fact that this man owned millions of dollars' worth of real estate. "This is the only vacant space left. It used to be a bakery, but the previous owners retired a couple of months ago and I haven't found anyone to replace them. I'm pretty hands-on with my tenants—they have my number and know they can call any time of day if there's a problem—so I like to find ones I click with."

*Dammit.* A great location, a nice landlord, *and* brick walls? It was the perfect space…if it didn't cost an arm and two legs every month.

"That's great." I swallowed the disappointment building in my throat. "I'll be honest, I love the space, I really do, but I can't afford it. I should've asked before you came all the way here." I gestured around the sun-dappled main room. "I'm sorry for wasting your time."

"You didn't. As someone who can't tell one type of lily from another, I'm impressed by what you want to do." Aiden examined me. "Do you have a lawyer? I'm happy to negotiate with them."

I had a feeling Cole's family law expertise didn't count. "No," I admitted.

Aiden frowned. He probably thought I was ridiculous, and I didn't blame him. People *planned* for milestones like this. Meanwhile, I just walked by the storefront one day and decided I wanted to rent it.

Heat prickled my skin.

"How about this?" he finally said. "If you pay a portion of the construction costs and agree to a longer lease period, I'll give you three months' free rent. It should help with initial costs while you get your shop off the ground."

My eyes jerked back to his. "Why would you do that?" Surprise had dissolved my normal filters, and I didn't have time to phrase the question in a more tactful way.

"Vacancy is expensive, and I'd rather not spend more time interviewing potential tenants than necessary," Aiden said. "Like I said, I want people I click with, and even though we just met, I can tell you're one of them. Pay your rent on time, keep the shop in good condition, and we'll get along swimmingly."

I drew my bottom lip between my teeth.

If something sounded too good to be true, it probably was. The last thing I needed was to get scammed into some ruinous real estate scam.

Aiden must've picked up on my hesitation because he added, "I know this is moving fast, but it's hard to find good tenants in the city. When I see one, I tend to snatch them up. I'll email you a lease with the amended terms so you can have a lawyer look it over. You don't have to decide now, but I would like an answer within the next two weeks." He held out his hand. "Deal?"

That sounded fair enough to me. I didn't want to use Dominic's lawyers, but one of my friends must know someone who could help me out.

I shook Aiden's hand, my stomach fluttering with nerves and a hint of excitement. "Deal."

---

"He wants to bang you," Isabella said the following night as we walked into Le Boudoir. "There's no way a *New York City* landlord would be *that* nice unless he has ulterior motives."

"No, he doesn't. He has his own business reasons for giving me free rent." I'd researched it after returning home from the tour yesterday, and it was a common "perk" landlords offered during negotiations.

"Yeah, but the fact he brought it up without you having to ask?" Isabella arched an eyebrow. "Suspicious."

"I agree." Vivian slid out of her lush faux fur coat and handed it to the coat check attendant. "Especially since he's around your age and single. You didn't see a wedding ring, right?"

During our walk to the restaurant, I'd told my friends what happened with Aiden and I already regretted it. Sloane was the only one missing from the gang-up because she was still in Europe.

"You guys are ridiculous," I said. "Not everyone has an ulterior motive. Besides, he hasn't sent the papers yet. Until I have a lawyer look over them, nothing's concrete."

I shot a quick glance at Dante and Kai, who were trying their best to pretend they weren't listening. They'd stayed several steps behind us on the walk over, but I knew they'd heard everything. Considering they were good friends with Dominic, the conversation must have been as awkward for them as it was for me.

Luckily, my friends' ridiculous assumptions about Aiden's motives dissolved into greetings and small talk as other guests came over to say hi.

Le Boudoir was the latest jewel in the Laurent Restaurant Group's crown, and most of Manhattan's elite had turned out for its exclusive soft opening. I'd stayed away from society events the past few weeks because I didn't want to face the inevitable questions about Dominic—no one gossiped more than the rich and idle—but my friends had convinced me to make an exception. It was a small event, it was hosted by Sebastian Laurent, and there was zero chance of Dominic attending since, according to Dante, he was supposed to be en route to London right now.

Key phrase: *supposed to be.*

My stomach plunged into free fall when I stepped into the main dining room and instantly spotted a familiar head of dark blond hair by the bar. I didn't even have to look for him; his presence was like gravity drawing me in whether I wanted it to or not.

"You said he was traveling to London," Vivian whispered, glaring at her husband.

"I said he was *supposed* to be traveling to London," Dante corrected. "It seems he, ah, had a change in plans."

I didn't hear the rest of their conversation. Everything—the music, the guests, the servers circling with trays of champagne—dulled into a muted roar when Dominic glanced up from his conversation with Sebastian. Our gazes collided, dark blue against light, and the impact almost knocked my knees out from under me.

My heartbeat slowed to a painful rhythm. We'd been married for a decade, yet seeing him here after last night was like laying eyes on him for the first time all over again.

*"You must be Dominic. I'm Alessandra, but my friends call me Ále." I smiled, trying to hide an unexpected spark of attraction.*

*Even with his glare and cold, stoic expression, Dominic was jaw-droppingly gorgeous. But beyond the chiseled bone structure and muscled build, there was something about him that tugged at my heart.*

*I recognized the suspicion lurking behind his eyes. It was the type of suspicion born from being let down one too many times by the people around him. My brother had carried the same chip on his shoulder for years before he found his crowd. Maybe that was why I had a soft spot for him even though we just met; his guardedness reminded me of Marcelo's, which used to be mistaken for standoffishness.*

*"Hello, Alessandra." Dominic's careful enunciation of my full name told me breaking down his walls would be a challenge. Luckily, I thrived on challenges.*

*But when he sat across from me, and a small swarm of butterflies erupted at the brush of his jeans against my leg, I realized I might already be in well over my head.*

Present-day Dominic's throat flexed. He wasn't paying an ounce of attention to Sebastian, and I wanted to look away, to act like everything was fine and I wasn't affected by his presence, but his gaze chained me to the spot.

I hated the effect he had on me. I hated how my eyes always went to him in a room full of people and how I couldn't stop thinking about him no matter how hard I tried. Most of all, I hated how I couldn't hate him, not even a little bit. No matter how many times he broke my heart, there would always be a piece that belonged to him.

A familiar ache unfurled behind my ribs.

Dominic shifted as if to walk toward me, but someone bumped into my side and finally dragged my attention away from the bar.

An iron grip closed around my elbow, steadying me. "Apologies." The low, cool voice sounded like the aural equivalent of a razor blade wrapped in silk.

"It's…" My sentence faltered when I looked up.

A brutally handsome man with green eyes, pale skin, and the sharpest jawline I'd ever seen stared back at me. Despite his good looks, something about him instantly put me on red alert.

He removed his hand from my arm and offered an apologetic smile that didn't reach those cold, flat eyes.

The hairs on the back of my neck rose. Before I could say anything else, he disappeared into the crowd and left me with an unsettling sense of foreboding.

The foreboding intensified when I returned my gaze to the bar only to find Dominic gone, like he'd never been there at all.

# CHAPTER 13

## Dominic

"WHAT THE *HELL* ARE YOU DOING HERE?" I SLAMMED
Roman up against the wall, my words dripping with venom in the
dark hallway.

Running into him last night could've been a fluke, but two
nights in a row? That wasn't a coincidence. Not when Roman was
involved.

I'd hired a private contractor I'd worked with in the past to
look into him the instant I left the bar, but they hadn't unearthed
anything yet. That in and of itself was concerning; they usually
had a full report for me within twelve hours, which meant Roman
was damn good at covering his tracks.

And the only reason someone would cover his tracks was if he
had something to hide.

"Attending a restaurant opening, just like you and your *lovely*
wife," he drawled, seemingly unfazed by my hostile greeting.
"My wedding invite got lost in the mail, but she's beautiful. I see
why you can't take your eyes off her."

Arctic needles of fear pierced my spine, followed by the slow
simmer of rage. "You touch a single strand of hair on her head,"

I said softly. "And there won't be a place on earth where I won't hunt you down and kill you so slowly you'll be begging for death."

My arm pressed tighter against his throat. He didn't flinch, but something flashed in his eyes before it submerged beneath pools of green ice. "You didn't find me all these years. Not until I showed up right in front of your face."

"I wasn't looking."

"No. You were too busy building your empire to remember your dear brother." His mouth curled with a mirthless smile. "How does the money taste, Dom? As good as you'd always dreamed of?"

*Goddammit.* I let out a low curse and released my hold, but I kept myself between him and the dining room. "I'll ask you again. What the fuck are you really doing here, and how the hell do you know Sebastian?"

I'd intercepted him on his way out of the bathroom after he ran into Alessandra. It was a role reversal from last night, when he'd left without answering any of my questions about where he'd been, how he found me, and why he'd showed up again after over a decade of silence.

"You're not the only one with connections." Roman straightened his jacket. He'd dressed up for the opening, but even in designer clothing, he exuded trouble. "We're a long way from Whittlesburg, aren't we?"

My jaw clenched, his presence and the mention of our hometown unearthing memories that were better left buried.

*"We'll both make it out of here one day." Roman's eyes glinted with a stony determination that belonged to someone older than his fourteen years. A dark bruise marred his face from where our foster mom had hit him. "And when we do, everyone will pay."*

Roman and I had been foster siblings in my fourth home. He was only a year younger than me, and he'd been the closest thing I had to an ally in that hellhole until he fell in with the wrong crowd and landed in juvie for arson my senior year of high school. I'd refused to provide him with a fake alibi; I'd just been accepted to Thayer, and I couldn't risk upending my future over someone else's criminal offense. I hadn't seen or heard from him since.

Until last night.

"Don't worry. I won't touch your precious wife. I simply wanted to say hi even if I shouldn't." The flash of earlier emotion resurfaced and disappeared as quickly as before. "If you don't want people to find you, you shouldn't splash your face all over the *Wall Street Journal* and society papers." Roman brushed past me. "Now if you'll excuse me, I have a dinner party to return to."

He made it to the end of the hall before I spoke.

"Tell me you're not in trouble again." I shouldn't care. We'd cut ties long ago, but a small part of me couldn't shake off my guilt over leaving him in Ohio. He'd made his choices, and I'd made mine, but once upon a time, he'd been the only real family I had.

Roman stopped, his frame falling so still he resembled a statue backlit by the restaurant lights.

"Don't act like you care," he said. "It doesn't suit you."

---

The first half of dinner passed without incident, but I barely tasted my food. I was too distracted both by Alessandra, who sat at one end of the table, and Roman, who sat at the other.

He was up to something. He had to be, and my suspicions only grew after Sebastian admitted he didn't know him personally. Someone on his team had sent Roman the invite.

Meanwhile, Alessandra was doing her best to pretend I didn't exist, though I caught her looking at me a few times when she thought I wasn't paying attention. It should've made me feel better. Instead, her proximity to Roman, who was smart enough to detect and exploit the tension between us, made me want to leave dinner and drag her with me to safety, etiquette be damned.

"Stop staring," Dante said without looking at me. "You're about as subtle as a sledgehammer."

"Look who's talking." He was infamous for his heavy-handed tactics when it came to punishing people who'd crossed him. Broken bones, comas, the whole shebang.

Nevertheless, I tore my eyes away from where Alessandra was laughing with Vivian and Isabella. We needed to talk about what happened at the bar, which would be easier if I could actually get her alone. I only came tonight to see her, but her friends were like bodyguards who refused to leave her side. I should—

A loud clatter broke through the hum of conversation, followed by a fit of choking and wheezing. It cut off abruptly, and the dining room quieted as I jerked my head toward the previous commotion.

One of the guests had collapsed face down in his plate. Blue suit, distinctive silver hair. Martin Wellgrew, the CEO of Orion Bank.

Sebastian was out of his seat in a flash. "What happened?" he demanded.

"I don't know. We were talking and then he…he just collapsed," the woman sitting next to Martin stuttered. "Is he okay? He's not moving. Oh God…what if…"

I could hear a pin drop while Sebastian checked Martin's pulse. He sucked in a breath, and I knew what he was going to say before he said it.

"He's dead."

There was a moment of stunned silence before pandemonium erupted. Half the guests rushed for the exit while the other half ran to the restrooms, presumably in case the food had caused Martin's sudden death. They nearly trampled each other in their haste, and

I lost sight of my friends in the mayhem. However, I was only interested in finding one person.

*Alessandra.*

I pushed through the crowd, my heart ricocheting in my chest. A familiar buzz drowned out the mounting hysteria in the room. I didn't know what happened with Martin, but I needed to see her and make sure she was okay. She could be hurt, trampled, unconscious...

The buzz sawed through my head with high-pitched frequency. Fuck, why was it so hot in here?

Sweat slicked my palms as I searched for brown hair and a red dress. *Come on, baby, where are you?*

The restaurant was small, and it was chaos as I tried to sort through the crush of people.

Black hair. Black dress. Gray hair. Navy suit. The guests blurred into a generic entity. Someone bumped into me, and I was about to push them off when I looked down and a familiar pair of blue-gray eyes met mine.

Relief knocked the breath out of my lungs. *She's okay.*

We stared at each other for a suspended second, our chests heaving with adrenaline, before another guest jostled us and spurred us into action again.

She didn't resist when I gripped her wrist and wrestled us toward the exit. The police had just arrived on the scene, but we managed to slip into a cab without them stopping us. I was sure they'd follow up with every guest later about Martin's death, but I had zero desire to wait around and play concerned witness at the moment.

Alessandra remained quiet when I gave the driver the penthouse's address. She seemed shell-shocked by the evening's jarring turn of events, and I didn't blame her. I'd attended hundreds of society gatherings over the years; none of them had ended in death.

Then again, none of them had had Roman as a guest.

I hadn't seen him since Martin's collapse. Not in the stampede toward the exit and bathrooms, and not outside the restaurant.

A tight knot of dread formed in my stomach. Between the SEC investigation into DBG and Martin's death, there was a suspicious number of crises involving the banking industry. I didn't know where Roman's sudden reappearance fit in, but it was a piece of the larger puzzle. I felt it in my gut.

"Well," Alessandra said as we pulled up to our building. I still thought of it as ours, even though it hadn't felt like home since she left. "That was the most memorable dessert course I've ever had."

Despite my trepidation, a smile ghosted my mouth. I'd missed her little quips. Her sense of humor was one of the many reasons I'd fallen in love with her, but it'd made fewer and fewer appearances over the years.

Contrition extinguished my temporary amusement.

"Sebastian is going to have a PR nightmare on his hands," I said. I wasn't a fan of Martin, who'd been notoriously corrupt and underhanded when he'd been alive, so I couldn't say I was too torn up over his death. However, its circumstances and timing would have massive ripple effects to come.

"I bet." Alessandra's fingers tightened around the edge of her seat. "Oh God. Someone *died*. He was sitting right across…he…"

Her breaths shallowed. *Fuck.*

I quickly paid the driver and ushered her into the building and up to the penthouse before she went into shock again.

"It was likely an allergic reaction." I doubted it, but if it made her feel better, that was what I was going with. "Unfortunate timing, but it happens. There was nothing you could do about it."

Still, I wrapped her in a blanket and brought her a mug of tea when we entered the penthouse. The staff had clocked out for the night, so the living room was silent as she curled her hands around the drink.

"You probably think I'm overreacting." She stared into the mug, her face unreadable. If she had any feelings about being home for the first time in weeks, she didn't show it.

Emotion tangled in my throat. "I don't. Seeing someone terminate in front of you is pretty traumatic."

Alessandra's brow arched a fraction of an inch. "Terminate?"

"It sounded better than *die* in my head." I rubbed a hand over my mouth. "It doesn't, does it?"

"No. Not really." Her soft laugh warmed the room. Our gazes lingered on each other, and her smile slowly faded as silence descended again. This time, it was a poignant silence, filled with memories and regrets and, perhaps, the tiniest bit of hope.

"Can I confess something?" Her voice was barely audible. "When the chaos erupted and everyone was running, you were the first person I looked for. I didn't want to, but I did."

My heartbeats pulsed like they were finally alive.

"Good," I said quietly. "Because I was looking for you too."

The rest of our unspoken words spilled around us, one spark away from igniting.

Alessandra's eyes darkened, and the spark flared to life. Flames of emotion surged through the air, incinerating any inhibitions or rational thought. The only thing left was a gnawing, insatiable desire to kiss her before I died of deprivation.

She must've read the intentions scrawled over my face because her breaths turned ragged. Her lips parted, and that was all the invitation I needed.

One second, we were sitting on opposite ends of the couch. The next, my mouth was on hers, her body was against mine, and we were stumbling into the elevator in a tangle of pent-up longing and heightened adrenaline. Thank god for the penthouse's private lift because there was no chance in hell we could make it up the stairs without injuring ourselves. Not when my blood was on fire and Alessandra was grasping my hair with a desperation that cut into my soul.

We somehow made it to the bedroom in one piece. I kicked the door shut behind us, and our clothes fell to the floor with little care.

Dress. Shoes. Shirt. Underwear.

They left a rumpled trail behind us as we fell onto the bed. I kissed my way down her neck and chest while my fingers found the heat between her legs.

So wet. So perfect. So *mine*.

Alessandra let out a small whimper when I closed my mouth around her nipple, licking and sucking until she pulled my hair hard enough to hurt.

"Please," she panted, bucked against my hand in a fruitless search for more friction. "More. I need more."

"More what?" I grazed my teeth over her nipples and soothed them with soft, leisurely licks. One hand forced her writhing hips still while the other played with her clit, lingering on the spots that drove her wild. "Tell me what you want, *amor*."

"I want...*oh God*." Her hands fisted the sheets as I continued my journey down her torso. My mouth trailed between her breasts, down her stomach and over the smooth rise of her pubic bone. Her skin was hot to the touch, and tiny trembles wracked her body the closer I got to her clit.

I paused at the juncture of her thighs and looked up, soaking in the sight of her flushed face and glazed eyes.

"I asked you a question," I said calmly. I pushed a finger inside her, eliciting another cry. "Tell me what you want, or I'll keep you here all night."

"I want you inside me," Alessandra panted. She squirmed, clenching around me with obvious need.

"I am inside you." I added a second finger, withdrew, then pumped inside her again with agonizing slowness. My body practically vibrated with the need to thrust inside her and taste her cries as she came, but I wanted to draw this out as long as possible and savor every second. "Be more specific."

"Fuck me." Her plea escaped as a gasp. "I want your cock inside me. Please."

Her words nearly undid me. I groaned, sweat beading my forehead as I pulled my fingers out and buried my face between her legs.

"Not yet." I circled her clit with my tongue, letting the taste and scent of her distract me from the ache in my cock. "I want you to come on my face first. Show me how much you want it."

Alessandra's pleas morphed into unintelligible sobs as I feasted on every inch of her. I loved the way she arched into me, greedy and searching. I loved how she panted my name and pulled on my hair. I loved *her,* and I'd missed having her in my arms so damn bad that I would give up every possession just to freeze this moment in time.

I gripped her thighs and rested her legs on my shoulders so I could thrust my tongue inside her. I locked her ruthlessly in place as I tongue fucked her, letting her sobs of pleasure drive me faster and harder until she finally came with a shuddering climax.

Her arousal drenched my senses, and I couldn't take it anymore.

A quick shift in positions and I was inside her, sinking in slowly for both our sakes. Her because she was hypersensitized from her recent orgasm, me because she felt so good I had to grit my teeth and silently run through the Yankees roster before I embarrassed myself.

I exhaled deep, ragged breaths each time I pulled out and pushed in, making sure to hit her most sensitive spots instead of pushing her into the mattress and fucking her brains out like my baser instincts screamed at me to do.

My wife was home, and I'd be damned if I wasted the night on a one and done deal.

Alessandra clung to me as I drove into her, harder and faster, until she was gasping for air. My hands fisted on the mattress; my breaths grew choppier. The headboard slammed against the wall with each thrust, and even though I should've known better, I made the mistake of looking down at where we were joined.

It was the end of me because seeing my cock slide in and out of her—seeing how perfectly we fit and how fucking well she took me—was so fucking hot and primal that my orgasm peaked without warning. It climbed up my spine, snapping my restraints and driving me to fuck her deeper with long, savage strokes until she fell apart with another scream.

It'd barely faded before my own climax exploded. It flayed me raw, contracting my muscles and heightening my senses to the point where I might die from the stimulation. Alessandra's nails clawed at my back, prolonging our waves of pleasure, and as we rode them out together, I had the dim thought that if I did die, I would do so happily because I was exactly where I belonged: with her.

# CHAPTER 14

## Dominic

IT SMELLED LIKE LILIES AND RAIN MIXED WITH GOLDEN warmth. It smelled like *her*, and it was so damn intoxicating I couldn't bring myself to open my eyes even though the strength of the sun on my skin told me it was late morning.

I was usually in the office by six, but I didn't want to wake up and find out last night had been a dream. There'd been too many of those, and too many subsequent showers where I'd washed off my disappointment over Alessandra's absence in real life.

Snippets from the previous evening floated past my mind's eye. Seeing her at the restaurant, bringing her home, our kiss and what came after...

A niggling feeling told me I was forgetting an important piece of the puzzle, but I'd deal with that later. She was home where she belonged, and I—

The soft rustle of clothes dragged me out of my slumberous bliss.

I cracked my eyes open, my stomach hollowing when I saw the bed beside me was empty. Another rustle wrenched my attention to the corner where Alessandra was pulling her dress over her head. The sunlight bathed her in an ethereal glow—hair shot through with gold, skin a deep bronze against red silk. She had her back to me, but she was etched so thoroughly in my brain I could picture every flicker in her expression. Feel every curve, map every dip and valley I'd spent hours worshiping last night.

Her dress spilled over her thighs, and she zipped up the back with agonizing care. She didn't want to wake me, which meant...

My stomach hollowed further. "Where are you going?"

My question echoed like a gunshot in the silence. Alessandra froze for a second before she resumed dressing. "Back to Sloane's. I have a lot of work to do."

"I see." I got out of bed, my movements slow and precise. Controlled, unlike the dread and anger flaring in my chest. "Were you planning to say goodbye, or were you going to sneak out like I'm a one-night stand you regret?"

No reply.

*Goddammit.* I'd thought we were making progress, but I could feel her slipping away before I truly had a chance to have her again.

"What happened last night—"

"Was a mistake." Her fingers shook as she smoothed the front of her dress. "And so was what happened at the bar."

"It didn't sound like a mistake when you were screaming my name and begging me to let you come." My silken response didn't match the thorny vines creeping through my chest. The more seconds that passed, the deeper they gouged.

Scarlet washed over Alessandra's face. "It was just sex." Her voice wobbled on the word *sex,* but her body remained stiff and unyielding as I crossed the room to stand in front of her. "It didn't mean anything."

"Bullshit." I'd seen the way she looked at me and heard the way she whispered my name. Neither of us did "just sex," much less with each other.

"Our sex life wasn't an issue, but we can't *solve* our issues with sex." Alessandra finally met my eyes, her expression locked tight behind a steel wall. "I was drunk at the bar, and we were caught up in the adrenaline of what happened at Le Boudoir last night. There were too many emotions flying around that had nothing to do with *this*." She gestured between us.

Le Boudoir. Roman. *Fuck*. That was a whole other mess, but I'd deal with it later. For now, I focused all my energy on breathing through the strangling knot in the back of my throat. Beneath it, a fresh ember of anger sparked, and I grasped at it like a drowning man at rope.

"So what? You're going to walk out and pretend like nothing happened? What are you going to do, Alessandra?" I bit out. "Run to your fancy divorce lawyer and ask him to do your dirty work for you again because you're too scared to face me yourself?"

An audible inhale. "Fuck you."

"You already did."

I saw it coming, but the crack of her palm against my cheek hurt more than I'd expected. The fire spread from my face to my chest, where it ate away at the pieces of my heart while Alessandra and I stared at each other, our breaths jagged.

"I'm…I didn't mean…" She faltered, looking stunned.

My anger drained so quickly I didn't have time to register its loss, and the cold shock of remorse took its place.

This wasn't supposed to happen. Broken relationships belonged in the past with the old Dominic, who had nothing to keep people around. No one had cared about me until I made something of myself. The more money I accumulated, the more people gravitated toward me. It was a law of human nature. I wasn't supposed to lose the only person I cared about keeping now, when I was richer than I'd ever been.

"*Get out of my classroom.*"

"*You stupid, stupid boy. No wonder your own mother abandoned you…*"

"*Your current foster parents have requested you be moved to a different home…*"

I forced the memories at bay. I didn't live in that world anymore, and I would rather die than return.

I touched my cheek. The aftermath of Alessandra's slap stung less than the chasm between us. She stood less than a foot away, but we might as well be on different continents.

In a distant part of the house, the sound of a vacuum started up and severed the spell keeping us frozen. Alessandra turned, and I grasped her wrist before she could leave.

"Don't." My heart fought to break out of my chest with vicious blows. "I'm sorry, *amor*."

I'd been an asshole, but when my only choices were pain or anger, my instinct was to seek shelter in the latter.

She exhaled a shuddering breath. "Let me go."

My grip tightened. She wasn't talking about just this moment, and we both knew it.

"I wish I could." It would be easier if I never fell for her. I went into our first meeting determined to hate her, not knowing she would be the one who showed me what real love was instead. I might not have expressed it as often as I should've, but she'd always been the sun keeping my world in orbit.

Alessandra shook her head, her cheeks shining with wetness. "Dominic, it's over. Accept it. You're only dragging out the inevitable."

Accept it, my ass. This couldn't be it. Not for us, not after last night.

"Then why can't you look at me?" I demanded.

She shook her head again, her shoulders trembling with silent sobs.

"Dammit, Ále." A small, humiliating crack split her name in half. I was breaking into a million pieces, and she couldn't even be bothered to notice. "Can you honestly look me in the eye and tell me you don't love me anymore?"

"Loving you was *never* the problem!" She finally met my eyes, her expression equal parts infuriated and anguished. "I've loved you for eleven years, Dom. I loved you so much I lost myself. Everything I did, everything I gave up and endured was for *you*. The late nights, the missed dates, the canceled trips. I believed in you and wanted you to succeed, not because I cared about the money, but because *you* did. I thought one day, it would be enough, and you would be happy with what we had. But you'll never be happy, and I'll never be enough."

A bitter laugh mixed with her sob. "Do you know that there were times when I *wished* you had a mistress? At least then, I would have something concrete to fight. But I can't fight what I can't see, so I went to sleep every night in an empty bed, and I woke up every morning to an empty house. I faked my smiles for so long I couldn't remember what a real one felt like, and I hate myself because despite all that, I couldn't let go of what we once had." Alessandra's voice broke. "You're right. I do still love you. A part of me always will. But you're not the person I fell in love with anymore, and all this time that I've spent trying to pretend you are? It's killing me."

The room blurred, and a painful roar filled my ears as I dropped her arm.

I couldn't draw enough oxygen into my lungs. Couldn't think clearly. Couldn't *breathe*.

Throughout it all—the long weeks, the ignored calls, even the damn divorce papers—I'd thought we would make it. After all, perseverance had gotten me this far. The unwanted foster kid from Ohio turned king of Wall Street. The pauper turned billionaire. The unlovable turned husband.

But perseverance crumbled in the face of truth, and Alessandra's truth smashed any excuses I might've had to smithereens. So I went with my own truth, the only one that had remained indisputable since the day she walked into my life.

"You're the only person I've ever loved." I didn't recognize my voice. It was too raw, too laced with emotions I'd sworn I would never feel. "Even if I didn't show it. It's always been you."

A fresh tear slid down her cheek. "I know."

*But it's not enough.*

I knew her well enough to hear the unspoken words, and if it was possible to die multiple deaths, I would've visited hell a thousandfold in that one moment.

"If you really loved me," Alessandra whispered, "you would let me go. Please."

Silence echoed, deep and mournful. There was nothing left to say.

A strange, watery film obstructed my vision, so I relied on muscle memory to navigate to the nightstand. Shards of glass wedged between my ribs with each step, but an icy numbness enveloped me as I opened the top drawer.

I retrieved a pen, slid a sheaf of documents out from the waiting manila envelope, and, after one last, agonizing heartbeat, I signed our divorce papers.

# CHAPTER 15

*Alessandra*

IT WAS OFFICIAL. I WAS DIVORCED.

The papers went through exactly six weeks after Dominic signed them. Most divorces took three to six months in New York, but Cole managed to pull some strings and expedite the process.

I thought I would feel different. Lighter, freer, *happier,* but I only felt numb as I went through the motions of setting up my shop.

I'd had a lawyer look over the lease Aiden sent and it all looked good, so things had moved as quickly on that front as they had for my divorce.

"Ále. *Ále!*"

I startled at my name. The coffee I was pouring overflowed from its mug and spilled onto my temporary desk.

"*Merda!*" I cursed and scrambled to shove papers out of the way before they got soaked. My friends helped, though I suspected their tangible worry had less to do with ruined order sheets and more to do with me.

Isabella was drafting her next novel in the shop since the construction noise "helped her focus," and Vivian and Sloane had dropped by on their lunch breaks. It was out of the way for both of them, but they'd been extra solicitous since the divorce.

"Here." Vivian ripped a paper towel off a nearby roll and handed it to me so I could wipe the coffee off my skin. "Are you okay? Do you need ice?"

"I'm fine." Luckily, the liquid had already been lukewarm when I poured it. "I just got lost in thought."

She exchanged glances with Isabella and Sloane. The sounds of drills and construction from the bathroom filled the silence. Workers had been coming in and out for the past two weeks, renovating the old interiors and installing new tiling. The store wouldn't be ready for at least another three or four months, but at least the prep would keep me busy through the holidays.

My first holiday season without Dominic in a decade.

"Thinking about him again?" Isabella asked softly during a lull in the noise.

"It's inevitable." I forced a smile. "We were married for so long. It'll take me time to adjust."

My friends tried their best to take my mind off him. We went out dancing, took a weekend road trip to see the fall colors in New Hampshire, and gorged on popcorn with jalapeño peppers while watching Sloane's much hated/loved rom-coms. It worked in the moment, but when I was alone, the hollow in my chest returned with a vengeance.

"Exactly. You need to adjust." Sloane tossed her empty salad bowl into the trash. "Which is exactly why you should jump into the dating pool again. The best way to forget the old is to move on with the new."

Vivian shook her head. "It's too soon. Let her enjoy being single."

"Dating *is* part of the single experience," Sloane countered. "I'm not saying she should jump into another relationship, but she should at least get a feel for what else is out there. It'll help take her mind off—"

"*She* is standing right here." I interrupted before she could say Dominic's name. I hadn't gone on a date with anyone else in so long that the mere thought made me itch with anxiety. "Don't I get a say in this?"

"Of course you do." Sloane's phone buzzed. She glanced at it, her fingers flying over the screen as she dealt with whatever new PR crisis had just popped up. "But you've spent *eleven years* with the same man. It's time to broaden your horizons. Think about it."

Despite my best efforts, her words echoed in my head for the rest of the afternoon. I'd gone on a handful of dates that never went anywhere before Dominic, but I'd never been a one-night stand person. I needed an emotional connection for sex. Then again, I wasn't twenty-one anymore. Maybe Sloane was right and I *should* broaden my horizons. There was no harm in trying, right?

The construction workers left, and I was preparing to lock up when the door opened and Aiden walked in. He wore his standard uniform of flannel and jeans, and his warm smile flashed white against his beard.

"I was in the area and thought I'd drop by," he explained. He handed me a to-go cup from the coffee shop down the street. "Matcha. Figured you don't need espresso this late in the day."

"Thank you." I took a grateful sip and examined him over the paper rim.

Aiden hadn't been joking when he'd said he was hands-on with his tenants. He checked up on me frequently, not in a creepy or overbearing way but in a helpful way—probably because he knew I had zero experience opening a retail store—and he'd referred me to his trusted contractors when I was overwhelmed by the choices.

"How are things going?" he asked. "The guys aren't giving you a hard time, I hope."

"No, they've been great. They said everything should be ready after New Year's." It would be sooner if the holidays didn't slow everything down. I wasn't complaining; as much work as I put into the shop, the prospect of actually *opening* it made me want to throw up.

What if I didn't get in-person customers? What if I accidentally set the place on fire? What if it got vandalized or a pipe broke or…or I got held up one night during closing time? It was a safe neighborhood, but still. Running a brick-and-mortar store was a lot different than running an online business, and I'd jumped headfirst into it without much planning or forethought.

"Good," Aiden said. "I'm sure it'll be a hit. The cafe was a good idea."

Since I doubted I would get much foot traffic hawking flowers alone, I'd added a few elements to my original business plan. Once it was finished, the space would be part gallery, part flower shop, and part cafe.

"Yes. Nothing draws New Yorkers like a good…" I trailed off when I caught a glimpse of blond hair outside the window.

Tall frame. Tailored suit. *Expensive.*

My heart leapt into my throat. Then the man turned, and it crashed to earth again.

Not Dominic. Just someone who bore a passing resemblance to him.

I wished I could say it was the first time I mistook a stranger for my ex-husband. I hadn't seen him since he signed the papers, but the specter of his presence haunted me on every corner.

Was there a support group for this type of thing? A Divorcees Anonymous where we could exorcise the ghosts of marriages past? My mother was the only divorced person I knew, and her advice was less useful than a paper umbrella in a rainstorm.

"Alessandra?" Aiden prompted, bringing my attention back to him.

"Sorry. I thought I...I thought I saw someone I knew." I took another sip of my drink and took solace in its earthy warmth.

Bringing me matcha instead of espresso had been a thoughtful gesture, not that I was surprised. Aiden was *always* thoughtful. Why couldn't I have married someone like him instead? He was nice, attentive, and seemed content with his life. Granted, my interactions with him had been limited to discussions of plumbing and the best local takeout so far, but maybe they didn't have to be.

*You've spent eleven years with the same man. It's time to broaden your horizons.*

Sloane's advice crept through my head again, and I took the leap before I could chicken out.

"By the way, do you have any plans for tomorrow night?" I asked, hoping I sounded casual instead of jittery.

*Breathe. You can do this.*

Aiden's brows rose an inch. "Nothing concrete. I usually catch a game with friends at a bar, but that's flexible."

I may not have dated in years, but even I recognized a deliberate opening when I saw it.

"Do you want to grab dinner? A friendly one," I rushed out. I wasn't ready for a real, official date yet, but this was as close as I could get for now. "I want to thank you for referring me to the contractors. I would've spent weeks trying to find good ones if it weren't for you."

Surprise flickered in his eyes, followed by a pleased grin. "I would love to get dinner with you."

———

This was a mistake.

It'd been less than twenty-four hours since I'd invited Aiden to dinner, and I already wanted to kick my past self for her foolishness.

We'd said it was a platonic date, but I'd gotten my hair done and he'd cleaned up in a dress shirt and non-denim pants.

He looked nice, *really* nice, but everything seemed wrong. The scent of his cologne, the way he guided me through the restaurant with his hand on my arm instead of the small of my back…it was like trying to force a puzzle piece into the wrong slot.

*Stop overthinking things. You had years to get comfortable with Dominic, and you barely know Aiden. Of course it'll feel weird at the beginning.*

"I've never been to this restaurant," Aiden said as we sat at our table. "But I've heard great things."

"Me too."

An awkward silence descended. We conversed so easily at the shop, but outside the box of our previously defined relationship, I couldn't think of a single interesting thing to say.

Should I talk about the weather? The upcoming holidays? The article I'd read about a rat infestation on one of the subway lines? Probably not. It was New York. There was always a rat infestation.

Luckily, our server arrived soon after and saved us from drowning in the tension.

"We'll have the merlot. Thank you," Aiden said when the server presented the wine list and I told him to choose. After all, it was his thank you dinner.

"Don't you…" I bit back the rest of my sentence.

Dominic always ordered a cabernet, our mutual favorite, but I wasn't on a date with him. I would never go on another date with him again.

The burn that spread behind my eyes was so fierce and sudden I didn't have time to steel myself. One second, I was thinking about pasta and dessert; the next, I was on the verge of tearing up over a complimentary basket of garlic bread.

*Get a hold of yourself.*

I was having a perfectly palatable dinner with a perfectly nice, handsome man. I should *not* be thinking about my ex-husband. But despite my moving out, Dominic signing the papers, and Cole's call informing me everything had gone through without a hitch last week, it hadn't hit me that I was *divorced* until that moment.

No ring. No marriage. No Dominic.

I grabbed my water and chugged it, hoping it would wash away the taste of my failed relationship. It didn't.

"You okay?" Aiden asked gently. Our server had left, and he watched me with a cautious expression that made me want to cry all over again. "We can take a rain check if you're not feeling well."

He was tactful enough to give me an out that didn't involve mentioning my teetering meltdown. *I'm the worst dinner date in the world.*

"No. I'm fine." I cleared my throat. "I just had something in my eye." I could stick it out for one meal. It was food and conversation, not torture. "You recently came back from upstate, right? How was that?"

Whether it was the wine, impeccable pasta, or my utter determination to salvage the evening, Aiden and I finally hit our stride during the main course.

"Honestly, my dream is to retire upstate," he said. "I'm not a big city person. If it weren't for business, I'd be in a cabin somewhere, drinking beer and soaking in the fresh air. Fishing, hikes on the weekend. The good life."

"That sounds wonderful." I hadn't gone hiking in a while, but my brother and I used to go all the time during our summers in Brazil. I missed it. "I hope you don't take this the wrong way, but when I first saw you, I thought you looked like, well…" I coughed, second-guessing my moment of truth. "Like a lumberjack."

Aiden's boisterous laugh turned every head in the tiny trattoria and cooled the blush heating my cheeks.

"Nah. It's a compliment. And if we're on the subject of honest first impressions…" He leaned forward, his face softening. "When I met you, I thought you were the most beautiful woman I've ever seen."

In theory, his confession should've given me butterflies. In practice, it made me feel…nothing. He might as well be a robot reading me the ingredients off a can of soup.

I took a gulp of wine, trying to think of an appropriate response that wouldn't lead him on.

"Aiden, I—"

"Alessandra." The deep, cold voice sent goose bumps scattering over my arms.

My glass froze halfway to the table. *No.* After six weeks of radio silence, this couldn't possibly be the night I ran into him again. The universe wouldn't have such a sick sense of humor.

But when I glanced up, there he was. My ex-husband in all his infuriating blond, chiseled glory. He wore a crisp buttondown, an expensive watch, and a stony expression as he rested his hand on the back of my chair with an intimacy he no longer had rights to.

"Dominic." I didn't bother hiding my displeasure.

Across the table, Aiden flicked his eyes between us with dawning comprehension. I'd mentioned the divorce to him in passing, and I could practically see him putting two and two together.

"What a coincidence running into you here," I said stiffly. "We're in the middle of dinner, so if there's something you'd like to discuss, we can do it later."

"I see that." A muscle ticked in Dominic's jaw. "Camila found some of your books in the library the other day. You should pick them up."

"I'll send someone next week." There was no way in hell I would step inside the penthouse again. The last time I had gone home with him, we'd...

A flush crept beneath my skin. I craved another sip of wine for courage, but I refused to let him see the effect he had on me, so I kept my hands planted on the table, where my ringless finger looked especially bare against the white tablecloth.

"There's also the matter of your art and kitchen goods," Dominic said. "You need to pick out which ones you want."

"I don't want any of them."

"That's not what your lawyer said."

"My lawyer was overzealous." I pasted on a smile. He was obviously stalling; if the home goods were so important, he would've reached out about them *before* tonight. "You can keep everything. I'll buy new items. Fresh start and all."

His jaw ticked again.

"Sebastian is waiting." I nodded at where his friend sat a few tables down, watching us with a curious expression. The normally suave French billionaire looked a little worse for wear. The Laurent brand had taken a beating since Martin Wellgrew's death at Le Boudoir. He'd been allergic to peanuts, and the medical examiner had officially ruled it death by anaphylaxis due to traces of peanut in Wellgrew's supposedly nut-free dinner, which wasn't great for the restaurant it had taken place in. "Like I said, we can talk later."

I forced myself to meet Dominic's gaze as he stared down at me, his eyes unreadable. Then, just when I thought he'd refuse to leave, he released his hold on my chair and walked away without another word.

My breath escaped in a painful rush.

"I'm sorry about that." I faced Aiden again and attempted a smile. "He can be a little...intense."

"That's all right." Concern and a hint of amusement glinted in his eyes. "I'm guessing that was the infamous ex-husband."

"What gave it away? The rude interruption or the weird fixation on kitchen items?"

"I don't think it's the items he's fixated on."

I hated the tiny jolt that followed his words. I'd begged Dominic to let me go, and he had. In the long run, it was a good thing, but in the short run, part of me twisted uncomfortably at the prospect of him moving on. It was hypocritical, considering I was the one on a quasi-date, but emotions weren't rational.

Aiden rubbed a hand over his mouth. "I hope I didn't make you uncomfortable with what I said earlier. I meant it, but I'm also not expecting anything from this dinner other than a nice evening out with someone whose company I enjoy. You just went through a divorce and I'm, well, I'm in no place to start a relationship either. Maybe things will change down the road, but for now, let's take things at face value. How does that sound?"

He had an uncanny knack for saying exactly what I needed to hear. "That sounds perfect."

Without the expectations that'd tainted the first half of dinner, I finally relaxed. Conversation flowed easily, and by the time dessert arrived, I could almost ignore the dark blue stare burning a hole in my side.

Aiden excused himself to use the restroom while I finished my tiramisu. He hadn't been gone for more than thirty seconds before a familiar clean, woody scent filled my senses.

I stiffened again, my eyes locking with Dominic's as he took the other man's vacated seat. Aiden filled it naturally, but Dominic overpowered it. Broad shoulders, cool eyes, sculpted jaw. Every inch of him oozed arrogance and intensity.

"That seat is taken."

"Was that your new landlord?" Dominic ignored my pointed remark.

"How...never mind." Of course he knew Aiden was my landlord. He probably knew the man's Social Security number, home address, and preferred breakfast items too. Dominic was meticulous about digging into the people in his life, no matter how peripheral. "Whether he is or isn't is none of your business. We're not married anymore. I can go on a date with whoever I want."

"Is that what this is?" The tiniest flicker passed through his eyes. "A date?"

"Yes." A platonic one, but he didn't need to know that. I lifted my chin, challenging him to push back.

"He's not your type."

"I'm trying new types. The old one didn't work out so well for me."

He tried to hide it, but I didn't miss the fissure in his cool expression or the trickle of hurt that leaked through.

*Don't feel bad for him. He deserves it.* I curled my fingers around the edge of my chair so hard they hurt.

"You can go on as many dates as you want, *amor*," Dominic said softly. "But no one will love you like I do. *Você e eu. Não tem comparação.*"

The words curled through me, warm and aching and filled with nostalgia for days past.

My smile hid the painful thrum behind my ribcage. "That sounds like a good thing to me."

"Is there a problem?" Aiden returned, his expression decidedly less friendly when he saw Dominic in his seat.

"No problem." I didn't take my eyes off my ex-husband. "He was just leaving. Weren't you, Dominic?"

The curve of his mouth lacked humor. He stood, his body

unfurling with a lethal grace that drew several admiring glances, both male and female.

"Enjoy the rest of your dinner." He tapped the spot next to my wineglass on his way past. "He should've ordered the cabernet."

The intimate murmur brushed a shiver down my spine. I held my breath until Dominic returned to his seat across from Sebastian, who appeared unconcerned that his dinner partner had abandoned him halfway through the meal.

"You okay?" Aiden touched my shoulder.

"Yes." I forced another smile. "I'm done, so let's get out of here."

As expected, he tried to pay for the meal, but I'd had the foresight of paying ahead of time. I really did need to thank him for his help with the contractors, and after so many years of depending on Dominic for money, it felt empowering to pay my own way.

Aiden and I parted ways with a friendly, semi-awkward goodbye, and I managed to hold myself together throughout the ride to Sloane's apartment. I'd found a new place near her, but my lease didn't start until January, so I was staying with her through the holidays.

It was only after the cab dropped me off in front of her building that I sagged. I leaned against the exterior and sucked in a lungful of cold air as I tried to clear my senses of all things Dominic. The sound of his voice, the smell of his cologne, the soft brush of his suit against my skin.

I was trying to get over him, but that was hard when everything reminded me of him. The city was a monument to our relationship—our first getaway, our home, our demise.

*Tu e eu. Não tem comparação.*

The streetlights cast a warm glow over the sidewalk. People hurried past, dressed up for a night out or eager for a night in. Across the street, a line stretched outside a new Brazilian steakhouse. It made me think of my brother, who was busy living it up in São Paulo. I envied him. He wasn't married, he wasn't dating, he wasn't heartbroken. He was free and enjoying life the way he deserved. If only…

I straightened, my skin tingling with a sudden burst of inspiration.

If everything in the city reminded me of Dominic, maybe it was time to get out of the city.

I hurried into the lobby and dialed a familiar number.

"Hey," I said when my brother picked up. "I have an idea."

# CHAPTER 16

*THWACK!*

I smashed my racket against the tennis ball. It sailed over the net and came within inches of slamming into Dante's face.

He returned it with a scowl. "Are you playing tennis or trying to send me to the hospital?" he demanded. "That's the third time you've almost broken my nose. I'm starting to take it personally."

"Quit if you can't handle it." I delivered another shot, my breaths even despite the sweat pouring down my back. "I won't hold it against you."

Dante responded with a powerful backhand that echoed across the grounds. He and Kai vented their frustrations through boxing, but our tennis matches were almost as therapeutic.

The sun beat down on Valhalla's outdoor tennis courts. It was an unusually hot day for mid-November, and we were taking full advantage of it before the weather slid into the depressing gray that characterized New York winters.

For once, I didn't have a lunch meeting, but I'd skipped "getting some rest" as my chief of staff suggested and dragged

Dante to the club. I needed to keep busy because every time I closed my eyes, I saw Alessandra.

Alessàndra, her face streaked with tears.

Alessandra, on a date with that fucker Aiden and his stupid fucking beard.

Alessandra, laughing and talking with him like she was already moving on when I'd been slowly dying inside for the past six weeks, five days, and four hours.

Part of me had hoped she'd call the whole thing off after I signed our divorce papers. It'd been a foolish hope, but it'd been hope all the same, and there'd been a moment—one tiny moment—when she'd hesitated. Then she'd taken the papers and walked out.

I'd signed countless contracts that had brought me riches beyond imagining, but for once, I'd had to sign one giving up the most important person in my life. Something wrenched at my chest as the ball sailed toward me. This time, I hit it with so much force the impact reverberated through my entire body. It went wide and smashed into the water pitcher on the sidelines. Glass shattered, followed by the clatter of Dante's racket on the ground.

"That's it," he said. "We're done for the day."

"Glad you can finally admit you're a quitter, Russo." Alessandra's face shimmered in the heat waves dancing over the court before I blinked it away.

I'd thrown myself into work even deeper than usual since our divorce, but no matter how many meetings I took or how many numbers I crunched, I couldn't keep her off my mind. She was always there, taunting me. Torturing me. Making me wish I could turn back time when time was the one thing I had no power over.

Part of me craved any glimpse of her while another part dreaded it because it reminded me too much of what I'd lost. Seeing her unexpectedly was bad enough; seeing her with fucking

Aiden nearly killed me. It'd taken all my willpower not to punch him in his smug, bearded face.

"I'm not a quitter. I'm pragmatic. I have a dinner date with Vivian, and if I miss it because you can't aim properly, we'll *both* be pissed," Dante said, drawing my attention back to the present. He flicked a glance at where a club staffer was already cleaning up the shattered glass. "You've been on edge the entire damn game. It's Thanksgiving week. Lighten up."

It was ironic that the notoriously grumpy Dante was telling me to lighten up, but marriage changed everyone, I supposed.

"Fuck Thanksgiving." There wasn't much to give thanks for. Besides running into Alessandra on her date last week, I had to deal with my missing foster brother. Roman had disappeared since the restaurant debacle in October, and even the shadier side of my network couldn't find him. But he was still in New York. I could feel it. Rather than reassuring me, his radio silence loomed like the ominous calm before a storm.

"I thought you and Vivian were headed to Paris tonight." I switched subjects before I spiraled down into the shit show of my personal life. "Or are you staying in town for the weekend?"

"Alessandra's goodbye drinks are tomorrow, so we postponed—" Dante cut himself off, but it was too late.

I stilled. "What goodbye drinks?" The quiet words bounced off the clay courts.

The other man's face shuttered.

"*What goodbye drinks?*" I repeated, strangling the handle of my tennis racket. A familiar buzz drilled into my head, and my heart picked up a pace that would give my doctor a coronary.

"Alessandra's leaving for Brazil tomorrow morning," Dante finally said.

I relaxed an inch. "For the holidays." She always visited her mom and brother for Christmas. Not so much for Thanksgiving since that wasn't a holiday in Brazil, but maybe she needed another getaway this year.

"Not exactly." Dante looked like he would rather be anywhere but here. "It's a one-way ticket. Vivian doesn't know when she'll be back."

---

*One-way ticket...doesn't know when she'll be back.*

Dante's words haunted me through the night and into the following morning, when I sat at my desk and stared at the market numbers on my computer without really seeing them.

The office was a ghost town the day before Thanksgiving, which made it one of my favorite days to work. However, I couldn't focus on the SEC investigation into DBG or any of the investment accounts in my portfolio.

Alessandra couldn't be *moving* to Brazil. My private contractor had confirmed she was headed to Buzios, where her mother owned a house, but she'd just rented a storefront in Manhattan, for Christ's sake. One did not break a commercial lease in that neighborhood without paying an arm and a leg. Still, the idea of her flying thousands of miles away with no return date made my throat close.

How had I ever willingly spent so many hours away from her when I would give up my fucking kidney for a moment alone with her again? Why had I been more afraid of losing everything else instead of losing her?

I'd given Alessandra space since the divorce because it was too early to reach out. The emotions were too raw for both of us, and I needed time to figure out how to win her back. I'd signed the papers, but that didn't mean I'd given up on us. Not by a long shot.

Every end came with a new beginning. I just had to make sure we started over together.

My cell rang, dragging me from my thoughts. I cursed at the caller ID. *That damn unknown caller again.* I should stop picking up, but curiosity got the better of me every time.

As always, silence greeted me.

Annoyance flared, and I gritted out a warning. "If you don't stop calling, I—"

"Keep an eye on your brother." The voice was so distorted, I couldn't distinguish its gender. "Or you'll be next."

The soft *click* of the call ending filled the line before I could answer. I cursed again and tossed my phone on the desk.

I'd had my guy look into the calls, but whoever was behind them was skilled enough to make them untraceable.

Fucking Roman. It had to be him. He'd used to pull similar stunts all the time until our foster mother had whipped him within an inch of his life for racking up the phone bill. I also wouldn't be surprised if he'd picked up some black-hat tech tricks over the years. He was a fast learner. It was too bad most of what he learned involved some type of lying, cheating, or manipulation. I didn't know what game he was playing at now, but I was damn sick of it.

A knock sounded at the door.

"Sir?" Martha entered, her expression hesitant. Her behavior had been much more subdued since I'd chewed her out for the way she'd treated Alessandra. "Your eleven o'clock is here."

"I'll be out in a few minutes."

I'd forgotten about my meeting this morning. The thought of sitting and smiling through an hour of bullshit suddenly made me want to crawl out of my skin.

I loved the city. The noise and people drowned out the voices in my head; the breakneck pace prevented me from dwelling on any one moment too long. I found safety in the chaos, but Alessandra's absence and Roman's presence had upended my neat, ordered world. The only reason I wasn't in a constant panic was because I had a discreet security team guarding Alessandra in the city and another one watching out for Roman.

*It's Thanksgiving week. Lighten up.* Dante's advice echoed through my head. The bastard was a pain in my ass half the time, but he occasionally had good insights. After all, he was the one who'd inspired part of my Win Alessandra Back plan.

I waited until the door closed behind Martha before I opened a new tab on my browser.

I couldn't believe I was even contemplating doing what I was about to do. It was so far-fetched, so out of character, that I felt like someone else was piloting my movements as I navigated to a familiar website.

But dammit, I wanted my wife back, and if that meant taking drastic action, then so be it.

For the first time in my life, I didn't overthink or dwell on the fact I've never missed a single work meeting before. I simply clicked on the blue button, input my payment details, and bought a one-way ticket to Brazil.

# CHAPTER 17

# Alessandra

"IF WE DIE HERE, I'M BLAMING YOUUUU!" THE ONCOMING wave crashed over me and swallowed my last word. The world silenced, and for an endless moment, I hung suspended underwater.

Then I resurfaced, spluttering, to Marcelo's raucous laughter.

"You're out of practice, *irmã*." He lay on his board, his face shining with brotherly teasing. "You used to out-surf me."

"That was *years* ago." I dragged in a lungful of sweet air, my body aching from the force of my wipe out. "Manhattan isn't exactly known for its waves."

Despite the humiliation of eating it in front of everyone on the beach, my blood buzzed with adrenaline. The water, the sunshine, the salt-laced air...it was good to be home.

Even though Marcelo and I grew up in New York, where our mother had lived for the majority of her modeling career, we'd spent every summer and holiday in Brazil as kids. It was only after I got married that my trips had tapered off to once a year.

Still, I'd always considered Brazil my second home, and I was glad I'd convinced my brother to join me in Buzios for a last minute but long overdue sibling vacation. We'd arrived on Wednesday and spent the past two days eating, swimming, and catching up. New York felt like worlds away.

Marcelo observed me, his amusement fading into something softer. "You look much happier than when you landed. The vacation has been good to you."

"Yeah." I glided my fingers through the water, watching the sunlight sparkle on the surface. "I should've done this a long time ago."

I didn't know why I'd felt like I couldn't visit without Dominic. God knew he went on enough trips without me. Perhaps if I had, I would've gained the clarity to speak up sooner.

Would things be different if I'd put my foot down the first time Dominic missed an important date? Maybe. But I couldn't change the past, so there was no use dwelling on what ifs.

"Perhaps," Marcelo said. "You sounded sad the last few times we spoke on the phone."

How I'd sounded hadn't compared to the sadness I'd felt, but I kept that to myself. "It's an adjustment period, which is why I'm here. Adjusting."

It was working. Sort of. I'd only thought about Dominic a dozen times a day since I'd arrived instead of the usual two to three dozen.

*Baby steps.*

"Hmm." My brother didn't look convinced. "And what happens when you go home?"

"I'll cross that bridge when I get there."

I hadn't booked my return flight to New York yet. Luckily, the upcoming holidays meant construction work on the store was slowing down, and I'd put the online shop on hiatus. Isabella had offered to keep an eye on things while I was gone. She'd worked for Floria Designs before she'd gotten published, and she still helped out occasionally when I needed an extra hand. She was one of the few people I trusted to manage the contractors in my absence.

"I don't want to push, but we have to discuss the elephant in the room sometime," Marcelo said gently. "When was the last time you talked to Dominic?"

I flinched at the mention of his name. My brother and I had avoided the topic of my divorce like the plague since we'd arrived, but he was right. We had to talk about it, and I guess he'd been waiting for the right time to bring it up—aka a time when we were relaxing in public so I couldn't lock myself in my room or use our activities as a deflection.

"Last week," I admitted. "Before I called you. We were at the same restaurant, and he saw me on a...he saw me when I was having dinner with a friend." I returned Marcelo's scrutiny with a hesitant look of my own. "I'm sorry. I know you guys are close."

Marcelo and Dominic had hit it off right away, partly because they'd shared similar struggles with dyslexia growing up and partly because my gregarious brother could charm a rock if he needed to.

I was protective of Marcelo, who'd been bullied relentlessly in his younger years, and though I'd already loved Dominic when they'd met, their easy friendship had made me fall even harder.

"Don't apologize. It's *your* relationship," Marcelo said, his voice gentling further. "I liked Dom a lot, but we'll never be as close as you and me. You're my sister. I'll always have your back."

A lump formed in my throat. "Don't get all sentimental on me, Marcy. It's still your turn to take out the garbage tonight."

His laugh made a quick return. "Fine. I should've known buttering you up wouldn't work," he teased. "But seriously, don't worry about me. Do what's good for you, and this..." He swept his arm around the beach. "This is good for you. You jumped straight from taking care of me to your marriage. It's time you enjoyed life without worrying about others."

"I didn't mind taking care of you."

"I know. But that doesn't make what I said less true. You skipped your own senior trip to help me study for an *English test*. You've spent your life living for others. Now you can finally live for yourself."

I watched other beachgoers splash around us while Marcelo's words replayed in my head.

I'd never thought of it that way, but he had a point. Our mother had spent our childhood working, partying, and dating increasingly rich but dubious men. I was the result of a one-night stand with someone she'd been too drunk to remember; Marcelo was the son of a married Brazilian businessman who'd threatened our mother with bodily harm if she ever told people about their affair.

We were half-siblings, but despite being born only two years apart, I'd acted more like his mother than his sister until we were both adults. I couldn't rely on our actual mother to parent him properly, so I'd done it myself.

Perhaps that was why I'd slipped so easily into the role of Dominic's spouse. I was used to being the support instead of the star in my own life.

I was trying to change that with Floria Designs and my divorce, but all big changes took time.

"Enough maudlin stuff." I swallowed the emotion crowding my throat and nodded at the horizon. "You want to talk about living? Talk about that giant wave that's coming toward us."

Marcelo cursed, and soon, all thoughts of Dominic, neglectful mothers, and absent fathers drowned beneath the exhilaration of *living*. New York would always be there; this moment wouldn't.

Once we got tired of surfing, we retired to the sand for sunbathing and drinks. We stayed at the beach for another two hours until golden hour painted the sky with oranges and yellows and exhaustion tugged at my eyelids.

"I think it's time to call it a day." A yawn split Marcelo's face. "We'll repeat tomorrow. Or not. I might just pass out and sleep."

"No sleeping. We're on vacation." I packed up our towels while he took care of our cooler.

"Isn't the point of vacation to sleep?" he grumbled, sounding like a preteen again.

"Not when you're with me."

"Fine." Marcelo rolled his eyes. "Take the girl out of a relationship, and she's suddenly a party animal."

"Hey, I'm rediscovering myself, okay? It's like *Eat Pray Love,* but without the pray or the love."

That earned me a loud snort.

I glanced at a couple kissing near the shore on our way back to the villa. The woman's red hair blazed like fire against the sunset, and the guy had the lean, muscled build of an athlete or outdoors enthusiast.

I watched as he broke the kiss halfway through, threw his girlfriend over his shoulder, and walked deeper into the ocean with admirable ease.

"Josh, don't you dare! I'm going to kill you!" she screamed a second before he tossed her into the water. She grabbed him at the last minute and he fell in with her, their laughs and curses echoing across the empty beach.

A wistful smile pushed through the ache in my chest. God, I missed those heady days of young love. I was only thirty-one, but I felt like I'd lived a lifetime in terms of relationships. Jaded, worn out, heartbroken. What a prize after ten years.

Whoever the couple was, I hoped they'd have a happier ending than I did.

Marcelo and I arrived at our street right as twilight melted into dusk. Our mother owned a vacation home in Buzios in addition to her apartment in Rio, where she'd moved after retiring from modeling, but she rarely used the villa. I was convinced she'd forgotten it existed.

"What's for dinner?" I asked. Marcelo and I had subsisted on alcohol and snacks all day, and since my cooking skills were subpar at best, he was in charge of the food while I handled the cleanup.

"Feijoada," he said, naming a traditional black bean and pork stew. "I'm too tired to come up with anything more creative."

Since it was a heavy dish, most people ate it for lunch, not dinner, but I would never say no to my brother's feijoada regardless of the time of day.

"Well, you know I'll never turn down…" My sentence trailed off when a cab stopped a few feet away from us. A man got out of the backseat and retrieved his suitcase from the trunk.

It was too dark to see his face clearly, but his height and build looked alarmingly familiar.

*Stop. It's not him. You're in* Brazil, *for Christ's sake. Not New York*.

Marcelo squinted into the evening. "Is it just me or does that look a lot like Dominic?"

Sweat coated my palms. *Breathe.* "Don't be ridiculous. Not every tall—" I interrupted myself when the cab pulled away and its headlights cast the man's face into sharp relief.

Blue eyes. Chiseled face. A casual expression as he approached us like he hadn't popped up out of nowhere in freaking Buzios wearing…were those *shorts*? I hadn't seen Dominic in anything more casual than a T-shirt and jeans in years, and even that was rare.

"Hi." He stopped in front of us, looking relaxed and devastatingly handsome. "Beautiful night, isn't it?"

"What are you doing here?" This couldn't be happening. I must be hallucinating after getting heatstroke from our beach day. "Are you *following* me?"

"I'm on vacation," Dominic said calmly. "I'm long overdue for a break, and since it's Thanksgiving, I figured I'd head somewhere sunny. New York is pretty miserable this week."

"Thanksgiving was two days ago."

"Yes, but it's still Thanksgiving *weekend*." His smile, though brief, hit me harder than I cared to admit. "It counts."

I crossed my arms, grateful for any barrier that separated us. "And of all the places in the world, you *happened* to vacation here?"

A shrug. "I love Brazil." His simple reply didn't conceal the intimacy of his meaning.

I love Brazil. *I love you.*

The unspoken words wrapped around me, holding me captive long enough that Marcelo cleared his throat. Loudly.

I startled and tore my eyes away from Dominic. I'd forgotten my brother was there.

"So, uh, where are you staying?" His gaze darted between me and his ex-brother-in-law.

This time, Dominic's smile contained a hint of devilishness. "At Villa Luz."

Villa Luz belonged to a Brazilian socialite who occasionally rented it out to VIP guests when she wasn't using it. It was famously large, lavish, and decorated to the nines.

It was also located smack dab next to our own villa.

## CHAPTER 18

### *Alessandra*

*FUCK.*

# CHAPTER 19

## Alessandra

"HE LOOKS LONELY."

"That's none of our business." I stared at my drink and forced myself not to look next door. "He chose to go on a solo vacation."

Marcelo and I were having homemade caipirinhas on the rooftop deck while the feijoada cooked. I shouldn't ingest any more alcohol after our boozy beach day, but I needed to take the edge off after my run-in with Dominic.

"True," Marcelo said. "Still, it's kind of sad."

Curiosity played tug of war with my better instincts. The former won, and I glanced to my right, where Dominic was sitting by his pool. Six-foot hedges separated our villas, but my high vantage point gave me a direct view of his backyard.

He was scrolling on his phone and eating the saddest-looking sandwich I'd ever seen. Lantern lights swayed in the trees, casting a soft glow over his features.

The cynical part of me wondered if he was eating by the pool because he'd heard us on the rooftop and wanted to gain our sympathy. The empathetic part of me couldn't help but feel a pang in my chest.

Marcelo was right. He *did* look lonely.

My brother followed my gaze. "The town feels a whole lot smaller, doesn't it?"

"It's big enough. He does his thing, we do ours." I kept my voice low, but Dominic looked up at that exact moment like he'd heard me. Our eyes locked, and a shiver of electricity ran beneath my skin.

I tore my gaze away before it intensified into anything more dangerous.

"You feel bad for him, don't you?" I said when Marcelo frowned. "What happened to always having my back?" I was only half joking.

My brother owed a lot to Dominic, who'd gotten him his first job as a junior chef in one of the Laurents' restaurants before he graduated to his current role as executive sous chef. I didn't expect him to shun him just because we were divorced, but his obvious soft spot for Dominic made me uneasy simply because I could see myself sliding toward the same feelings.

I was too susceptible to others' opinions. I didn't want to be, but I couldn't help it.

"It's still true, but I also feel bad for him," Marcelo said. "We both know why he's here, and it's not for vacation." He nodded at the man in question. "When was the last time Dominic *willingly* took time off work?"

Never. Even when we were married, I had to force him to stay in Brazil for longer than a few days between Christmas and New Year's.

It suddenly struck me how massive a deal his appearance was. This wasn't a night off or a rescheduled meeting; he'd left the office, flown to another continent, and, judging by how comfortable he was making himself at Villa Luz, he intended to stay awhile.

My stomach twisted into knots. *Don't let him fool you.* Dominic would do anything to win, but the prize only mattered before he obtained it.

"Come on," I said, sidestepping Marcelo's question. "The food is going to be ready soon, and I need to take a shower."

"You showered an hour ago."

"I need to shower again," I lied. "The humidity's a killer."

Marcelo slid a knowing glance at me but didn't argue. While he checked on the feijoada, I halfheartedly rinsed off, letting the hot water wash away my lingering sympathy for Dominic.

By the time I toweled off and entered the dining room, Marcelo was already setting the table.

"Here. I'll help." I grabbed the plates from him. "Why are you looking at me like that? I didn't take *that* long this time."

He always teased me about my long showers, but I'd been in there for thirty minutes, tops.

"I know." He scratched the back of his neck, his expression equal parts scared and apprehensive. "So, uh, here's the thing. While you were—"

Someone came up behind him and interrupted him. "Where did you put your cocktail glasses? I don't see—" Dominic stopped abruptly when he noticed me. He'd changed into a linen shirt and pants, and he held a bottle of cachaça in one hand and his phone in the other.

Heat suffused my skin, erasing the shower's aftereffects. There was only one reason why he would be in our house, holding that bottle, and looking for *our* cocktail glasses.

Marcelo had invited him over for dinner.

Forget sibling vacations. Tomorrow, I'd be an only child because I was going to *murder* my brother.

My soon-to-be-dead brother cleared his throat. "Dominic came over and asked if he could borrow some sugar. Turns out

Luz didn't stock the house with condiments and the store in town is closed, so I asked if he'd like to join us instead. I made too much food anyway."

"If you're uncomfortable, I can leave," Dominic said when I remained silent. "I'm not that hungry anyway. I had a sandwich."

"It's fine." I forced a smile. I refused to let him see how he affected me.

Another awkward beat passed before Marcelo cleared his throat again. "The glasses are in the lower cabinet, second from the left. Easy to miss if you're not looking for it."

Dominic nodded and disappeared into the kitchen again. The instant he was out of eyeshot, I glared at Marcelo, who backed away with his hands in the air.

"*What were you thinking?*" I whisper-shouted. "Borrowing sugar? Seriously? You fell for that?"

"I panicked, okay?" he hissed back. "What was I supposed to do? Turn the poor guy away?"

"*Yes.*" I flapped a hand in the general direction of the kitchen. "You invited my ex-husband to dinner! We divorced two months ago, and he *followed me to Brazil*!"

"You know I don't deal well with interpersonal pressure! He smelled the feijoada and...fuck, he's coming."

We clammed up again when Dominic returned with the cocktail glasses. He raised an eyebrow when I grabbed one and made myself another, hasty caipirinha before we sat down, but he wisely refrained from saying anything.

Dinner was, as expected, quiet and stilted. Marcelo carried the conversation while Dominic and I ate in silence. I felt like I was living out an absurdist film about marriage and divorce. Everything, from the location to Dominic's presence to the music Marcelo put on for "atmosphere enhancement," seemed surreal.

This couldn't be my life right now.

"How's your shop going?" Marcelo asked after he finished rambling about Brazil's latest soccer game, or football as it was called everywhere except the U.S. "Everything on track for the grand opening in the new year?"

"Yes." I rapped my knuckles against the oak table so I didn't jinx it. "I haven't received any emergency texts from Isabella, so I assume the store hasn't burned down."

"You once said you'd never open a physical store." Dominic's quiet observation had my shoulders tensing. "You said it'd be too stressful."

"That was in college." I didn't look up from my food. "A lot has changed since then."

I'd majored in business at Thayer but focused on e-commerce. Instead of starting my own company after graduation like I'd originally planned, I'd helped Dominic build his. However, I'd stepped back after he'd hired a permanent team, and the retail landscape had shifted so much since college that creating Floria Designs was like starting from scratch. Most of what I'd learned in school was outdated, and the past two years had been a never-ending learning process.

Opening a physical store scared me to death, but I needed something solid. Something I could look at, touch, and call mine, that proved beyond a doubt that there was still some fight left in me.

"What about you?" Marcelo asked when Dominic remained silent after my reply. "How's, uh, work?"

"It's fine. The markets change but Wall Street doesn't."

Another long silence.

"How long are you staying in Brazil?" My brother made another valiant attempt at conversation.

"I'm not sure." Dominic took a casual sip of his drink. "I haven't bought a return ticket."

I nearly choked on a mouthful of beans and pork. Across from me, Marcelo's jaw unhinged, revealing a half-chewed piece of meat. It was deeply unflattering and something he would've called another person out for, but Dominic's admission had knocked us both for a loop.

Him flying to Brazil was shocking enough. Him flying here without a return date was so unthinkable I almost reached over to check if he was suffering from a high fever or a personality transplant.

"How?" Marcelo finally found his words. "What about work?"

Dominic flicked a glance at me. I looked down and pretended my meal was the most fascinating thing I'd ever seen while my breath stilled in anticipation of his answer.

"Work will always be there," he said. "Other things won't."

No one spoke again for the rest of the meal.

After dinner, Marcelo excused himself to do the dishes even though it was my turn to clean up. He ignored my death stare as he hastened into the kitchen with an armful of plates and cutlery, leaving me and Dominic alone in the dining room. We stared at each other, held captive by uncertainty. It was a new dynamic for us, and I didn't know how to handle it.

Dominic was many things—ruthless, irritable, ambitious—but he'd never been uncertain. Since the day we'd met, he'd been a force of purpose, propelled by single-minded goals and ambition. Graduate. Start his own company. Become so rich and successful he silenced every person who'd ever doubted him.

Even as a broke college student, Dominic had exuded such confidence one couldn't help but look at him and see someone destined to achieve everything he set his mind to. Success was his true north, but now he appeared lost, like he was adrift at sea without a compass.

"Ále—"

"It's getting late. I should go to bed." I stood, my heart rattling for reasons I didn't want to examine, but I didn't make it two steps before a hand closed around my wrist.

"Please."

The rawness of that one simple word dissolved some of my willpower. I stopped and faced him, hating how his touch sent butterflies soaring in my stomach and how his voice made my heart beat just a little faster. I wished I could sign away my feelings as easily as I had our legal marriage, but our relationship on paper was worlds different from reality.

"You shouldn't be here." A strange mix of fatigue and adrenaline coursed through my veins. "This isn't healthy for either of us. We just got divorced. We can't move on if you insist on following me everywhere."

Dominic's eyes flickered beneath the lights. "That's the thing," he said softly. "There *is* no moving on. Not for me."

My entire body tensed, but no amount of steeling myself could blunt the impact of his words.

"You haven't tried."

"Do you want me to try?"

*Yes. Maybe. Eventually.* I blinked away the image of Dominic attending some fancy gala with a glamorous blonde on his arm or, worse, cuddling up next to her on the couch. It was the intimate moments I yearned for, and I envied the slices of life he'd eventually share with someone else.

*Don't dwell on it. This is what you wanted. Remember?*

"You signed the papers." I pulled free from his grasp. The imprint of his touch burned, and it took all my willpower not to touch my wrist.

"I signed the papers because you asked me to, not because I wanted to."

"And yet you're here against my wishes."

A small smile touched his lips while his eyes remained solemn.

"You never told me you *didn't* want me here, so I'm technically not going against your wishes."

I sighed, exhaustion outpacing adrenaline. "What do you want, Dominic?"

"I want you back."

My pulse spiked. Thank God he was no longer holding me or he would've felt the exact moment his words sank in.

"You can't have me back." Maybe if I said it enough times, he would believe it, and I wouldn't feel this dull ache behind my ribcage.

"I know."

"Then what—"

"Specifically, I want a fresh start for us." Dominic didn't take his eyes off mine. "You said we didn't know each other anymore, and you were right. You said I neglected you and took you for granted during our marriage, and you were right. I lost my perspective of what was most important. I can't change what I did in the past, but I can do things differently in the future. Give me a chance to prove it to you."

"How?" The question scraped out in a whisper. I couldn't help it. I was too curious, too ensnared by the intimate honesty reflected on his face. It was honesty that had been missing from our relationship for years, and in that moment, he wasn't Dominic Davenport, the king of Wall Street. He was simply Dominic, the beautiful, smart, tortured boy I'd fallen in love with so many moons ago.

"By not pushing me away." His throat flexed. "That's all I ask. A chance for us to talk and get to know each other as we are now. I want to know what makes you laugh, what makes you cry, what your dreams look like when you sleep and what keeps you up when you can't. I'll spend however many lifetimes I need to rediscover those parts of you, because you're it for me. In every iteration of every life. Things may have changed since we got married, but you and me? We were always meant for forever."

# CHAPTER 20

## Dominic

SEEING ALESSANDRA AND NOT BEING ABLE TO HOLD her was a special kind of torture. It'd been two days, thirteen hours, and thirty-three minutes since our dinner together, and I had spent every waking moment since replaying it. She was right next door, but I was afraid that if I didn't etch her into my mind deeply enough, she would slip away like grains of sand through my fingers.

Fortunately, Buzios was small, and we ran into each other everywhere. At the beach. At the boardwalk. At the supermarket shopping for fruits and vegetables. Unfortunately, our interactions in those places were limited at best.

Alessandra was still wary of me. Her response to my plea on Monday night had been a mere "I need to go," and she eyed me like I was a cobra waiting to strike every time she saw me. It made me feel like shit because I knew she had every right not to believe me, but at the same time, I loved watching her in the quick moments before she realized I was there. The flash of her smile, the glow of her face, the untouchable, intangible *something* that harkened back to the girl who'd taken me under her wing at Thayer and hadn't let go until I could fly on my own.

———————

*"Here's your coffee. Black with no sugar or cream. Just the way you like it, for whatever reason."* Alessandra was the first person I saw when I walked out of Professor Ruth's classroom. She handed me the cardboard cup, her expression a mix of anticipation and trepidation. *"So, how did it go?"*

*"Fine."* I took a sip, savoring the bitterness she always wrinkled her nose at. *"Professor Ruth didn't imprison us until we could recite Shakespeare's full body of work by memory, which I count as a win."*

*"Ha ha. Very funny."* She pinned me with a droll stare even as her mouth twitched. *"I'm talking about your final exam, smartass. Did you...did you pass?"*

Alessandra looked so nervous, I abandoned my original plan to drag this out and fuck with her a little longer.

*"Seventy-eight."* I couldn't stop the slow spread of a smile. *"I passed."* It wasn't the best grade in the class, but fuck it, it was leagues better than what I'd gotten the last time I took English comp. Thanks to Alessandra, I'd done fairly well on my midterms, and I'd needed at least a seventy-five on the final to pass the class.

*"You passed? Oh my God, you passed!"* Alessandra squealed and threw her arms around me, nearly knocking me over. I hastily tossed the coffee into a nearby trash can before I spilled it over both of us. *"You did it! I never doubted you for a second."*

*"That's why you looked like you wanted to throw up when you asked how I did, right?"*

*"Well, my reputation as a tutor was on the line. I couldn't ruin my one-hundred-percent success rate, you know."* She pulled back, her eyes sparkling with pride. My stomach clenched. She was the only person who'd ever cared about my accomplishments. Hell, she probably cared more than me, and I had no idea how to deal with that sort of thing. *"But seriously, I knew you could do*

it. You're one of the smartest people I know, Dominic. You just show it in a different way."

Heat singed my cheeks and neck. "Thank you." I cleared my throat and disentangled myself from her. Alessandra felt alarmingly good in my arms, and I was afraid that if I didn't break free now, I'd never let her go. "I'm glad you didn't give up on me even when I was being an asshole, because I couldn't have done it without you."

The sentiment came out easier than expected. I'd always had a hard time saying thank you, but maybe that was because no one had truly deserved it until now.

Alessandra's face softened. "You *did* this, not me. I merely guided you on the way."

"Right." I rubbed my hand over the back of my neck, the heat escalating. "Well, I guess this is it. Thanks again for everything. Maybe I'll see you at graduation."

There was no reason for us to see each other again. My classes next semester were all finance and economics, which I could pass with my eyes closed, and despite our many late-night study sessions, I wasn't naive enough to think we were friends.

Alessandra blinked, seemingly caught off-guard by my abrupt goodbye. "Oh. I mean, you're welcome." She tucked a strand of hair behind her ear and glanced around at the stream of students passing us. "Um, I guess I'll see you at graduation then."

If I didn't know better, I'd think she was disappointed.

"Right. See you." I sounded like a broken record. Why couldn't I come up with more words?

She hesitated like she was waiting for me to say something else. When I didn't, she gave me an awkward wave and turned to walk away.

My heart kicked against my ribcage. She was at the end of the corridor. Soon, she'd be lost in the crowd, and who knew if we *would see each other again? Granted, Thayer was a small campus and I had her number, but instinct told me I was letting something special slip through my fingers if I didn't stop her right fucking now.*

*She was almost out of sight.*

*Panic spurred me into action. I broke into a flat-out run and caught up with her right as she turned the corner. "Wait! Alessandra."*

*·She stopped, her brow knitting with confusion at my flushed face. "What's wrong?"*

*"Nothing. I mean…" Just spit it out. "When are you heading home for the holidays?" Classes didn't officially end until next week, but a lot of students went home early if they didn't have mandatory in-person exams.*

*Her puzzlement visibly mounted. "Tuesday. Why?"*

*"I was wondering…that is…" Fuck. I sounded like an inexperienced schoolboy asking his crush out for the first time. What was wrong with me? "Do you want to grab dinner on Saturday? Just the two of us."*

*Alessandra's confusion melted, replaced with a familiar teasing smile that kicked my heart rate from a canter into a gallop. "Dominic Davenport, are you asking me on a date?"*

*Hell, if I was going to do it, I might as well go all in. No ifs, ands, or buts. "Yes."*

*Her smile widened. "In that case, I would love to have dinner with you."*

---

The memory of our first official step toward dating distracted me enough that I almost walked past the diving center. I doubled back, trying to shake off the pang in my gut.

Although I was in Buzios for Alessandra, I really did need a vacation. I couldn't mope around town the entire time; that was too pathetic even for my current circumstances. I was taking virtual meetings and working early in the mornings, but I trusted my team to keep things running while I was gone.

I gave them Thanksgiving off but had to prep them for my extended absence the following day. It was the only reason I hadn't flown to Brazil the same morning as Alessandra.

The problem was, I'd never gone on a solo vacation before. Now that I was here, I didn't know what to do, so I'd booked every activity that looked interesting. Scuba diving today, a boat tour tomorrow.

And if I just so happened to have booked the same scuba diving class as Alessandra after Marcelo slipped up and told me about it during our grocery store run-in yesterday...well, it was a small town. There were limited options.

I checked in at the front desk and joined the small group of first-time divers out back. My gaze skipped over the silver-haired man, the pair of giggling coeds, and the couple whispering furiously to each other under their breath. It landed on a glossy brown ponytail at the edge of the group...and stayed there.

When was the last time Alessandra had put her hair in a ponytail? I couldn't remember. It was such a small detail, but it was yet another sign of how far we'd grown apart over the years. We'd used to play tennis together; she was the one who'd introduced me to the sport, and she'd worn the same ponytail and all-white outfit every time.

She was checking something on her phone, but she must've felt the heat of my stare because she looked up and froze. She didn't utter a word, but she didn't have to; her expression said it all.

"Small world." I stopped opposite her. "Good morning, Alessandra."

"Good morning." She didn't return my smile. "What a coincidence we're signed up for the *same* dive excursion at the *exact* same time."

"Like I said, it's a small world," I drawled, ignoring her

pointed tone. My gaze skimmed over the curve of her shoulder and up her neck to her face. "You look beautiful."

Her hair had lightened into a sun-kissed brown, and she'd developed a healthy tan from the beach. A tiny constellation of freckles scattered over her nose and cheeks, so faint they would've been unnoticeable had I not been so familiar with her features that even the slightest change stood out. Most of all, the stiffness that had cloaked her in New York had melted away, revealing a relaxed easiness that did more than any makeup or fancy dress could.

Alessandra was always stunning, but here she glowed in a way that made my chest ache—partly because she was so beautiful, I couldn't believe she was real, and partly because it took her leaving the city, leaving *me,* to find happiness again. Out of everything, that hurt the most.

Regret formed a jagged rock in my stomach, and emotion flickered across her face before she looked away.

It was only then that I realized the rest of the group had fallen silent. The silver-haired man was on his phone, but the coeds and couple were watching us with avid interest.

"*Bom dia!*" Our diving instructor interrupted the awkward tension and approached us with a toothy grin. He looked like one of those twenty-somethings who spent their days stoned or surfing, which already irritated me. Then his gaze lingered on Alessandra for an extra beat, and the irritation ignited into sudden, fierce possessiveness. It took all my willpower not to punch him in the fucking face.

"I'm Ignacio, your diving instructor today. It's our beginner's course, so it'll be nice and easy." He spoke in Portuguese first before translating into English. He stood way too damn close to Alessandra as he droned on about our itinerary and the safety protocols. He made a stupid joke about whales that made her laugh, and my fantasy evolved from punching him to ripping his tongue out.

After an eternity, we boarded the boat and headed out to the dive site. Maybe I'd get lucky and Ignacio would fall off the side and get eaten by a shark. Stranger things have happened.

"You okay? You look like you want to kill our instructor," Josh, the guy half of the couple in our group, joked. "If you do, wait until we've returned to shore. Jules is scared of sharks."

We'd introduced ourselves earlier. Josh and Jules, the couple, were a doctor and lawyer from Washington, DC. The older man was a businessman visiting from Argentina, and the coeds were students taking a long weekend off from the University of São Paulo.

"I'm not *scared* of them." Jules notched her chin up. "I simply have no interest in meeting them."

"That's not what you said when we were watching Shark Week."

"Excuse me for not liking creatures with that many teeth. At least I don't cry over Disney movies..."

I tuned out their playful bickering and refocused on Alessandra, who stared out at the ocean with a pensive expression.

"Nervous?" I asked softly. She was fine with surface-level activities like swimming and surfing, but she was terrified of going under the ocean. She'd refused to go scuba diving during our honeymoon, which was why I'd been surprised when Marcelo had told me her plans for the day.

"I'll be fine. I've gone diving before." She didn't look away from the water.

A fresh wave of surprise rippled through me. "When?"

"Last year when I went to the Bahamas."

I vaguely remembered her girls' trip in the Caribbean. That was the same weekend I'd flown to London to close a deal, and I didn't recall us ever discussing our respective trips with each other after the fact. I hadn't asked; she hadn't offered.

The regret expanded and filled my lungs.

"How did it go?" She must've been terrified.

Shame soaked through me. If I hadn't been so damn oblivious during our marriage, I would've been the one she went scuba diving with for the first time. I would've held her hand on the boat ride over, distracted her with jokes, and just fucking been there.

We'd stood at the altar and vowed to share our milestones together, but how many had I missed since I had uttered that promise?

*Too many.*

Alessandra shrugged. "It went well enough that I'm doing it again."

"Good." I tapped my fingers against my seat. Nerves twisted through my gut; I felt like a freshman trying—and failing—to talk to the most popular girl in school. "What made you decide to take the plunge? No pun intended."

*Oh, for fuck's sake.* The line was so corny I wanted to snatch it back before it fully left my mouth, but at least it got her to look at me. A shadow of amusement crossed her face, and I decided I would deliver as many corny jokes as she wanted if it meant she would look at me with anything other than sadness or wariness.

"I wanted to try something new," she said. "It was about time. Besides, I stopped being so afraid of the ocean a while ago. I don't plan on breaking any dive records, but the basic stuff…it's not so bad. We all have to face our fears eventually, right?"

Some of them. Other fears were better left intact.

"I'm sorry I wasn't there to see it," I said quietly. I should've been there. I should've been a lot of places on a lot of occasions over the years.

My gut churned in time with the engine behind us.

"It's fine. I was used to it." Alessandra's tone was matter of fact, which cut deeper than if she'd spoken out of anger.

Hatred, I could battle. But indifference? That was the death knell for any relationship.

The boat stopped at the dive site. I tried talking to Alessandra again, but she either didn't hear me or was actively ignoring me as we prepared to go into the water.

Frustration chafed at my skin. The waters surrounding Buzios contained incredible marine life, but I was so focused on Alessandra I barely paid attention to my underwater surroundings.

It was hard to believe she was the same woman who'd lost all color when I'd suggested diving during our honeymoon in Jamaica. Now, she lingered by the corals, marveled at a passing sea turtle, and swam alongside a school of yellow fish. The only time she freaked out was when an eel brushed her shin, but overall, she handled herself with such grace I couldn't help but smile.

I hated that we'd grown apart, but I loved how much more at ease she was with something that had once terrified her. I was so fucking proud.

The entire excursion lasted four hours, including transport to and from the dive center. By the time we made it back to land, the group was equal parts exhausted and exhilarated.

The businessman immediately left while the students crowded around their phones, giggling at the pictures they'd taken. The couple, Josh and Jules, announced they were getting drinks at a nearby beach bar and that we were free to join before splitting off.

"Are you hungry?" I asked, falling in step with Alessandra as we walked into the main building. "There's a good restaurant down the street for lunch."

She shook her head. "I'm eating at the house with Marcelo."

"Why wasn't he on the dive too?"

"He woke up late."

"Typical." Alessandra was a morning person, but her brother was a night owl. One time, he'd visited us in New York and hadn't woken up before noon the first three days.

We lapsed into silence as we entered the dive center.

"What about dinner?" I tried again. "I can get us a table at the new restaurant near Tartaruga Beach. Including Marcelo." The restaurant was booked out during high season, but I could easily pull a few strings.

Alessandra stared at the floor. "I haven't decided yet. We might eat in tonight too."

"Right." I rubbed a hand over my face. "Well, if you change your mind, let me know. You have my number, or you can...I mean, I'm right next door."

The familiar heat of humiliation crept beneath my skin.

I hadn't stumbled over my words so badly since my high school English teacher had forced the class to take turns reading *Hamlet* aloud. It'd taken me an eternity to get through one sentence while everyone else snickered behind their hands.

"I know." Alessandra's voice softened a smidge. It wasn't much, but I'd take anything I could get. "I have to go. I'll, um, see you around."

I watched her walk away, deflated. I hadn't expected her to jump back into my arms simply because we were on the same excursion, but I'd expected...fuck, I didn't know. *More.* More talking, more progress.

Then again, perhaps I didn't deserve more.

Instead of staying in town, I returned to the villa and caught up on the news by the pool. The latest job data, market fluctuations, and press conference held by the new head of Sunfolk Bank, whose previous CEO died of cancer a couple of months ago. Between Sunfolk and Orion, there'd been a lot of bank CEO deaths lately, but none of the news was interesting enough to capture my attention or distract me from the woman next door until I spotted a name that hit me like a punch in the gut.

*Thayer University Regents approved naming a wing of*

*Carter Hall to honor former professor David Ehrlich, who died in 2017. The David Ehrlich Wing is home to Thayer's Department of Economics, which served as Ehrlich's academic home for more than twenty years.*

I read the paragraph twice, partly to make sure I was understanding it correctly and partly because I couldn't believe Ehrlich's name was resurfacing again after so long.

It was about damn time. He'd been one of the best professors at Thayer and the only teacher who'd treated me like I was a normal student instead of an annoyance they (barely) tolerated. We'd kept in touch after graduation, and his death had devastated me.

———————

*"You have to eat." Alessandra came up behind me, her voice gentle. "You can't subsist on alcohol alone."*

*"I'm not hungry." I stared out the window, where rain poured from the sky in a relentless river of grief. It was late afternoon. It'd rained nonstop since the morning, and it seemed fitting that Ehrlich's funeral had taken place during the most miserable day of the year.*

*The procession, the casket, the eulogy. They'd been a blur. All I remembered was the ceaseless, biting chill in my bones.*

*"Two bites." Alessandra handed me a sandwich. "That's it. You've barely eaten since…"*

*Since I got the news that Ehrlich had died of a stroke two weeks ago. If it weren't for her, I'd have drowned at the bottom of a bottle by now.*

*Some people might have wondered why I was so torn up over the death of a former professor, but I could count the number of people I cared about who also cared about me on one hand.*

*If Ehrlich hadn't pushed me into tutoring, I would've never met Alessandra, and if he hadn't leveraged his connections to help me the past few years, I wouldn't be opening my own company next month.*

*He'd been a friend, a mentor, and the closest thing I'd had to a father figure. He'd worked so hard on Davenport Capital with me, and he would never see it come to fruition.*

*A boulder lodged itself in my chest and blocked the flow of oxygen to my lungs.*

*"One bite." Alessandra brushed her fingers through my hair. "Last offer."*

*I had zero appetite, but I took a bite for her. I'd been so surly and irritable the past two weeks I was surprised she hadn't left, but she'd stayed by my side through the mood swings, late nights, and restless mornings.*

*I didn't know what I'd done in my past life to deserve her. I wish I did so I could repeat it on a loop and ensure we found our way to each other in every lifetime.*

*"See? That wasn't so bad," she teased, taking the empty wrapper from my hand and tossing it in the trash.*

*I glanced down, surprised to see I'd eaten the whole sandwich. "You tricked me."*

*"Don't blame me. I said one bite. You're the one who kept going." Alessandra laughed. Her expression gentled as she slid onto my lap and looped her arms around my neck. My hand settled on her hip, savoring her warmth.*

*"We'll get through this," she said. "I promise."*

*"I know." Grief ebbed and flowed. I wouldn't drown forever, but Ehrlich's death would always echo.*

*"I actually have something for you." She reached into her pocket and retrieved a small silver object. She pressed it into my free hand, her eyes so tender it wrenched at my heart. "A reminder. No matter how dark it gets, you can always find a light."*

_____

The sun had set, cloaking the town in shadows. Alessandra and Marcelo's house was dark and quiet; they'd gone out for dinner after all.

The click of my lighter was the only sound interrupting the stillness. I stared at the flame as it danced against the night and illuminated the words engraved in silver.

> _To Dom_
> _Love always, Ále_

# CHAPTER 21

*Alessandra*

NO MATTER HOW SOLID THE ROCK, WAVES WOULD eventually erode it through sheer persistence. It was a law of nature, unstoppable and inevitable.

I feared the same phenomenon was happening with me and Dominic. Every run-in crashed against my defenses; every conversation, no matter how short, chipped at my willpower.

I was nowhere close to forgiving him, but I didn't run in the opposite direction when I saw him either. I couldn't decide whether that meant I was coming to terms with our divorce or if I was in danger of sliding back into his orbit.

Either way, I needed to regroup and figure out how to deal with his continued presence. Even if I left Buzios, he'd be there in New York. We had mutual friends, and our chances of running into each other were high. I couldn't brush him off forever. It was too stressful.

"A drink for your thoughts," Marcelo quipped, handing me a mini coconut shell.

"That's dangerous. I've had three already." Nevertheless, I accepted his offer. Batidas de coco—made with coconut milk, sweetened condensed milk, coconut water, and cachaça—were simply too good to resist.

Plus, it was Marcelo's last day on the island before he had to return to work, so we were having a last hurrah at our favorite beachfront bar. I was sad he was leaving so soon, but I couldn't count on my brother to stay by my side forever. One of the reasons I'd left Dominic and the city was to find my autonomy again, and that meant independence from *everyone,* not just my husband.

*Ex-husband,* a voice that sounded suspiciously like Sloane's corrected.

I downed my drink.

"You sure you're going to be okay here by yourself?" Marcelo asked. "Mom's apartment in Rio is empty if you want to head there instead. She's in Tulum. Or Hawaii. Or L.A." He shook his head. "Actually, I don't know where the hell she is."

"Hey, who's the older sibling here?" I nudged his ankle with my foot. "I'll be fine. I'm not ready to give up the island life yet."

Other than the uncertainty cast by Dominic's arrival, Buzios was paradise. I was tanned and toned from hours of surfing, swimming, and sailing. My arms were stacked with beaded bracelets I'd created at a jewelry making workshop, and my physical tension had gradually melted thanks to daily beach yoga.

I'd spent the past two weeks picking up new hobbies I wasn't necessarily good at but enjoyed—hello, drawing—and reaffirming the things I *didn't* enjoy, like trying to keep up with twenty-year-olds at the bar.

For once, I was living for myself, at my own pace, and I loved it.

"Mm-hmm. Looks like someone else isn't ready for you to give it up either." Marcelo nodded at someone behind me. "Incoming."

I turned, my heart skipping a beat before I saw the brown hair and professionally whitened teeth.

"Hey. Alessandra, right?" Ignacio, my diving instructor from Thursday, walked over with a wide smile. "Tudo bom?" How's it going?

"Good. How are you?" I replied in Portuguese. I chalked the pinch in my chest up to alcohol, not disappointment.

"Can't complain." He cast a curious glance at Marcelo, who held out his hand.

"Marcelo. I'm Alessandra's brother."

We made the requisite small talk before Marcelo excused himself to use the restroom. He ignored my glare on his way past. "He's not bad looking," he whispered. "Have fun."

Great. Now my own brother was trying to pimp me out to a semi-stranger.

"So, how long are you staying in Buzios?" Ignacio asked.

"Probably for another week. I haven't decided." I brushed a strand of hair out of my eye.

He nodded and flicked a glance at my left hand. I expected him to back off when he saw my ring until I remembered I didn't have a ring anymore.

My chest pinched again.

"If you need anyone to show you the best hidden gems in town, I'm your guy." Ignacio leaned closer and dropped his voice to a conspiratorial whisper. "I've been coming here since I was kid. I have it all mapped out."

I didn't mention that I'd visited Buzios almost every other year since I was a kid too. "Yeah? What kind of spots?" I teased.

He was too young for me, but a little harmless flirting never hurt anyone. Besides, I needed the reminder that other men existed as romantic potentials besides Dominic. He wasn't the end-all be-all. Not by a long shot.

Ignacio's smile widened. "Well, there's this secret beach…"

We flirted for a while without mentioning Marcelo's extended absence. It was light, pressure-free, and exactly what I needed. We weren't interested in starting a relationship or even hooking up, though I strongly suspected Ignacio wouldn't say no to sex. We were simply having *fun*.

The music shifted from mellow pop to an upbeat samba song. The other bar patrons erupted into cheers. Chairs and tables were pushed aside to make room for a dance floor, and the afternoon's lazy contentment morphed into raucous debauchery.

I shook my head when Ignacio held out his hand. "I'm too tipsy to dance. I'll look like an idiot."

"Come on! Drunken dancing is the best kind of dancing." He gestured around the bar. "Look at everyone here. Do you think they'll judge you?"

Oh, what the hell. If I had to make a fool of myself, I might as well do it on vacation.

I laughed when Ignacio dragged me onto the dance floor and spun me until I was dizzy. We weren't exactly sambaing, but I didn't care. I was enjoying myself too much.

"Oof!" I slammed into him on my last spin.

"Careful." Ignacio steadied me, his laughter blending with the music. "No more drinks for you today."

"I'm not—" My sentence abruptly cut off when I glimpsed a flash of distinctive blond hair.

In the breath between my heart stopping and restarting, Dominic shouldered his way between me and Ignacio and pinned the other man with a stare so cold it sent shivers down my spine.

To his credit, Ignacio didn't back down. "Hey man, what's the deal?" His tone was friendly, but wariness filled his expression. "We were dancing."

"And now you're not," Dominic said, his tone deadly calm.

Ignacio's eyes narrowed. "Do we have a problem?"

"No." I answered for my ex-husband. "Dominic was just leaving. Weren't you?"

He didn't budge.

Anger washed away the remainder of my buzz. "If you don't leave us alone right now," I said quietly, "I will never talk to you again."

It was the first ultimatum I'd ever issued, and I meant every word. I usually wasn't this dramatic, but I refused to let Dominic barge in like a jealous rhino every time he saw me with another man. He'd lost the right to *any* opinions on my personal life weeks ago.

His eyes snapped to mine. Shock flitted through them, followed by a quick flash of betrayal, then hurt.

I would be lying if I said his reaction didn't pull on at least one heartstring. Despite everything that'd happened between us, I didn't want to actively hurt him, but I couldn't let him walk all over me either.

My conviction must've been scrawled all over my face, because after what felt like an eternity, Dominic turned and walked away without a word.

However, the moment was already ruined. No matter how hard I tried to laugh, dance, and focus on Ignacio again, my mind was stuck on the man who held more shares of my attention than he should. He was gone but still *there*, his gaze a warm weight on my skin, his presence a black hole that drew every inch of awareness toward him.

I couldn't take it anymore. I lasted one more song before I made an excuse about needing another drink and left Ignacio on the dance floor.

I stormed toward the bar, where Dominic sat like a king surveying his empire. I stopped inches away from him and jabbed a finger at his chest. "Enough."

His eyebrows rose. "I didn't do anything."

"You're *here*."

"It's public property, *amor*. I have as much right to be here as you do."

"You know what I mean. And stop calling me *amor*." My heart threatened to pound out of my chest. "It's not...I'm not..."

"You're not what?" Dominic's voice dipped a decibel.

"I'm not your wife anymore." I shouldn't have drunk so much. My head swam, and my palms were clammy with sweat.

"No." He didn't take his eyes off mine. "But you're still my love. That hasn't changed."

*Damn him.* Damn him to hell.

He said the right thing every time...when he cared enough to say it. His confession after Monday's dinner had been stuck on a permanent loop in my head for the past week.

*That's all I ask. A chance for us to talk and get to know each other as we are.*

I knew better than to fall for it, but sometimes, resisting him was like a falling stone trying to resist the pull of gravity.

My phone vibrated against my hip. I wrenched my gaze from his, eager for a distraction while my pulse pounded at triple speed. It spiked even more when I saw who was calling, but I pressed *accept* anyway. Anything was better than being alone with Dominic. We might be surrounded by people, but when he was there, no one else existed.

I turned away from him and pressed my phone tight against my ear. "Mom? Is everything okay?"

The last time my mother called me out of the blue like this, she'd lost her passport and missed her flight to New York after partying too hard at some billionaire's chateau in Europe. She had been the guest of honor at a major fashion event in the city the following day, and I'd scrambled to get her an emergency passport *and* a new flight so she could make the event. If it hadn't been for the Davenport name, I might not have succeeded.

"Everything's wonderful," she trilled. "In fact, I have *amazing* news, darling. Are you ready?"

Disbelief coasted through me when she delivered her bombshell. I shouldn't have been surprised, but the timing was absurd, even for her.

"*This* Tuesday? Are you kidding?"

"Why would I kid about something like that? This is a big deal! Of course, you and Marcelo *need* to be there. You're family, and family is nonnegotiable."

"Yes, but—"

"Oops, I have to go. Bernard is waiting for me in the hot tub." She giggled, which was a deeply disconcerting sound coming from one's fifty-seven-year-old parent. "See you soon! Don't forget to moisturize and hydrate. You want to look good for the big day."

"Mom, you can't—"

Dead silence interrupted my protest. She'd hung up.

"What is it?" Dominic asked when I faced him again. A frown was etched in his brow; my end of the conversation was enough to indicate something was wrong.

I was too stunned to hold on to my earlier anger or do anything except tell the truth.

"My mom's getting married again." I looked up, seeing my stupefaction reflected in his eyes. "The wedding is in three days."

## CHAPTER 22

*Alessandra*

IN HER HEYDAY, FABIANA FERREIRA HAD BEEN KNOWN for her curves, her beachy waves, and the small, endearing mole above her upper lip. She'd commanded almost as much money per day as Naomi Campbell, Linda Evangelista, and Christy Turlington, the so-called Holy Trinity of supermodels in the nineties, and she'd graced the covers of every major publication from *Vogue* to *Mode de Vie* to *Cosmopolitan*.

However, outside of her modeling accomplishments, she was even *more* famous for her string of failed relationships, including three marriages (and divorces) by the time she turned forty.

She was almost sixty now, but she could pass for someone twenty years younger as the makeup artist put the finishing touches on her face. It'd been seventy-two hours since her call, and here I was, helping her get ready for her fourth wedding in Rio.

"Thank you, darling," my mother said when I handed her a bottle of coconut water. "I'm *so* glad the dress fits you. Lorena is a genius." Lorena was her longtime stylist and best friend.

"Me too," I said dryly. Considering the tight timeline, I'd have to make do even if the dress hadn't fit.

After my mother's call, Marcelo and I had scrambled to pack and prep for the wedding. I'd been so frazzled I'd forgotten about bus tickets until Dominic stepped in and offered to book us a private driver. His jet was in Rio, and it was easier to get from Buzios to the city by road than by air. Under any other circumstances, I would've said no, but I'd had enough on my mind without stressing over tickets and potential delays. I'd accepted, which meant he was in attendance today since it would've been rude *not* to invite him after he did us a favor, but I'd deal with that later.

At the moment, I was more concerned about my mother's impending marriage to someone I didn't know and hadn't heard of until three days ago.

"How did you and Bernard meet?" Between the fittings, photo-shoots, and last-minute cake tastings, we hadn't had a chance to discuss her relationship until now.

Apparently, Bernard was a big shot in the telecommunications space, which explained how he had the money and resources to pull together a luxury wedding with less than a week's notice. According to Mom, he'd proposed the day before her call.

"At a boutique on Avenue Montaigne. Isn't that just perfect?" My mom sighed. "I was shopping for a new pair of shoes and he was buying jewelry for his mother's birthday. It was love at first sight. He invited me to dinner that night—we went to a restaurant with the most *fabulous* foie gras—and the rest, as they say, is history."

Buying jewelry for his mother? Likely story. I bet the jewelry had been for his girlfriend at the time, but I kept my mouth shut. I'd learned a long time ago that there was no use arguing with my mother when it came to her love life.

"And when did this perfect meet cute happen?" I asked.

"During Paris Fashion Week." My mother examined her reflection with a critical eye. "I need more powder here, here, and here." She pointed to a few flawless spots on her face. "I don't want to look like a melting ice cream cone in photos." The makeup artist obliged even though the base was already perfect.

I was stuck on *Paris Fashion Week*. "The one in September?" I stared at her. "You don't think it's…" *Foolish. Idiotic. Bonkers.* "Imprudent to marry a man you met *two months* ago?"

"When you know, you know. You can't put a timeline on love." She fluffed her hair. "Look at you and Dominic. You got married a year after you met."

My chest squeezed at the reminder. "There's a difference between two months and a year. Besides, we're not married anymore."

Most people would have enough tact not to bring up someone's marriage so soon after their divorce, but my mother and tact were casual acquaintances at best. She wasn't malicious, merely oblivious, which was somehow worse.

"I suppose not. What a shame. There aren't many men who are as rich and handsome as he is." My mother pursed her lips. She'd been skeptical of Dominic until he'd made his first million. She'd softened further after his first hundred million and was all in by the time he'd hit his first billion at the tender young age of twenty-six. "Isn't he your date today? Things can't be that bad if you brought him with you."

"Mother, we're divorced. You can't get any worse than that."

"Then why is he here?"

"Because he flew me and Marcelo here *at the last minute*." I gave her a pointed look.

She ignored it and slanted an uncharacteristically knowing look in my direction. "Alessandra, darling, it's only a three-hour flight from Buzios to Rio. A nice gift would've been a perfectly acceptable thank you. You didn't need to invite him to the wedding."

I stared at the array of creams and lipsticks on the table.

For once, she was right. Having Dominic attend an intimate

family event was one of the worst ideas in the history of bad ideas, but I couldn't bear the thought of attending the wedding solo. I had Marcelo, but he was busy playing groomsman and feeling out our soon-to-be stepfather to help. He wasn't as resigned to our mother's terrible choices in men as I was.

The prospect of sitting through yet another Fabiana Ferréira wedding alone had snuffed out my irritation over Dominic's jealousy and stubborn persistence. He was one of the few people who understood my complicated relationship with my mother, and despite what had happened between us, my first instinct was to turn to him for comfort.

The ceremony started in an hour. Wrangling my mother was like wrangling a toddler—I had to confiscate her hidden flask of alcohol, soothe her temper tantrum when the poor makeup artist finally put her foot down about changing her contour, and shower her with compliments and reassurances as I pulled her away from her reflection—but eventually, I got her to the altar in one piece.

Luckily, unlike her first two lavish weddings (the third had been a drunken affair at an Elvis chapel in Vegas), this one was relatively short and understated. There were about two dozen guests in attendance, which was decent considering the uber last-minute notice. Besides Lorena, I recognized Ayana, my mother's supermodel protege, Lilah Amiri, a famous fashion designer, and a handful of magazine editors.

Dominic sat on the bride's side of the aisle, wearing an exquisite black suit and a solemn expression. The heat of his stare warmed my skin as I walked past him carrying a bouquet of calla lilies.

I was my mother's only bridesmaid this time around, but the walk, the flowers, and the processional music excavated memories of another wedding from long ago and far away.

The doors to the chapel opened. Wagner's "Bridal Chorus" soared, and butterflies caught on the frayed nerves in my stomach.

I was getting married today.

Me, Alessandra Ferreira. Getting married.

I couldn't wrap my head around the concept. I'd fantasized about my Prince Charming here and there as a child, and I'd lingered on pictures of pretty wedding dresses on Pinterest when I came across them as I got older, but I'd never imagined I would marry this young. I was only twenty-three, fresh out of college and trying to navigate the post-school world. What did I know about marriage?

The skirt of my white satin gown rustled with each step. It was a simple ceremony with no more than fifty guests in attendance, much to my mother's chagrin, but neither Dominic nor I had wanted any extraneous fanfare.

Dominic. He stood at the altar, his hands clasped in front of him and his posture ramrod straight.

White jacket. Black pants. Rose boutonnière pinned to his lapel.

Devastating.

And when his gaze caught mine, holding it captive, my nerves fell away like autumn leaves in the wind. His muscles were visibly tense, but his face radiated so much love I could feel the warm tendrils wrap around me from halfway across the room.

People looked at him and only saw the harsh edges and cold exterior. They ruminated over why the daughter of a famous supermodel was dating a "nobody," and they whispered about us getting married too young, too soon, and too quick.

I didn't care. They could gossip all they wanted; I didn't need their validation or extra time to know he was the one.

*"Perfect," Dominic whispered when I reached the altar.*

*I gave him a shy smile, my chest full to the point of bursting. Life contained few certainties, but at that moment, I was sure that I was the luckiest girl alive.*

---

I stopped at the present-day altar. I couldn't breathe past the tears lodged in my throat, and it took every ounce of willpower to force my memories back into the padlocked box where they belonged.

*Don't look at him.*

If I looked at him, I would break down, and the last thing I needed was to embarrass myself at my mother's wedding.

I was so focused on not crying, I only half paid attention to the ceremony. God, this was a bad idea. What had made me think I could do this so soon after my divorce?

*Don't look at him. Don't look at him. Do. Not. Look. at him.*

I would've been a horrible daughter if I'd skipped the event altogether, but I should've insisted on attending as a regular guest. I'd played bridesmaid enough times, and the wedding was so low-key, my mother didn't need someone to stand there holding a bunch of lilies while she recited her vows in English and Portuguese.

The familiar cadence of the words broke the padlock. Memories escaped again, flooding my brain with echoes of my own vows to Dominic.

*"I promise to support you, inspire you, and, above all, love you always—for better or worse, in sickness and health, for richer or poorer. You are my one and only, today, tomorrow, and forever."*

I'd never broken my last vow. Not when I'd moved out, not when I'd served the divorce papers, and not when I'd pushed him away. I'd promised to love Dominic always and I did, even when I shouldn't.

A tear trickled down my cheek. I wiped it away, but in my haste, I made my biggest mistake of the day.

I looked at him.

And once I did, I couldn't look away.

# CHAPTER 23

I WAS IN BRAZIL, SURROUNDED BY CURRENT AND former fashion models, but there was only one person I couldn't take my eyes off of.

Alessandra stood at the altar, resplendent in a pale orange dress that made her glow despite the overcast skies. Wisps of hair framed her face, and a delicate glint of gold gleamed around her neck.

If I were a bride, I would never let her in my wedding party because she outshone everyone around her. Every time, a million times over.

Orange instead of white. Rio instead of DC. Bridesmaid instead of bride.

It wasn't our wedding, but seeing her up there, looking so damn beautiful I couldn't believe she was real...it was an excruciating reminder of what I'd had.

And what I'd lost.

*"I promise to be your best friend, your confidante, and your partner in all things big and small. You will never face the world alone because I'll be there for you, always and forever."*

I'd meant my vows when I'd said them. I still did. But intentions couldn't replace actions, and somewhere along the way, I'd mistaken the former for the latter.

Loving someone wasn't enough if I didn't show it. Appreciating them wasn't enough if I didn't express it.

I'd been so used to Alessandra's unquestioning support that I hadn't realized what a toll being the emotional anchor of our relationship had taken on her. She was strong, but even the strongest needed someone to lean on. I'd promised that someone would be me, and I'd broken that promise more times than I could count.

A fist crushed my heart to pulp.

Alessandra stared straight ahead as her mother walked down the aisle and the real ceremony commenced. I could tell by the tightness of her expression and her stranglehold on the flowers that she was holding back tears.

I didn't know every part of her anymore, but the parts I did know, I knew intimately. Her tears weren't for her mother; they were for us.

The fist squeezed harder. Even if she hated me with the fire of a thousand suns, that wouldn't compare to how much I hated myself in that moment.

A crystal droplet snaked down her cheek. She quickly wiped it away, but our gazes collided when she looked up again. Her eyes shone with pain, and if I hadn't been sitting, the impact would've knocked me flat on my ass.

I'd spent my life building an empire, but in that moment, I would've happily dismantled the entire fucking thing if it meant making her smile instead of cry.

Past and present blurred into one as we stared at each other, caught in the web of a thousand memories and regrets. The buzz had returned to my ears, drowning out the rest of the ceremony. It wasn't until the other guests stood and filed into the reception hall that I realized the actual wedding was over.

Alessandra's eyes lingered on mine for a final beat before she glanced away. It was a small movement, but it felt, irrationally, like I was losing her all over again.

I swallowed past the jagged shards in my throat.

Luckily, the wedding was small, so it was easy to find her in the crowd after she finished her bridesmaid duties. I made it halfway to her before Marcelo stopped me.

"Hey. Can we talk?"

Wariness crept through my chest. He'd been friendly enough in Buzios despite the divorce, but he seemed uncharacteristically guarded as he led me to the quietest corner of the room.

"Whatever you're thinking of doing, don't." Marcelo cut straight to the chase. "Not today."

My eyebrows winged up. "What, exactly, do you think I'm planning to do?"

"I don't know, but I know it has to do with Alessandra." He nodded at his sister, who was talking to a model I vaguely recognized from the billboards in Times Square. "It's not the time, Dom. You know how much our mother stresses her out. She doesn't need you adding to that."

"I just want to talk to her. I'm not going to hurt her."

"You mean, more than you already have?"

I flinched. That shouldn't have hurt as much as it did, considering it was the truth, but that was precisely why his words stung. I had no defense.

Marcelo sighed and rubbed a hand over his face. "Look, I like you. You were a good brother-in-law, and you've done a lot for me over the years. But Ále is my sister. I'll always choose her over anyone else."

I suppressed another flinch at the word *were*. I'd never thought there'd be a day when a simple past tense would sting, but the past two months had been eye-opening in more ways than one.

"I should've kept my distance in Buzios. I was too…" Marcelo shook his head. "Fuck, I don't know. We were brothers for ten years, and it was hard to switch that off. I want you both to be happy, and I thought if you worked out your issues, everyone would win."

"That's still possible." My hand flexed in lieu of reaching for my lighter. It was the only thing I had left from Alessandra that I could hold, and the compulsion to check that it was in my pocket every other minute was growing untenable.

"No," Marcelo said softly. "I saw her face during the ceremony when she looked at you. You broke her heart, Dominic. It would take a hell of a lot more than a trip to Brazil to fix that."

———————

Marcelo's words echoed in my head throughout the reception.

He was right. Taking time off work and coming to Brazil was a drop in the ocean of what I needed to fix things with Alessandra, but it was hard to make progress when she kept running from the shore.

After Marcelo left to take care of something with the caterers, I caught up with Alessandra near the bar, where she watched her mother and new stepfather dance with equal parts exhaustion and amusement.

"Fourth time's the charm, right?" I came up beside her, my senses coming alive with the scent of lilies and rain.

"God, I hope so. I don't think I can sit through another one of my mother's weddings without shaking her." Alessandra stared at the creamy surface of her passion fruit sour. "I didn't get a chance to say it earlier. Thank you again for flying us here. I appreciate it."

"Anytime."

We lapsed into silence. I typically avoided parties unless they were useful for networking. Too many people, too much noise, too few inhibitions. They were overstimulation hell, but they were always more tolerable when Alessandra was next to me. She was the only reason I'd soldiered through as many society events as I had over the years.

"I should—"

"Do you want to—"

We spoke again at the same time. I gestured for her to go first.

"I should check on the food," Alessandra said. "The cake is, um, delicate."

"Your brother is doing that now."

"Then I should check with the DJ on the setlist. It's tough to balance a mix of Brazilian and American music. I don't want anyone to feel—"

"Ále," I said in a low voice. "If you want me to leave, I'll leave. You don't have to make up excuses to avoid me."

She'd always had a tough time with her mother, who had paid more attention to her revolving door of boyfriends and husbands than she had her children. Fabiana should have been the one taking care of Alessandra, but whenever they were together, Alessandra slid right back into her role of caretaker. Even now, I could see her mentally calculating how long it would take before she had to cut Fabiana off from alcohol so she didn't embarrass herself at her own wedding.

She had enough to worry about without worrying about me.

Alessandra fiddled with her glass without looking at me.

I paused, a tiny kernel of hope kindling in my stomach. "Do you want me to leave?"

An eternity passed before she gave a tiny shake of her head.

I wasn't naive enough to think she wanted me here because

she was ready for reconciliation. Besides Marcelo, I was the only person in attendance who understood her wariness when it came to her mother and who was here for *her*, not Fabiana.

It didn't matter. She could ask me to stay and mop the fucking floor and I would do it.

"Come on." I held out my hand. "The reception's over soon. You can't leave without at least one dance."

To my surprise, Alessandra didn't argue. She set her glass on the bar and slid her palm into mine.

I guided her to the dance floor, where I rested my free hand on her hip as we swayed to the music. My pulse thrummed with nerves.

*Don't fuck this up.*

"Do you remember what happened during our reception?" I murmured. "Someone hacked the DJ's booth..."

"And started playing nineties rap during our first dance," Alessandra finished. She let out a small laugh. "I've never seen you look so panicked."

"I'm talented at many things, but freestyling isn't one of them, I'm afraid."

Our DJ had wrestled control back fairly quickly, and we'd never figured out who was responsible for the unexpected musical diversion. However, it made for a good story, and I would never forget how willing Alessandra had been to roll with it. If I hadn't already loved her more than I could fathom, I would've fallen head over heels right then and there.

"If I could rewind time and go back ten years, I'd do a lot of things differently," I said. "Including beefing up the DJ's security." *And loving you the way you deserve.*

The DJ statement was a joke, but everything else wasn't. Despite the billions in my bank accounts, I couldn't buy the only thing I wanted.

A second chance with her.

"If only." Alessandra gave me a sad smile. "But there's no use living in the past."

"No. There isn't." My throat constricted. The drum of my heartbeat intensified behind my ribcage. "Go on a date with me."

She sighed. "Dom..."

"We've never had a real date in Brazil. Every time we've visited, we've spent it with your family."

"That's not a good enough reason."

"I don't need a reason to be with you, *amor*. But I'll give you ten thousand if it means you'll say yes."

A visible swallow slid down her throat. "You always know what to say."

"Not always." I wish I did. I wish I'd said a thousand things and asked a thousand questions instead of glossing over them. "I don't expect you to jump into a relationship with me again, or even go on a second date," I said. "I just want to spend time with you for as long as you'll let me."

Alessandra remained quiet.

"It won't make up for the nights we lost or the dates I missed, but I..." A mix of frustration and misery scraped my words raw. "I'm so fucking sorry. For everything."

Eloquence had abandoned me, but if I stripped away the frills, they were the only words left. Every ounce of regret, shame, and guilt distilled into two words.

*I'm sorry.*

The current song ended. We'd stopped dancing long ago, but we stayed rooted to our spots while my heart thumped to a painful beat.

"One date," Alessandra finally said. My shock of relief cut off a second later when she added, "But that's all it is. It doesn't mean we're dating, and I'm free to see other people. If I do, you can't follow me, threaten the men, or do anything else that'll ruin the dates."

Every muscle coiled at the thought of her dating someone else, but I fought back my visceral reaction. I was smart enough to recognize a test and a punishment when I saw them, and I was desperate enough to take them as they were given.

I dipped my head in agreement before she could walk back her concession. *One date.* I could work with that.

"Deal."

# CHAPTER 24

*Alessandra*

"YOU *WHAT*?" SLOANE'S FACE FILLED MY SCREEN WITH disapproval. "Why would you agree to go on a date with your ex-husband? Are you high? Do I need to fly down for an inter-vention?"

"It's not as bad as it sounds. I told him *one* date and that it doesn't mean we're dating, which means we can see other people."

"Are you actually seeing other people?"

"Not yet," I admitted. "But I will once I'm back in New York."

It'd been two days since my mother's wedding, and I was catching my friends up on everything that'd happened over the past week. My mother had left for her honeymoon yesterday and Marcelo had returned to São Paulo that morning because he couldn't miss any more work—he'd only been granted an extra day off because of the wedding—which meant I was alone in my family's Rio apartment.

I hadn't decided when I'd return to the city yet. It was already mid-December, so I might as well stay here through the New Year. According to Isabella, everything was progressing smoothly with the physical store, and my online shop was still on hiatus. I didn't *need* to be in New York.

"You're dating someone you divorced two months ago," Vivian said gently. "We're just worried you're…"

"Backsliding," Isabella supplied. "A rich, hot guy flying all the way to Brazil to win you back? I don't blame you for caving, but it doesn't solve your core issues. Right?"

"No, and I'm not caving." My response contained the ring of a half-truth. "I know Dominic. He won't give up until he gets what he wants. This way, I can go on a date with him and call it a day."

I made it sound far easier than it was, but Dominic had too much pride to stand by and beg for attention while I dated other men. I gave him a month tops before he bowed out.

"Maybe." Isabella didn't look convinced. "I hope you know what you're doing, babe. We don't want you to get hurt again."

"I won't. I promise."

A knock interrupted our call. There were no groceries in the fridge, so I'd ordered in for breakfast.

I promised my friends I'd update them on the Dominic situation and hung up. I crossed the living room and opened the front door, expecting to see the delivery guy with my açaí bowl.

Instead, broad shoulders and lean muscles filled the doorway. My eyes traveled over white cotton and the strong, tanned expanse of his throat to meet a pair of dark blue eyes.

"Did you eat yet?" Dominic asked before I could ask what the hell he was doing at my mom's apartment at nine in the morning.

"My food's on the way."

"Let me guess. Açaí from Mimi Sucos?"

I crossed my arms. "Maybe." I wasn't *that* predictable. Was I?

"Cancel it," he said with so much self-assurance I almost pulled up the delivery app right then and there. "We're going somewhere better."

"Where?" Mimi Sucos had the best açaí in town.

A hint of mischief creased his cheeks, and my heart fluttered with reluctant anticipation. "You'll see."

---

I'd expected Dominic to take me to a fancy brunch spot or a nice beach for a private picnic...and he did.

In Florianópolis.

Located an hour and a half south of Rio by plane, Floripa (as it was known by locals) was a mecca of hidden coves, stunning beaches, and lush hiking trails. Half of it lay on the mainland, the other half on Santa Catarina Island, and it was my favorite place in Brazil along with Bahia.

Dominic's jet touched down in Floripa two hours after he showed up at my door. A private car met us on the tarmac and whisked us to the city's most luxurious resort.

"Much better than Mimi's, isn't it?" he said as two servers arranged a veritable feast on the table.

We sat on the balcony of the presidential suite overlooking the beach. Sunbathers dotted the white sand like ants, and the wind carried the faint sound of waves and laughter toward us.

"You're unbelievable." I shook my head even as my stomach grumbled at the smell of fresh scrambled eggs and straight-out-of-the-oven pastries. I'd had a snack on the plane, but there was nothing like a basket of buttery pao de queijo to tempt a girl into carb overload. "This is too much. A simple brunch in Rio would've sufficed."

"Not for our first date." A light breeze swept past, ruffling Dominic's hair. He'd acquired a tan since he'd arrived in Brazil, and he looked relaxed and casual in a white T-shirt and shorts. "You deserve the best," he said simply.

Temptation battled with self-preservation. I should keep my guard up, but it was hard when I was surrounded by the things I loved.

Food. Sea. Sun. *Dominic*.

I banished the last thought as I grabbed a cheese bread and ripped it in two. *Remember. No caving*, I warned the butterflies crowding my stomach. I would eat the free food, enjoy the free trip, and leave. That was all.

"It was either Florianópolis or Bahia, but it's been longer since you've visited Floripa." Dominic nodded a thank you at the servers, who retreated and closed the balcony doors with quiet discretion. "So here we are. We can make a long weekend out of it."

I drowned the swarming butterflies with a gulp of orange juice and switched topics. "Don't you need to go back to New York soon? You've been gone for a while."

Except for client meetings, he could do his job remotely, but Dominic liked to know exactly what was happening in his office. Davenport Capital was his kingdom, and he ruled it with an iron fist. I didn't believe for a second that he'd leave it in others' hands for this long.

"I'm staying on top of things while I'm here," he said, confirming my belief.

"Right."

We ate in silence for a while. It was a tentative quiet, the type that sprouted from uncertainty rather than discomfort. How did you act during a first date with someone you'd been married to for ten years?

Talking about the weather was too mundane; talking about anything else was too dangerous. Every time I opened my mouth to make conversation, something about the topic reminded me of *us*.

Hiking trails in Florianópolis reminded me of the time we'd hiked in upstate New York.

The latest action blockbuster reminded me of our popcorn-fueled *Fast and Furious* marathons during the early days of our relationship.

My mother's Instagram stories from her honeymoon in Fiji reminded me of *our* honeymoon in Jamaica. We couldn't afford anything fancy back then, so we'd rented a cozy, semi-rundown cottage by the ocean and spent the week swimming, eating, and having sex. It'd been one of the best weeks of my life.

Aching nostalgia threaded its way through my heartstrings. I'd told Dominic there was no use living in the past, but I'd give anything to turn back time so I could savor our happy days second by second.

That was the irony of life. People always reminisced about the good old days, but we never appreciated living *in* those days until they were gone.

"I ran into my brother recently," Dominic said, his voice quiet.

My head jerked up at his abrupt and unexpected shift in tone. He'd had many foster siblings growing up, but there was only one he'd ever referred to as his brother.

"Roman?"

Dominic rarely talked about his family. I knew his father was dead, his mother had abandoned him when he was a baby, and he'd hated every foster home he'd been placed in. He'd mentioned he and Roman had been close before the latter went to juvie for arson, but that was about it.

"Yes. I ran into him at the bar after you left the bathroom…" My cheeks heated at the reminder of what we'd done in said bathroom. "And he was at the Le Boudoir opening."

My heart stuttered beneath the blow of surprise. I'd been acquainted with pretty much everyone at Le Boudoir. The only person I hadn't recognized was…

An image of cold green eyes and pale skin surfaced in my mind's eye.

"The man who bumped into me." Realization chilled my skin. I'd pushed him out of my mind, but few people disconcerted me as quickly and thoroughly as he had. "*That* was Roman?"

Based on Dominic's previous descriptions, I'd pictured a lanky boy with a buzz cut and sullen expression, not someone who looked like they moonlighted as a killer. Then again, he hadn't seen his brother since they were teenagers. Of course Roman was different now.

Dominic gave a curt nod. He gave me a quick rundown of their interactions since they had run into each other, which wasn't much. "I haven't seen or heard from him since the dinner. I have someone tracking him down, but there's been nothing yet."

"Maybe he finished his work in the city and left," I suggested.

"He hasn't left the city," Dominic said flatly. "If he had, he wouldn't be this hard to track."

True. If someone with Dominic's money and resources couldn't find him...A niggle of unease wormed through my stomach. "He wouldn't hurt you though, would he? You two were close."

"*Were* being the operative word. I don't think he ever forgave me for not being his alibi when he was arrested." A shadow crossed Dominic's face. "I looked for him a few times over the years, but he was a ghost. I thought he'd died."

I picked up on the tiniest kernel of guilt in his tone.

Dominic didn't have many close friends, but he was loyal to those who were loyal back. He'd mentioned once that Roman had taken the rap for him multiple times when they were young. One time, Dominic had stolen cash from his foster mother for a bus ticket to a nearby college tour. Roman had covered for him and said he'd taken the money for a date. In retaliation, their foster mom had hit him with a belt so hard he hadn't been able to sleep on his back for days.

Dominic never said it, but I knew he harbored regrets over how things with Roman had ended.

"Do you want a relationship with him again?" I asked gently. "It's been a long time since you were brothers. You're not the same people anymore."

"I don't trust him." He evaded a direct answer. "I want to know what the hell he's doing in New York and what he's been up to since he got out of juvie. That's all."

I had a feeling Dominic wasn't telling me everything. He had a lot of unresolved issues with his brother, but even if we had still been married, it wasn't my place to help him heal that part of his past. Some journeys were meant to be taken alone.

A loud peal of laughter drifted up from another balcony and dispelled the brooding aftermath of Dominic's statement.

He wiped a hand over his face with a rueful laugh. "I'm sorry. This wasn't the conversation I'd planned for our first date, but you asked about New York and…" His Adam's apple slid up and down his throat. "You're the only person I've ever been able to talk to about these things."

"I know," I said softly. "You don't have to apologize."

This was the Dominic I missed. The one who opened up and *talked* to me instead of hiding behind his masks and money. He was afraid people would leave if they saw behind the curtain, but the parts hidden there were what made him human. Some wanted the myth and legend of Dominic Davenport; I wanted the man.

Used *to want. Past tense*, a stern voice reminded me. *Don't forget this isn't a real date.*

I didn't forget. But it also wasn't a coincidence that, in a day filled with private jets and lavish meals and luxury suites, my favorite part had been a simple conversation about Dominic's family.

The opulence didn't touch my defenses, but the vulnerability chipped at my walls until a tiny section of them crumbled.

# CHAPTER 25

## *Alessandra*

DOMINIC AND I SPENT OUR FIRST DAY IN FLORIPA LAZING around the resort. He had someone bring me a suitcase full of new clothes and makeup since I hadn't packed for an overnight trip, and he'd booked a second suite in case I didn't want to stay in the same one as him, but I'd settled for separate bedrooms. The presidential suite was so big, I wouldn't see him unless I wanted to, anyway.

I'd expected a full itinerary of activities during our stay, but he was surprisingly hands-off about what we did here. Other than mealtimes, which we shared, he kept a respectful distance—almost too much so. By the time the next morning rolled around, I felt like I was on a work trip with a colleague instead of a date.

"Isn't that a good thing?" Isabella asked. I'd called her to check on the status of the store since we hadn't gotten the chance to discuss business during yesterday's group chat. "You can lie by the pool, go home, and call it a day. That's what you wanted."

"Maybe. It's not like him to be so passive." Why would Dominic fly us to another city only to leave me to fend for myself?

"I don't know. People change. Either way, enjoy yourself and don't think about work too much, okay?" Isabella said. "Sloane has the grand opening party under control, and I'm loving the construction noise while I write." She was the only person I knew who'd say something like that and mean it. Isabella thrived in chaos. "I don't want to hear a peep from you this weekend. If there's an emergency, I'll call you."

I laughed. "Sounds good. Thanks again, Isa."

I'd lucked out when I'd met Vivian, who'd then introduced me to Sloane and Isabella. I'd lost touch with my college friends years ago, and though I had casual friends in New York, I'd never felt like part of a group until Vivian took me under her wing.

Happy hours, shopping trips, girls' nights...our friendship made me realize how much I'd lost during my marriage, not only in terms of close confidantes but also in the small things that rounded out a normal, healthy life.

Abandoning my goals in favor of someone else's wasn't healthy. Replacing my hobbies with societal obligations because the latter were better for my husband's business wasn't healthy. Taking a supporting role instead of a main role in what should've been an equal partnership wasn't healthy.

Dominic had his faults, but I wasn't blameless either. I should've stood up for myself and what I wanted far earlier than I had. Younger me had thought love was enough to solve any problem, but growing up meant recognizing the importance of loving yourself as much as you did someone else.

I hung up and changed into a sundress before wandering into the suite's living room. Sunlight spilled through the glass wall and drenched the pale oak floors with golden hues. My stomach rumbled with hunger, but I couldn't decide whether to order room service or wait for Dominic.

I made a left toward his room. I lifted my hand to knock, but his voice bled through the door before I made contact.

"...can't make it back to New York this weekend." His deep

timbre sent a shiver of pleasure down my spine. "I don't care. Tell Grossman he'll have to wait." A short pause. I couldn't see him, but I could picture the irritation stamped on his face. "That's what I pay you for. Take care of the problem, Caroline, because I'm not leaving Brazil until Alessandra does."

The mention of my name plunged my stomach into free fall. I knew Dominic was giving up a lot of business opportunities to be here, but there was a difference between understanding something in theory and hearing it in practice.

I was still finding my equilibrium when the door opened and he nearly walked straight into me. Surprise erased the lines of annoyance from his brow.

"Alessandra? What's wrong?"

An unexpected tinge of sadness tugged at my heart at his assumption that I was only seeking him out because something was wrong.

"Nothing." I fiddled with my bracelets. "Did you have something planned for us today besides meals?"

"I'd rented canoes for this afternoon," Dominic said cautiously. "Why?"

"So nothing in the morning?" I ignored his question.

He shook his head.

"Good." I made an executive decision on the spot. "Because we're going to the market."

---

## Dominic

Florianópolis's Public Market occupied an old colonial building right in the city center. A walk down any of its aisles revealed dozens of vendors selling clothes, food, ceramics, and local handcrafts. The air was alive with the sounds of English and Portuguese as tour guides led their groups through the maze and locals bartered in their native languages.

Alessandra and I grabbed a quick breakfast of coxinhas (chicken croquettes) and ate them while browsing the stalls.

"Which one do you like better?" She held up two scarves. "I can't decide."

I stared at them. They looked exactly the same. "That one." I gestured at the one on the right.

"Perfect. Thanks." She bought the one on the left. "Why are you laughing?"

"No reason." I knew she'd choose the left one. When it came to shopping, she always went with the option I discarded. I suspected she didn't trust my taste in women's fashion, and I would've been offended had I not agreed with her.

I snuck a glance at her as we moved on to the next stall. I'd deliberately kept our schedule open in Florianópolis. I didn't want to overwhelm her or force her to spend every minute with me while we were here. We had several days here; I figured we'd take it slow and see what she wanted to do, which was why I'd been pleasantly surprised when she proposed visiting the market.

I preferred the Michelin-starred chefs and gourmet restaurants, but Alessandra loved street food.

"Did you have work this morning?" she asked. "I heard…um, I thought I heard you talking to Caroline."

"I had a quick call." Caroline was my eyes and ears while I was gone, and she delivered detailed reports over the phone every week. One of my clients was in New York this weekend, but I wasn't flying back to appease his ego when I would much rather be in Brazil with Alessandra.

"Speaking of work, how's the store going?" I asked. "I hear

Isabella is in charge while you're here." Kai was nothing if not meticulous when it came to relaying information.

"Yeah, her and Monty." Alessandra laughed. "I think her snake almost gave one of the contractors a heart attack the other day, but apparently, it's a great taskmaster. Everyone's too scared to slack off with a python glaring at them."

Ball pythons were one of the friendliest species of snake, but I supposed the average person only saw the *snake* part.

"I don't know much about pressed flowers, but if you need any help on the business and finance side, let me know." I should've offered when she'd started her online shop two years ago, but my head had been so stuck in the sand I hadn't realized she'd created an entire fucking business until weeks after it launched. She hadn't said a word, probably because she'd thought I was too busy to care. Kai was the one who'd mentioned it to me.

Alessandra's chin lowered. "Thank you."

"I should've been there for the original launch." Shame held me hostage. "Starting a company is a big deal."

"It's okay. It was just an Etsy shop at the time. It's not like I was entering the Fortune 500."

I didn't smile at her joke. It wasn't okay, or our relationship wouldn't be where it was right now.

"I mean it. If you need anything at all, call me. If I'm in a meeting, my office knows to put you through." Considering how well Floria Designs was doing, she didn't need my help, but the overture was there.

An ember of pride flared to life. I hated missing a milestone as big as the launch of her first business, but I was so fucking proud of what she'd built.

"Why pressed flowers?" I asked, desperate to keep the conversation flowing. If we stopped, she'd withdraw again, and I wanted to prolong this moment for as long as possible.

"Honestly, I was bored and needed a hobby." Pink tinted Alessandra's cheeks. "I've always loved flowers, and I came across a DIY tutorial on how to press them. I tried it, it was fun, and, well." She shrugged. "The rest is history."

"What made you decide to turn it from a hobby into a business?"

"I don't know." Her face took on a far-off expression. "I guess I wanted something I could call my own. Everything we had belonged to you. Our house, our cars, our clothes. Even if I bought them, you paid for them. It got to a point where I..." She swallowed. "Where I felt like I wasn't my own person anymore. I needed something to remind me I mattered. Me, as an individual, not as a wife or daughter or sister."

We'd stopped walking. I didn't know when we'd stopped or how long we'd been standing there, but I couldn't move if I'd wanted to.

I knew Alessandra had been unhappy with our marriage. After all, we were divorced. But I hadn't realized how deep-seated her unhappiness was, not just with our relationship but with herself.

I'd thought covering all our expenses and ensuring she never wanted for anything would make us happier. We'd struggled so fucking much in our early years, and I never wanted us to fall back into that hole again. What I hadn't accounted for were the things we'd needed that weren't material.

Time. Attention. Consideration.

They couldn't be bought, and in my rush to bury any possible problem with money, I'd completely lost sight of that fact.

"You matter," I said. "Always."

She was the *only* person who'd ever truly mattered. Even if she didn't love me anymore, even if all my efforts to win her back failed, she would always be the sun anchoring my universe.

Alessandra's eyes glossed. She quickly looked away, but a telltale hitch disrupted her otherwise bright voice. "Well, that's enough heavy talk for today. It's not even noon, and we have a lot of stalls to get through before the boating trip."

We stuck with safe topics for the rest of the morning—sports, food, the weather. But I never forgot the look on Alessandra's face when she'd explained why she'd opened Floria Designs.

After we exhausted the market, we ate lunch at a nearby oyster bar (since she'd picked breakfast, I picked lunch) and made our way to the canoe rental. Alessandra and I had gone canoeing during our honeymoon, and I thought it'd be a nice throwback to happier days.

We were good together once. We could be good together again.

Unfortunately, neither of us had gone canoeing in years, and our skills were…rusty, to say the least.

"Maybe this wasn't the best idea," Alessandra said as the boat wobbled. She glanced around us with trepidation. The nearest boaters were mere pinpricks in the distance. "We should've asked for a guide."

"We don't need a guide." I shifted, the canoe rocking with my movement. "We're perfectly capable of maneuvering a little wooden boat."

She glanced back at me. "Is this another one of those man things? Like how you guys refuse to ask for directions when you're lost, but now you're refusing to ask for help when you're in danger of tipping over."

"We're in the middle of a lagoon," I pointed out. "The time for a guide has long passed." Besides, I wanted Alessandra to myself; I didn't want a random third wheel ruining our date. "Trust me. It'll be fine."

"If you say so." She sounded doubtful.

Despite her misgivings, our canoe steadied the farther we went. My tension eased, and I settled back to enjoy our surroundings. I understood why Alessandra loved Florianópolis so much. It was—

"Oh my God!" She gasped. "Is that a dolphin?"

"I don't think there are—Ále, no!" It was too late. She twisted her body to the right, and the canoe tipped over, dumping us into the cold water.

Her scream and my curse warped the peaceful air. Then water closed in overhead, and all was silent until we resurfaced with a chorus of coughs and splutters. Luckily, we'd dislodged ourselves during the fall and avoided getting trapped under the boat, but treading water in the middle of a fucking lagoon hadn't been part of my game plan.

I let out another, more colorful curse.

I glanced at Alessandra, whose shoulders shook as she covered her face.

Alarm edged out my annoyance. "What is it? Are you hurt?" Had she hit her head on her way down? It would take a while to right the canoe, and we were at least—

A familiar sound leaked between her fingers. Was she... *laughing?*

She removed her hands from her face. No, she wasn't laughing. She was fucking *howling* to the point where her laughter no longer made a sound.

"I'm fine," she gasped, tears of mirth filling her eyes. "I just... you look like..."

I narrowed my eyes even as my mouth twitched. I didn't find our situation particularly funny, but it was impossible to see her smile and not want to smile too. "Like what? A dolphin?" I asked pointedly.

"No," she said with zero apology. "You look like a drowned rat."

Shock submerged me more thoroughly than the water when we'd tipped over. "I sure as fuck don't."

"I'm sorry, but you do." Alessandra's laughter finally subsided, but amusement lingered on her face. "You can't see yourself. I can, so my observation carries more—" She squealed when a splash of water hit her in the face. She wiped the droplets from her eyes and stared at me. "Did you just *splash* me?"

I shrugged. "It was an accident."

The words had barely left my mouth before she retaliated, and we ended up in a splashing war. Laughter and shrieks filled the air.

We were acting like children let loose on the beach, and I could barely breathe past her watery assaults, but there was something exhilarating about not giving a shit. It didn't matter that we were acting silly and immature; it was fucking fun.

By the time we called a truce, we were so drenched we looked like we'd taken a shower in our clothes. Twice.

Alessandra's mascara formed twin black tracks down her cheeks. Her hair was tangled, and not a single trace of her lipstick remained.

"I know," she said when she caught me staring. "You're not the only one who looks like a drowned rat."

"That's not what I was thinking."

"Then what were you thinking?" The volume of her voice tapered off as I closed the distance between us.

I brushed a stray droplet of water from her forehead before it reached her eye. "I was thinking..." My hand lowered and lingered by her cheek. "That you're the most beautiful sight I've ever seen."

Our breaths rose and fell over the soft laps of the water. The last echoes of our laughter disappeared and gave way to warm, heavy anticipation.

Alessandra's lips parted. She didn't pull away as I gathered her hair in a gentle fist and dipped my head, inch by agonizing inch, until our mouths touched.

Some kisses were a product of passion. Others were an

outpouring of emotion. But this one? This one was a fucking revelation.

Because when Alessandra angled her chin up and kissed me back, I finally understood, if only for a moment in time, what true contentment felt like.

No yearning, no chasing, no worries. Just her and us.

It was all I needed.

# CHAPTER 26

## *Alessandra*

I'D KISSED MY EX-HUSBAND.

I'd kissed my ex-husband and *liked* it.

What the hell was wrong with me?

I buried my face in my pillow with a groan. My alarm clock had gone off three times already, but I couldn't bring myself to get out of bed. Getting out of bed meant facing the aftermath of yesterday's choices, and I was content to stay in my bubble of delusion.

Sadly, the universe didn't agree. Less than a minute after I settled on the decision to loiter beneath the covers all morning, my phone rang. I ignored it. It rang again.

Another groan traveled up my throat. I almost wished I hadn't stored it in one of the canoe rental's lockers before we'd rowed out. Otherwise, it'd be at the bottom of the lagoon, and I wouldn't have to talk to anyone at—I peeked at the digital alarm clock— eight fifteen in the morning.

I pressed *answer* and put the caller on speakerphone without lifting my head or checking their identity. "Hello?"

"Good morning!" Isabella chirped. "Sooo, how's it going? Having the time of your life, I hope."

"It's complicated." The pillow muffled my response.

My kiss with Dominic had lasted both too long and not long enough. In reality, we couldn't have embraced for more than a few minutes, but his heat and taste had imprinted themselves so thoroughly on my senses that I could still feel him a day later.

The soft, firm pressure of his mouth. The expert sweep of his tongue against mine. The delicious tingles running down my spine when he'd tugged on my hair.

Goose bumps peppered my skin.

"Right, right." Isabella sounded distracted. "Um, out of curiosity, are you at your hotel right now?"

"Yes. I was sleeping," I said pointedly, which was half-true. Honestly, I was surprised she was calling this early. Isabella wasn't a morning person.

*Wait a minute.* Why *was* she calling this early?

I popped up, my adrenaline spiking with sudden alarm. "Why? Is something wrong?"

"Well…" She inhaled an audible breath. "A pipe burst overnight. The entire store is, um, flooded."

Shock punched through the tatters of my grogginess. *Flooded.* The word pulsed beneath my skin like a frantic heartbeat.

"How bad is it?" My voice remained surprisingly calm despite the panic short-circuiting my brain.

There were other questions I should ask—things I should do—but dread rendered me immobile as I waited for Isabella's answer.

"Pretty bad. The water damaged a majority of the inventory, and some of the electronics are toast. It happened overnight, so we're still getting a sense of the full scope of the damage. Kai called in someone who's assessing the situation right now." Guilt leaked over the line. "I'm *so* sorry. If I'd showed up earlier…"

"It's not your fault. There's nothing you could've done." Isabella was already doing me a huge favor by looking after the store while I was gone, and she wasn't a plumbing professional. Even *I* didn't know what to do in the case of a burst pipe.

"Don't worry. We'll take care of everything," Isabella said. Her guilt was still palpable. "Kai's on it, and the pipe will be fixed within the next two hours, but I figured you'd want to know."

"Thank you." My own guilt formed knots between my shoulders. The store's grand opening was in less than two months. Sloane had been working her ass off on the party, and she'd already sent invites to dozens of high-profile guests—the ones I depended on to spread the word and keep the business afloat. Managing a physical shop required more strategy and publicity than an online one; I couldn't fuck this up.

I knew that, and yet I'd been hiding in Brazil for the past two weeks. Yes, I'd needed a break from the city, but at this point, I was actively avoiding my return. Brazil was fantasy; New York was reality, and it was time I stopped running from my problems. It wasn't fair or right to make my friends shoulder the burden of managing *my* business. Isabella had a book to write, and Kai had a multibillion-dollar corporation to run. They shouldn't be fixing my plumbing issues.

"Tell Kai I'll handle it," I said. I glanced at my suitcase, which lay open on the luggage rack across the room. "I'm flying back to New York."

———

I asked Dominic for help out of necessity. I couldn't find any last-minute direct flights to New York, and when I explained the situation, he checked us out of the hotel and had us in the air within two hours. No follow-up questions required.

*The perks of owning a private jet.*

We didn't discuss our kiss during the flight. When we weren't eating or sleeping, we were working. I researched how to handle burst pipes, ordered extra inventory, and emailed my current contractors since they couldn't resume their work until the mess had been cleaned up. Dominic did whatever the CEOs of financial conglomerates did.

He tried to help me, but I declined. The flight was enough; I hated asking him for favors.

By the time we landed in New York that night, I felt marginally better...until I saw the store.

The place was soaked through. One of the drywall panels was so drenched it'd collapsed, and several pressed flower pieces had been pummeled into pulp from the force of the water. Luckily, the cafe equipment hadn't been delivered yet, but my work computer, printer, and various other devices were out of commission.

All my projects and gallery pieces, ruined. All my plans, upended. It would take thousands of dollars and God knew how many hours to ensure the space was ready for the grand opening.

Unshed tears crowded my throat. The burst pipe wasn't anyone's fault. It was simply bad luck, but it also felt like an omen. The universe's way of telling me I wasn't cut out for this, that I was better suited for building others' dreams instead of my own.

I stared at the waterlogged floor, where shards of glass glinted like the broken pieces of my life.

My divorce. My business. My relationship with my mother. Every fear, doubt, and insecurity I'd suppressed during the lost years of my life, when I'd lived without living. They cracked the glaze in my eyes, and tears poured through, blurring the carnage with a film of defeat.

I was so lost in my distress that I didn't resist when Dominic's arms closed around me and pulled me into his chest. He'd insisted on accompanying me to the store since it was so late, and I hadn't argued. I didn't have the energy.

I pressed my face against his chest, my soft sobs permeating the silence. I was probably ruining his shirt with my tears, but he didn't complain. In fact, he hadn't said a word since we'd arrived; he didn't need to.

Actions spoke louder than words, and in that moment, I didn't care about the things he'd done or hadn't done during our marriage.

I simply leaned into him, breathed in the comfort of his familiar scent, and let him hold me together.

# CHAPTER 27

*Alessandra*

I ALLOWED MYSELF TO WALLOW IN SELF-PITY FOR one night.

After I surveyed the shop's damage, I went home, showered, and fell asleep feeling sorry for myself. However, sometime between Saturday night and Sunday morning, the self-pity crystallized into determination.

I'd spent *years* living on the sidelines. Now that I'd finally stepped out of my comfort zone, was I really going to let the first obstacle I encountered knock me down?

It was physical damage, not death or financial disaster. My problem was totally fixable. If worse came to worst, I'd push back the grand opening and take a hit on the nonrefundable expenses like catering.

With that in mind, I spent the rest of the weekend formulating a game plan and looking up costs for replacement furniture and inventory. Most of them made my stomach churn. I needed rush deliveries to fix the shop in time for the grand opening, and rush deliveries (especially during the holidays) were expensive. *Really* expensive. Renters' insurance covered some of the costs, but I would still have to pay a decent chunk out of pocket.

On the bright side, I wasn't responsible for any property damage. Aiden was, and he swung by the following Monday anyway to assess the situation.

"The good news is, it could've been worse," he said after his walk-through. He was unexpectedly calm, but I guess he dealt with burst pipes often as a landlord. "The electrical system is mostly intact, and the ceiling hasn't collapsed."

A weak laugh scraped up my throat. It was lunchtime. I'd been cleaning the debris since six in the morning, and I probably looked like death warmed over, but I was too exhausted to care. "Thank God for the small things. What's the bad news?"

I might as well face it all at the same time. One giant blow was better than a thousand small cuts.

"The bad news is, your fingers are going to bleed from how many flowers you need to press before the grand opening." Aiden rapped a gentle knuckle against the table where I'd dumped the ruined projects. "What's the damage?"

"Two dozen." I deflated. It took me at least a week to get each one exactly the way I wanted it. Recreating two dozen in the next two months was impossible unless I spent every waking hour on the project. I didn't have the luxury of doing that. Even with my virtual assistants' help, administrative tasks dominated half my workload.

"How about this? I'll handle—"

The jangle of bells above the front door cut Aiden off mid-sentence.

Sharp jaw. Golden stubble. Lean muscles and ruthless command wrapped in a custom-tailored charcoal suit. *Dominic.*

A cool rush of shock flooded me. It was the middle of his first day back to work. What the *hell* was he doing here?

His gaze found mine, warm with concern, before coasting to Aiden. It was like watching a switch flip. The concern vanished beneath a layer of frost, and a vat of tension-laced silence drenched the already-damp floors.

"Hey," Aiden said easily. His tone was cordial, but challenge flickered in his eyes. "You're Alessandra's ex, right?"

I flinched at his emphasis on the word *ex*. I didn't relish the prospect of cleaning up blood along with everything else because that was where we were headed if Aiden provoked Dominic any further.

A smile curved along Dominic's mouth, as dark and cold as midnight ice. "Have we met?"

"Yeah. I was having dinner with her and you interrupted us." Aiden's smile matched his. "Kind of like how you're interrupting us now."

"*Okay.*" I quickly stepped in between them before their testosterone overran their good sense. "As much as I'm enjoying this chat, I have a lot to do. Aiden, thank you for coming by on such short notice. I'll call you if I have any questions. Dominic, what can I do for you?" I asked pointedly.

"I'm here to assist with cleanup." He kept his eyes on Aiden, who didn't budge from his spot next to me. I stifled a sigh. *Men.* "Your grand opening is coming up. Every extra pair of hands helps."

The thought of Dominic engaging in manual labor was so absurd I almost laughed out loud. "You have work." I could only imagine how much had piled up during his time in Brazil. "I'll be fine. It's tedious, but I'll get it done."

"You also need to recreate your collection," Aiden told me. "That's a better use of your time than sweeping and taking out the trash. Dominic is right. Every extra pair of hands helps." He leaned against the counter and crossed his arms. "I'm happy to pitch in as well. I prefer physical tasks over desk work anyway."

It was another indirect barb at Dominic, whose chilling calm reminded me of the ocean before a storm.

"I've rearranged my schedule." Dominic acted like Aiden hadn't spoken. "I'll work and take meetings in the morning, but my afternoons are reserved for you."

His gaze found mine again. My heart wobbled as his words slid into the empty places lurking beneath my defenses.

I wanted to say no. Brazil was one thing; inviting Dominic back into my life in New York was another. That wasn't even touching on the Aiden issue.

But Aiden was right about me needing to recreate my collection. I couldn't open a pressed flowers shop with no pressed flowers on display, and the rest of the construction work was at a standstill until I fixed the damage from the burst pipe. I would be an idiot to turn down voluntary free labor.

"Fine." I sincerely hoped I wasn't creating more trouble for myself, but right now, restoring the shop trumped everything else. "If either of you would like to help, feel free to drop by whenever you can. *But…*" I held up a hand when they opened their mouths at the same time. "I don't want any arguing, insults, or passive aggressiveness. Please keep it civil."

"Of course," Aiden said. "We have no reason not to be. Right, Dominic?"

Dominic's smile held no humor. "Absolutely."

My gaze ping-ponged between the stubborn jut of Aiden's chin and the dangerous glint in Dominic's eyes.

I sighed.

This was going to be a long week.

# CHAPTER 28

*Dominic*

"YOU'RE IN MY WAY." I SHOULDERED PAST AIDEN WITH more force than necessary. Alessandra had warned us against passive-aggressiveness, but it wasn't my fault if I bumped into her landlord while I was taking out the trash. The asshole was standing right in my path.

He stumbled before regaining his balance and pinning me with a hard smile. "Perhaps you should find an alternate route. There's plenty of space around me."

"It's covered with trash." I dumped an armful of ruined flowers into a giant Hefty bag.

"Then wait." He resumed sweeping a pile of glass shards into a dustpan. "You're not the only one working."

My eye twitched. I'd been here less than three hours, and I already wanted to punch Aiden in his smug, bearded face. Alessandra said their relationship was platonic, but no landlord was *this* hands-on with his tenant unless he wanted something.

Thank fuck I was here to make sure he didn't do anything sleazy. I would've helped Alessandra clean up regardless, but

Aiden's presence ensured I didn't step foot outside the shop until after he'd left every day.

"No, but I'm the only one in this room working efficiently," I said coolly. "How long have you been sweeping the same glass?"

"It's not always about speed. Good work requires time and care," Aiden said. "You could learn a few things about that."

Red crept into my vision. It would be so easy to grab one of the bigger glass shards and—

"How's everything going?" Alessandra emerged from the supply closet, looking tired but more optimistic than she had when we first saw the damage.

"Great," Aiden and I chorused. He smiled at me. I smiled at him. We smiled at Alessandra together.

"We're making a lot of progress," I said, which was true. We'd cleaned up most of the debris over the past two days, and we could start arranging the furniture back to their original positions tomorrow.

Her eyebrows skyrocketed, but she didn't question our over-the-top cheerfulness. I think she was just happy she hadn't walked into a fistfight or, if I had my way, bloody murder.

Alessandra stayed on the main floor, so Aiden and I kept our mouths shut for the remainder of the afternoon.

My sweat-drenched shirt stuck to my skin, and my muscles ached from hauling giant stuffed trash bags out to the dumpster every hour. I worked out, but I hadn't undertaken basic physical labor since I started Davenport Capital. The mindless tasks were grueling but oddly soothing.

Thanks to my temporary new schedule, I had to cram a day's worth of client interactions and financial assessments into six or seven hours every morning. It was nice to show up at Floria Designs in the afternoon and not have to think about what I was doing.

My team wasn't happy about the changes, but they worked for me, not the other way around. As long as our portfolios were performing well, which they were, they had no valid reason to complain.

"Here." Alessandra handed me a glass of water at the end of the day. Aiden had left twenty minutes ago for a dinner reservation, and I'd slowed my pace so I could spend a little more time with her. "You look like you could use this."

"Thanks." My fingers brushed hers when I took the glass. A burst of electricity zipped over my skin, and Alessandra stepped back so quickly she almost tripped over a flattened cardboard box.

I wasn't the only one who'd felt the charge between us.

"Things are shaping up," I said huskily. "I think we'll be done by the weekend."

"I hope so." A pink flush decorated her face and chest. She looked so fucking adorable, I almost grabbed her and kissed her again, but we hadn't even discussed our kiss at the lagoon yet. The last thing I wanted was to push her too far, too fast. "Thank you again for helping me with this." She gestured around the store. "You don't need to."

"No, but I want to," I said simply.

Alessandra had supported me unfailingly through the years, and I hadn't done the same for her. Not as much as I should've. I could scrub every inch of the store every day for the next ten years and it wouldn't come close to what she deserved. It was why I'd helped her myself instead of hiring a crew to do it. She warranted attention, not delegation.

Our breaths fluttered in the air before they liquefied into silence.

Lawn mowing, dishwashing, working as a busboy. I'd spent the first half of my life serving others for figurative pennies. After I made my first million, I swore I would never clean up other people's messes again, but I would happily spend the rest of my life doing just that if it meant Alessandra would keep looking at me the way she did now.

Like maybe, just maybe, the tiny flame of hope I'd carried around for us since our divorce wasn't misplaced after all.

———————

As predicted, we completed our cleanup efforts on Saturday. I'd developed a baseball team's worth of calluses by that point, but it was worth it.

"You did it," I said when Alessandra collapsed into her chair with visible relief. "The store is officially back on track."

"Sort of. I have about a thousand flowers left to dry before the grand opening, but..." Her sigh melted into a small smile. "*God,* it'll feel good to walk in on Monday and not see a pile of trash waiting for me."

"To no trash." I lifted my can of Coke.

She laughed and clinked hers against mine. "Amen."

We sat on opposite sides of her desk, which groaned beneath the weight of our Chinese takeout. We couldn't decide what to eat, so we'd ordered a bit of everything—beef with broccoli, spring rolls, sesame chicken, crab rangoon, sweet and sour pork. The delivery guy couldn't hide his shock when he saw there were only two of us during his drop-off.

That fucker Aiden had tried to stay for dinner as well, but a quick call in the bathroom took care of that problem—he was currently dealing with a vandalization issue at another one of his properties. It was fascinating how much damage one rock could inflict on glass.

I'd exhausted my patience with him days ago. He was lucky I hadn't called in anything more destructive than a fucking rock.

"I bet this isn't your idea of the perfect Saturday night."

Alessandra stabbed at a piece of broccoli. "Be honest. Where are you supposed to be right now?"

I'd received invitations to two charity galas, a private museum exhibit, and a dinner party at the Singhs' townhouse for that night. I'd declined all of them.

"Nowhere," I said. "I'm exactly where I want to be."

Alessandra's gaze faltered. She lowered her food without eating it, and the silence stretched so taut I feared it would snap and break the fragile camaraderie we'd developed since Brazil.

Part of me wanted to sweep the tough topics under the rug and continue enjoying our night. The other part knew that would only be a Band-Aid, not a cure. Alessandra and I had plastered the cracks in our marriage with a shiny veneer. It'd worked—until it hadn't.

Sometimes, the only way to cross the highest mountain was to climb it.

"We should talk about what happened at the lagoon." The elephant had been sitting between us for too long. "Our kiss—"

"Was just a kiss." Alessandra pushed her broccoli around without glancing up. "We were on a date. Kisses happen on dates."

"Ále..."

"No. Don't make it into something more than it was." A tremor ran beneath her words. "You asked for one date, and I gave it to you. That's it."

"If it didn't mean anything, you'd be able to look at me." My food lay abandoned on my plate, but it didn't matter. I'd lost my appetite. "No more lying to each other or ourselves. We deserve that much."

"I don't know what you want me to say." Alessandra threw her hands up, her features painted with frustration. "Do you want me to say I enjoyed the kiss and I don't regret it even though I should? Fine. I did, and I don't. But physical attraction has never been the issue. When I look at you, I..." Her voice caught. "I think I could never love anyone more than you or after you. That you took everything I had to give, and I gave it freely because I couldn't imagine a world where we wouldn't be together."

Her face blurred beneath the ache tearing through my insides.

"But I'm living in that world right now, and I'm scared." Alessandra's chin wobbled. "I don't know how to live life without you, Dom. I haven't dated anyone else in over ten years, and I just...I can't..." Her voice dropped to a whisper. "I can't promise you anything more than I already have."

I tried to speak, but every time I grasped a response, it crumbled into dust. I could only sit there and listen as she shredded my heart methodically, piece by piece.

"I know you're trying. I know what you gave up to be in Brazil, to be here, and I truly appreciate it. But I'm not ready for anything more than what we have. I'm not sure I ever will be." A lone tear streaked down her face. "You broke my heart, and you weren't even there to witness it."

If I ever thought I'd been in pain before, I was wrong. Broken bones and my foster mother's whippings paled in comparison to the white-hot lance of Alessandra's words.

I'd never intended to hurt her, but impact trumped intention, and no amount of verbal apologies could make up for what I'd done.

"I understand." A stranger's voice carried my words. It was too rough, too raw to be mine, but it was the only thing I had, so I used it. "If you need time, take it. If you want to date other people, do it. I won't interfere. I didn't appreciate you when I had you, and that's my cross to bear. But you'll always be the love of my life, and I'll always be here, whether it's a month, a year, or a lifetime from now." The sound of her sob dampened my cheek with something hot and wet. "There are probably hundreds of men who'd line up for the chance to be with you. I only ask that you let me be one of them."

I was taking the biggest gamble of my life. She'd said we could date other people in Brazil, but that had been hypothetical; this was real. The thought of standing by and watching another man touch her without doing anything about it made it damn near impossible to breathe.

But I broke her heart once, and I'd let her break my heart a thousand times in return if it meant that one day, she found her way back to me.

# CHAPTER 29

## *Alessandra*

"HE REALLY SAID HE'S OKAY WITH YOU DATING OTHER people?" Isabella wrinkled her nose. "That doesn't sound like Dominic."

"He's obviously lying." Sloane tapped her pen against her notebook. "I bet he thinks Alessandra will go on a few dates, not like any of them, and run back to him." Next to her, The Fish peered out at us from his bowl, his bulging eyes devoid of thought.

For the first time in my life, I was jealous of a freaking goldfish. If only I could ditch my earthly worries and spend my life swimming and eating custom pellets instead. *He has no idea how good he has it.*

"Am I the only one who feels bad for him?" Vivian drew her bottom lip between her teeth. "It's been months, and he's obviously trying. Maybe he *has* changed."

I wasn't surprised she was the first of my friends to soften toward Dominic. Given her history with Dante, she knew exactly how it felt to have the person you love mess up—and whether forgiveness was an option. In their case, it worked out. My case was still pending.

However, she wasn't the only person who felt bad. My heart

twinged every time I thought about Dominic, but that wasn't enough for me to run back into his arms.

"Can we talk about something else?" I rubbed my temple. My friends and I had rehashed my time in Brazil and my conversation with him last night so many times I wanted to scream. "Viv, how was your meeting with Buffy Darlington?"

The four of us were curled up at Sloane's apartment. Technically, it was a movie night, but we'd been too busy gossiping to actually watch the chosen film (except for Sloane, who managed to juggle our conversation with writing her undoubtedly vicious review of the latest rom-com).

"Terrifying, per usual." Thankfully, Vivian accepted my subject change without argument. Buffy was one of the grande dames of New York society and notoriously picky when it came to her events. She'd hired Vivian to plan her annual holiday soiree, which Vivian had been stressing about for the past three months. "But everything's confirmed and ready to go for tomorrow."

"Buffy's party tomorrow, the Valhalla Christmas gala on Tuesday." Isabella yawned. "There's nothing like the holidays in New York."

"It's a terrible season," Sloane said. "The Christmas music. The cheesy movies. The reindeer sweaters. *God*, the sweaters. They make me want to die."

"You've watched every single one of those cheesy movies," I pointed out. "You must not hate them that much."

"Sometimes, you have to endure the awful to appreciate the mediocre, which a majority of modern films are."

Isabella, Vivian, and I exchanged amused glances. It was a not-so-secret ongoing joke between us that Sloane single-handedly kept the romantic comedy industry alive. For someone who allegedly despised rom-coms, she was committed to watching every new release the day it came out.

"Who wants another drink?" Isabella tossed a handful of popcorn in her mouth and reached for the half-empty bottle of rum on the coffee table. "I'm in editing hell for my second book, so I could use all the rum and Cokes I can get," she said, her voice muffled.

I shook my head. "No, thanks." I'd already had three. Any more and I'd do something stupid, like message someone on the dating app I'd impulsively downloaded that morning. I'd swiped through a dozen profiles before matching with one. It'd freaked me out so much I'd immediately closed out of the app and pretended it didn't exist.

Clearly, my dating skills were rusty.

"I'll drink after I finish this." Sloane's pen flew over the page as she muttered under her breath. I couldn't catch all of it, but I thought I heard the phrases *sickening cheesefest of unbearable length* and *so unrealistic it makes mother-daughter body swaps seem believable*.

"Viv?" Isabella turned to the last member of our group. "You've been drinking water all night. Live a little!" She shook the rum with a dramatic flourish.

"I'd love to, but I can't." Vivian tucked a strand of hair behind her ear. "Not for seven more months."

Sloane's head jerked up from her notebook. Isabella's jaw unhinged, prompting a kernel of popcorn to fall out onto the floor.

I was the first to speak. "Are you…"

"I'm pregnant," Vivian confirmed. Her smile blossomed into a full-blown grin when we erupted into screams and laughter. We tackled her in a group hug, our questions overlapping with each other in a stream of euphoria.

"Do you know the gender yet?"

"What baby names are you thinking of?"

"Can I be the godmother?"

"Holy shit, you're *pregnant*!"

Vivian and Dante had been married for three years, so it was only a matter of time before they had kids. I was genuinely thrilled for her, but I couldn't stop a wave of sadness from dampening my mood when I thought about my life compared to hers.

Dominic and I both wanted children. We'd discussed it at the start of our relationship, and we'd agreed we would wait until our finances and careers were stable before we tried for a child. Unfortunately, by the time that happened, he'd been so obsessed with work we hadn't tried in earnest.

I was glad we hadn't. As much as I wanted a son or daughter, I would've basically raised them alone, and I didn't want any of my children to feel neglected.

The doorbell rang.

"I'll get it." I rose and walked to the door while Sloane and Isabella continued to bombard Vivian with questions.

A twenty-something guy in a white polo shirt greeted me. "Alessandra Ferreira?" He carried a small, gift-wrapped box in his hands.

"That's me." A line of puzzlement dug between my brows. I hadn't ordered anything.

"Sign here, please." He handed me a tablet.

I scribbled my signature and, too curious to wait, tore open the wrapping paper immediately after he left. The white box underneath contained no hint of what was inside, but when I opened it, my heart came to an utter standstill.

---

*"You brought me a present on our first date? You must really like me,"* I teased, taking the gift bag from Dominic's hand.

*A hint of color glazed his cheekbones. "It's not for the date. It's for the semester."*

*"What…"* My sentence trailed off when I retrieved the item.

*The cheerful white mug had a gold handle and a red apple stamped with the words "World's Best Teacher" in bold black.*

*Emotion crested in my throat.*

*No tutee had ever bought me anything beyond a Starbucks gift card. It was so unlike Dominic, both in sentiment and in product, that it rendered me speechless.*

*He must've mistaken my silence for displeasure because his color deepened.*

*"I know it's cheesy, and you're a tutor, not a teacher," Dominic said stiffly. "But you said your favorite mug broke a few weeks ago and…fuck. Never mind." He reached for it. "I'll return it. You don't—"*

*"No!" I clutched the mug protectively to my chest. "I love it. Don't you dare try to take it back, Dominic Davenport, because I'm keeping it forever."*

---

That turned out to be untrue. The original mug broke during our move to New York. I'd been devastated, but the one in my hands was an exact replica of the one he'd gifted me on our first date, down to the apple and "World's Best Teacher" font.

*Our first date.* December 21, aka today. It was the first anniversary of ours that I'd forgotten. I'd been too distracted by the mess at the store and the complications of our *current* relationship.

I picked up the handwritten note tucked beneath the mug with a trembling hand.

*I'll always think of you on this day.*

There was no signature, but it didn't need one. The dark, messy scrawl was unmistakably Dominic's.

Pressure built behind my eyes.

"What is that?" Isabella asked. My friends had fallen silent and were eyeing me with curiosity.

I placed the note back in the box and closed it.

"Nothing," I said. I blinked past the blur in my vision and forced a smile. "It's nothing at all."

# CHAPTER 30

*Alessandra*

AFTER ISABELLA AND VIVIAN LEFT AND SLOANE RETIRED for the night, I wedged into the back of my closet, took out my phone, and messaged the guy I'd matched with on the dating app. He messaged back immediately, and by the following afternoon, I had a date for Tuesday night.

It happened so fast it made my head spin, which was exactly what I wanted. If I thought too hard, I'd sink into the pool of guilt puddling in my stomach. I'd made it clear I wanted to date other people, and Dominic had agreed. I had no reason to feel guilty, but it was difficult to shed old ways of thinking.

*He's not yours anymore. You're free.*

One day, my feelings would catch up with my logic. Until then, I forced myself to give my upcoming date a fair chance.

Dalton was charming, well-educated, and handsome in a generic Ralph Lauren model sort of way. He'd just moved to New York from Australia and worked in "business," a vague descriptor that hinted at a possible trust fund background, but other than that, our text conversations were perfectly lovely.

"You look great," Sloane said on Tuesday. "Stop worrying and have fun."

"It's my first real date in eleven years." I didn't count my dinner with Aiden, which fell in the gray zone somewhere between *platonic* and *romantic*. "What if I embarrass myself? Or we run out of things to talk about? Do people kiss on first dates nowadays, or am I supposed to wait for the third?"

I fiddled with my necklace. Dalton was taking me to a gala uptown—"much nicer than getting drinks at a bar," he'd assured me—and I'd dressed for the occasion in a midnight silk gown and gold jewelry. It seemed like overkill for our first date, but I supposed it was better than shouting to be heard over Christmas bar music.

Sloane placed her hands on my shoulders. "Stop. *Breathe*," she ordered. I did, simply because one never said no to Sloane Kensington. She would make a great military general if she ever felt so inclined. "You'll be fine. First dates are *meant* to be a little awkward. Just go, have fun, and if things truly go off the rails, call me."

"Right. Okay." I sucked in a deep breath. *I can do this*. I was an adult; I wasn't going to run to my friend at the first sign of trouble. "Wait, where are you going tonight? I thought you had work."

Most people took Christmas week off, but Sloane wasn't most people. She would physically glue her phone to her hand if it weren't so logistically complicated.

"I do." She removed her hands from my shoulders and crossed her arms, the faintest bloom of pink coloring her cheeks. Instead of her usual suits, pencil skirts, and business sheaths, she wore a shimmering gold dress and heels that took her from five-eight to six feet tall. "I'm meeting a client at a...at a private party."

Suspicions over Sloane's uncharacteristic stutter fell away when her phone and the doorbell rang at the same time. We said a quick goodbye and rushed to answer our respective calls.

"Wow, you're even more beautiful in person." Dalton's dark eyes sparkled with appreciation as he gave me a thorough once-over in the elevator. "I'm so glad you messaged me."

I smiled past a twinge of discomfort. "Me too."

A private car waited for us downstairs. It whisked us uptown while Dalton and I settled into a conversation about his impressions of New York so far and the differences between living in the U.S. and Australia.

"At least there aren't animals waiting to kill you around every corner here," I teased when he complained about the American tipping culture.

"True." He grinned. "But not every snake you see is venomous…"

I enjoyed our conversation, but like with Aiden, I didn't feel that elusive *spark* with Dalton. Still, the night was young. We had plenty of time to connect.

"You're going to love this place," he said when the car pulled up to a pair of guarded gates. "I thought the Sydney chapter was nice, but the New York one blows it out of the water. I guess that's why it's the flagship." He laughed. I didn't join him.

I recognized those gates. I recognized the long, winding drive up to the main building and the grand white marble that loomed above us. I'd attended events there many, many times over the past five years.

Dread curdled in my chest as we walked up the red-carpeted stairs.

*Maybe he won't be here.* Dominic hated parties and tolerated them only for networking purposes. It was two days before Christmas; he had better places to be.

But any hope I had of avoiding my ex-husband while I was on a date with another man vanished when Dalton and I stepped foot into the Valhalla Club's ballroom.

I looked up, and there he was. Broad shoulders, devastating face, and burning eyes that were fixed directly on me—and on the touch of Dalton's hand on my waist.

_Dominic_

"No murder before Christmas," Dante warned me. "Vivian says it's bad luck."

"I'm not murdering anyone." I didn't want to get blood on my suit. But maiming? That was a strong possibility—if I hadn't promised Alessandra I wouldn't interfere with her dates.

Possessiveness churned beneath my skin as I watched her dance with Dalton Campbell. Her dress hugged every curve, and she'd styled her hair in an updo that revealed the smooth, bare expanse of her back. Eyes, hair, smile, _everything_. She was so damn beautiful it defied reality.

I flicked my lighter on and off as Dalton said something that made her laugh. Jealousy burned green and hot.

Seeing Alessandra on a date with another man and not being able to do a thing about it was as close to hell as I could imagine. I didn't know much about Dalton other than the fact the Campbells made their fortune in mining and that he'd recently transferred from Sydney's Valhalla chapter, but I loathed his guts already.

"Good." Kai brought half my attention back to our conversation. The other half was stuck on Dalton's hand on Alessandra's waist. He was touching her too intimately for a public setting, and I wanted to chop the fucking thing off. "We're here to celebrate, so stop glaring at the poor man like you're plotting his demise."

Dante had announced Vivian's pregnancy last night. I was

happy for him—for the most part. The Russos had been married for three years and were starting a family. I'd been married to Alessandra for ten and had nothing left of it except for the diamond in my pocket and the broken pieces serrating my heart.

Perhaps I was a masochist for carrying her wedding ring around when it reminded me so much of our failures, but like the lighter, it was also one of the only memories of us I could hold.

"We haven't decided if we want the baby's gender to be a surprise yet," Dante said in response to Kai's question, which I'd missed. He grinned, his eyes sparkling with a mixture of pride, joy, and nerves. He looked so unlike his usual grouchy self, I would've never guessed this was the same man who'd hated his wife when they first met. "I want to be surprised, but Viv wants to prepare. You know she loves planning things…"

I tried to pay attention, but I couldn't take my eyes off Alessandra and Dalton. Vivian and Isabella were here with Dante and Kai, but they'd disappeared to God knew where at the start of the gala. They hadn't even seen Alessandra yet.

My jaw ticked when Alessandra laughed again at something Dalton said. I couldn't take it anymore; I needed to remove myself from the same room as them before I strangled someone.

"I'll be right back." I left Dante and Kai without waiting for a response.

Green fumes choked my lungs as I exited the ballroom and headed to the gardens. I'd left my coat inside, and the wintry air bit through the soft wool of my suit. Still, it did nothing to dispel the misery tunneling through my veins.

*On. Off.* The lighter's flame provided the only source of warmth.

From physical beatings to verbal abuse, I'd been subject to plenty of punishments as a child, but none cut more than the past hour. I was a ghost tonight, forced to watch but unable to act.

I stayed outside until my face turned numb and the ache of the cold sank into my bones. I would've left Valhalla altogether had morbid curiosity not dragged me back to the party.

I needed to know whether Alessandra and Dalton were still there. As much as it hurt to see them together, the *what ifs* if they left together would eviscerate me even more.

I stopped at the bathroom first. I'd just finished washing my hands when a laugh leaked from one of the stalls.

"Did you see the photo I sent?" The voice carried a heavy Australian accent. "Yeah…I know. She's *hot*. Rumor has it she's recently divorced too, so you know she's craving a good rebound fuck."

I went deathly still.

Another laugh echoed in the bathroom. It was empty save for me and the fucker in the stall, and I could hear every ounce of smugness in his tone. "Nah. No way I'm chaining myself to some chick this soon, no matter how hot she is. I bet her pussy is tight as hell, though…yeah, she messaged me first. Imagine how long it's been since her ex touched her if she's this desperate to go on a date with someone she just started talking to." The toilet flushed. "Yeah, secret camera's still at my place. I'll show you how she is at the game."

The stall door opened, and Dalton stepped out. A flash of surprise crossed his face when he saw me by the sink, but he displayed no awareness of what he'd just walked into.

"Hey man, you mind moving?" He nodded at the sink. "I need to get back to my date." His wink told me he knew I'd overhead him and that he thought we were part of the same fucking boys' club.

"Sure." I calmly wiped my hand with a paper towel and tossed it in the trash.

"Thanks. I—" His sentence broke off into a howl when I slammed my fist into his face. Blood spurted from his nose, and the satisfying crunch of bone chased away the ugly remnants of his laughter. "*What the fuck?*" He clutched his nose, his face screwed into a mask of pain. "I'm going to sue the fuck out of you, you—"

Dalton howled again when I hauled him up by his collar. "What you're going to do," I said calmly, "is walk back to the ballroom, apologize to your date for wasting her time, and never touch or contact her again. Then you'll go home and dismantle that camera of yours before the FBI gets an anonymous tip about your secret activities. If I find out you violated *any* of those rules, I'll hunt you down, chop off your tiny, pathetic dick, and make you choke on it. Understand?"

"You're crazy," Dalton spit out. "Do you know who my father—"

I tightened my hold until his face turned an ugly shade of purple and his words devolved into a helpless gurgle. "Understand?"

He nodded frantically, his eyes bulging from a lack of oxygen.

"Good." I walked out and left him a bleeding, crying mess on the floor. Rage distorted my vision with every step, but as much as I'd like to beat him unconscious for the way he'd talked about Alessandra, I'd already crossed a line. I didn't regret it one bit, but I had a feeling she wouldn't feel the same.

My suspicions were confirmed later when she glanced at her phone with a frown and slipped out of the ballroom. Dante and Kai had both disappeared, so I was alone at the bar when Alessandra returned a few minutes later, her expression incandescent with rage.

"You. Outside. *Now*."

I followed her to a quiet upstairs hall, ignoring the other guests' curious stares and whispers. Our separation had made a splash in the society papers, and I could see the headlines that would come out of tonight's events already.

*Campbell heir assaulted at the Valhalla gala!*

*Dominic and Alessandra Davenport spotted arguing. Is more trouble on the horizon for this divorced couple?*

"You punched Dalton in the face?" Alessandra waited until we were alone before she laid into me. "What is *wrong* with you? That's assault!"

"Let me explain—"

"No." She jabbed a finger at my chest. "You said you weren't going to interfere with my dates."

"I know. I—"

"That was three days ago, and the first thing you do when you actually see me with someone else is to attack them in the bathroom?"

"Ále, he—"

"This is exactly why I can't trust you. You keep saying one thing and—"

"He was going to videotape you!" My words exploded with frustration.

Alessandra fell silent. She stared at me, her eyes round with shock.

"I overheard him talking to a friend in the bathroom." I skipped the crasser elements of Dalton's conversation. She didn't need to hear any of that. "He was planning to take you home and secretly tape you having sex." A fresh shimmer of rage threaded through my gut. "Tell me, what was I supposed to do?"

"You could've told me."

"Would you have believed me?"

She didn't respond.

"I said I'll stand back and watch you date whoever you want, and I will," I said. "It's not my place to tell you what you can and can't do. But I *will not* stand back and watch you be disrespected." Emotion roughened the syllables. "I'll do anything for you, *amor*, but I can't do the impossible."

Alessandra swallowed. Her anger had visibly abated, and she suddenly looked small and tired against our ornate surroundings.

My fist curled against the need to touch her. "I'll let you get back to the party," I said when she remained quiet. "I'm sorry for ruining your evening, but you deserve better than someone like Dalton."

She deserved better than me too, but at least I knew it. There wasn't a single person in the world who was worthy of her.

I made it two steps down the hall before she stopped me.

"Dominic."

My heart ricocheted at her low tone. I turned, but I didn't get a chance to react before she closed the space between us, grabbed my shirt...

And kissed me.

## CHAPTER 31

*Alessandra*

I DIDN'T KNOW HOW IT HAPPENED OR WHAT MADE ME do it. One second, I was watching Dominic walk away. The next, my hands were fisting his shirt, my tongue was tangling with his, and my world had blurred into a haze of heat and sensation.

Alcohol and a roller coaster of emotions dragged my inhibitions past the point of no return. In half an hour, I'd experienced a full range of human emotion—fury, shock, desire, and a thousand shades in between—and I was *tired*.

Tired of feeling uncomfortable in my own skin. Tired of making small talk and wondering if the other person liked me. Tired of fighting against the tide when I just wanted to sink into oblivion.

So for one night, I did.

Dominic's tortured groan ignited deep in my core and spread outward, setting tiny fires ablaze until I was consumed with knee-weakening, mind-numbing lust.

I hadn't had sex since the night before he signed our divorce papers. It'd been almost three months, but his earlier confession, that Dalton had been planning to take me home and sleep with me, made me realize that I wasn't ready to be with anyone except him. At least not like this.

I stumbled backward, dragging him with me. Hands searched and fumbled before we finally opened a door along the hall and staggered inside for a breath of privacy.

His grip was tight on my waist as we moved through the room. I caught a glimpse of leather books and stained glass when I came up for air; we must be in the library.

Reason. Words. All of it had disappeared, leaving only need and desire behind.

Nothing between us was real, but it was all the truth we had. Our bond tugged at me, even as the jagged pieces of my heart worked to tear me apart.

My knees hit the back of a leather chaise. Dominic pushed me back, his body covering mine as he kissed me with toe-curling intensity. I was already wet from the first taste of his lips, and need pulsed heavier between my legs at his tortured groan.

"You have no idea what you do to me, Ále." Warm, strong fingers curved over my hips. "I would destroy the world if it would please you. I would ruin every man who thought he could have you." His stubble scratched against soft skin; his breath skated across my cheek, sending shivers down my spine.

In that moment, I was desperate, needy, and so very his.

"Fuck me like you mean that, Dom." It was a weak taunt. An arrow that was too blunt to hit the center, but it was enough to get what I wanted.

"What makes you think I don't?" Fire and fury ignited his eyes.

"Our divorce papers." The words felt bitter on my tongue. The ugliness that had poisoned the well of our love was always there. Neglect. Disregard. Complacency. *Apathy.* But I didn't feel the emptiness tonight that I'd felt so many nights before.

His voice dropped to a deadly whisper. "Do you think I couldn't tear those papers apart? That ink on a page means anything to me?"

"All you've ever cared about is contract after contract. Why would ours be any different?"

His jaw clenched and a growl tore through him. There was nothing more to say. Tonight was about need. My need for him. My need to forget the future he saved me from and the past he'd destroyed me with.

He grabbed my hands and pinned them to the arms of the chair. "Don't let go." *Or else.* A throbbing ache in my lower stomach flared at the implied words.

My palms gripped the smooth leather surface as he ran his hands up my thighs, bunching my dress and stealing my breath with every slow inch he moved up my bare skin.

For an instant, I saw him as he was on our wedding day, in an unguarded moment when he thought I wasn't paying attention. And he looked just like this—hungry, reverent, and in awe of the prize he'd won.

"Look at this sweet pussy," he murmured. "It's fucking dripping for me, *amor.*"

His pants were rough against my hypersensitive skin. I desperately wanted to touch him, bring him back to me. Instead, I was bared to him from the waist down. Cool air ghosted over my most sensitive spot, causing goose bumps to pepper my skin.

Dominic's hands found the top of my dress.

My breaths came in shallow pants. I was too keyed up to care how out of control I was in this situation and how in control my ex-husband was.

Shivers wracked my body, and I dug my nails into the leather armrests, wishing it were him I was touching.

I hated that, in this moment, his control was what I needed.

Nothing could center me the way his focus could, and I couldn't regret my choice to sleep with him.

"Dom." My lungs strained with anticipation.

Two quick flicks of his wrist and my dress was down around my waist. He lowered his head and tugged on my nipple with his teeth.

I cried out at the white-hot spear of sensation.

His tongue laved me, lighting my nerves on fire as I soaked the leather below me. Rough hands stroked and gripped my thighs, never giving me the thing I wanted most.

"Do you think I could live without the taste of you on my tongue? Without the sound of your whimpers in my ear as you take my cock?" His words painted my skin with dirty desires.

"Can you?" I whispered. This was honesty, not a challenge. This question gave voice to every second thought I had.

His reply was a ghost of a sound I didn't believe. I knew this was supposed to be nothing more than safety with a man who knew my body the best, so I held myself back from saying anything else.

I wanted to ask where he'd been all those nights. I wanted to ask why he still wore his wedding ring. I wanted to know how empty these words were compared to the promises he broke time after time. But my heart couldn't handle another cut tonight.

He pulled back before moving to my other breast. Biting, teasing. One hand pinched my nipple, causing me to cry out. It hurt so good. The other slid my thong to the side and rubbed my clit, working me to impossible wetness but never letting me come.

"Please," I begged. I squirmed against his hand. "Dom…" I choked out another gasp when he nipped my skin in warning.

"No, I want to feel you clench around me, *amor*." Lust roughened his voice. "I want to feel your tight pussy stretch and grip me. I want to feel you come all over my cock."

*God.* His words shouldn't turn me on so much, but they did.

He pulled back, and the soft rasp of a zipper was all I heard before I saw stars.

*Full.* I was impossibly full as he didn't wait, didn't tease—he thrust into me with one long, hard stroke, and my body bowed from the sudden, immense pressure.

"*Fuck,*" I gasped. My submission was an invitation I knew I shouldn't give. I was exposed and he was nearly fully clothed. Every pretense was ripped away when it was my skin against his. There was no hiding the way I cried out for him or the way he pushed my body higher.

My moans and cries mingled with his grunts as he fucked my brains out on the sofa. I couldn't see, hear, or think clearly. It was just us, our bodies sweaty and moving in a rough, timeless rhythm.

"I could die in this pussy, Ále. I could die right now, knowing that you are mine." His hand wrapped lightly around my throat, pinning me to the leather while he moved us into ecstasy.

I felt him swell in me as he picked up the pace. My own release was building as nerves shot down my spine. I'd ruined the couch, and my palms were slick with sweat as he held me in place.

His hips pumped into me like he was trying to grind some unknown truth into my body. When he put his forehead on mine, I saw the shadows that hid on his face. I saw the words I didn't want to believe swimming in his eyes.

Safety and fear coiled deep in my gut.

His wedding ring against my waist felt heavy in the purgatory I was happy to enter if it meant this stolen moment.

One more thrust and I fell apart, fluttering like confetti against the leather, bits and pieces of me embedding themselves in his skin. Warmth filled me as he came soon after with a shudder and a groan.

Silence settled, hot and languid. Our breaths slowed as our sex-fueled haze cleared.

*I just had sex with my ex-husband.* The clarity bit at me, but I wasn't ready to think about what it meant. I'd wanted him, and I'd let him have me.

Regret pushed at me before I shoved it away.

Dom stood up and straightened his clothes. He exuded elegance and power, but I saw the man I fell in love with. The man who worked three jobs but would still eat me out under the table while we studied. The man who made promises and kept them until he didn't anymore.

Our gazes consumed each other, communicating what words couldn't.

I'd just roused myself off the coach and fixed my clothes when a third voice rang through the room.

"*Shit.*"

Our heads jerked up toward the third floor, where Kai and Isabella had emerged from...*was that a secret room behind the bookshelves?*

We stared at each other, all four of us rumpled and tousled in a way that could only indicate one type of activity.

"Well," Kai said, his posh British accent sounding a tad too dignified for the situation. "This is awkward."

# CHAPTER 32

## Dominic

MY POST-SEX HIGH LASTED PRECISELY AN HOUR AND eight minutes. After our awkward run-in with Kai and Isabella in the library, a red-faced Alessandra left with the couple (I assumed she and Isabella had a lot to catch up on), and I went home with my blood buzzing.

I knew better than to assume sex meant anything more than a temporary melding of desires, but it was a modicum of progress in our relationship, and that was all I could ask for at the moment.

The penthouse greeted me with silence when I returned. I'd given the staff the week off for Christmas, and my footsteps echoed against the marble floors as I walked through the foyer to the living room. I should turn—

Something moved in the darkness.

A cold dagger of fear severed the last tendrils of my warm, Alessandra-induced haze, and I came to an abrupt halt.

A second later, a lamp flicked on, throwing relief over midnight hair and cool green eyes.

"Late night," my brother drawled. "Where've you been?"

My fear crisped, burning into anger. "How the fuck did you get in?"

Roman lounged on the couch like an emperor lounging on his throne. A silver dagger glinted against his all-black outfit, and he tossed it absentmindedly from hand to hand while surveying me with amusement.

"Your security system is good," he said. "I'm better."

My jaw tensed into granite.

I had the best system money could buy. I also employed the best tracker in the city, and he hadn't been able to dig up a single thing about Roman's past or where he'd been since Martin Wellgrew's suspiciously timed death at Le Boudoir.

*What have you been up to since high school, Rome?*

"Don't worry. I come in peace." He held up his hands, his tone half-mocking, half-sincere. "Wipe the suspicious look off your face. Can't a guy pay a friendly visit to his brother for the holidays?"

"A friendly visit means a knock on the door, not breaking and entering."

"No one was home when I dropped by, so a knock wouldn't have done anything, would it?"

"Don't bullshit me." I crossed the room, cognizant of both the dagger in his hands and the gun I'd tucked in the fireplace's concealment mantle. "You disappeared after Le Boudoir, and you wouldn't be here unless you want something."

His mouth sobered, and the dagger came to a standstill in his left hand. "Like I said, it's the holidays. They make me nostalgic."

"We had shitty holidays." Our foster family hadn't been big on gift-giving or Christmas cheer. The only present I'd received from them was a pair of hand-me-down socks.

Roman shrugged. "True, but they had their moments. Remember when we got drunk off eggnog for the first time and

trashed Mrs. Peltzer's garden gnomes? We could hear her screaming from half a block away."

"We did her a favor. Those gnomes were hideous."

"That they were." Shadows danced over his face. "I didn't
have anyone to celebrate Christmas with after you left. Juvie was
a hellhole. When I got out, I had no friends, no family, no money."

Guilt pressed in on all sides. While I'd been rubbing elbows
with classmates and professors at Thayer, Roman had been suffering alone. He'd made his choices and faced the consequences, but
that didn't ease the bitter heaviness in my throat.

Still, he was an adult now, a dangerous one, and I'd be a fool
to let sentimentality dampen self-preservation.

"You seem to be doing fine now." I stopped next to the fireplace,
my eyes trained on Roman, my senses on high alert for any surprises
that may leap out of the shadows.

"So it seems." He pressed the tip of his blade against his finger.
A tiny drop of blood welled, "I floated for a while after juvie until
I met John. He was a World War II vet and prickly as hell, but he
gave me a steady gig in his shop and a place to live. If it weren't
for him, I wouldn't be where I am today." The shadows darkened
further. "He died last year."

"I'm sorry." I meant it.

I didn't know the man, but I'd had a similar figure in my life,
and Ehrlich's death had unmoored me more than anything else
had up to that point.

"I told him about you, you know," Roman said quietly. "How
close we were. How you betrayed me, and how much I hated you.
That hatred kept me alive, Dom, because I refused to die while you
got every fucking thing you wanted."

The bitterness swelled. It was a hundred boulders tied around
my waist, dragging me down until I drowned beneath its weight.

"I would've helped you. If you'd asked me for anything else, anything except an alibi, I would've done it."

"Who's the one bullshitting now?" Roman rose from the couch, resentment carving deep cuts across his indifference until it lay in tatters on the ground. "You wouldn't have done a single thing because Dominic Davenport always looks out for number one. How many times did I cover your ass when we were younger? Dozens. How many times did I ask for your help? *One*."

Flames of frustration licked at my guilt. "There's a difference between lying about underage drinking and fucking *arson*!"

"You want me to believe you give a shit about the law?" His anger bounced off the marble with teeth-rattling volume. "Don't tell me you haven't done shady shit since I last saw you. You'll do it to enrich yourself, but you won't do it to help anyone else." Animosity blazed through his eyes. "It wasn't about the alibi. It was about loyalty. You didn't even try to stay. You saw how my trouble threatened your precious get-rich plan, and you turned your back on the only family you ever had."

The buzz returned with a vengeance. It was deafening, a cacophony of noise I couldn't block out no matter how hard I tried.

"It seems to be a recurring pattern." Roman's expression smoothed with his kill shot. "Where's your wife, Dom? Did she get sick of your shit and finally leave?"

The tight, hard knot that'd been building inside me since the night I came home and found Alessandra gone finally exploded.

A snarl ripped through the air as I charged forward. Fist met bone, eliciting a sharp hiss. Roman was caught off guard only for a second before he tossed his dagger to the side and returned my hit with so much force it knocked the breath out of my lungs.

A vase shattered on the ground as we attacked each other the way only brothers could, with hostility more potent because of our shared past. I didn't go for my gun; he didn't reach for his blade. Our confrontation had been fifteen years in the making, and we weren't letting weapons soften our blows.

This was fucking personal.

Sweat and fury soaked the air. Skin split, pushing rivulets of blood down our faces. My vision flashed black, and the taste of copper filled my mouth. Somewhere, bone crunched.

It wasn't the first time Roman and I had physically fought. As teenagers, we were quick to anger, and we often tussled our way to cuts and bruises. However, the years had ramped up our capacity for brutality, and we might've both died that night had we not clung so fiercely to our reasons for living.

Alessandra for me, something unknown for Roman that he would never share.

Finally, at some point between the grunts and blows, our energy depleted. We sank onto the floor, bruised and exhausted, our chests heaving from the aftermath of the storm.

"Fuck." I spat out a mouthful of blood. It stained the edge of the twenty-thousand-dollar rug I'd bought in Turkey, but that was the good thing about being rich. Everything was replaceable. *Almost everything.* "You're not a scrawny little shit anymore."

"And you finally learned how to fight without cheating."

"Fighting smarter instead of harder isn't cheating."

Roman snorted. Deep purple blotches were already forming on his face, and dried blood painted rusty streaks across his skin. One eye was swollen half shut.

I bet I didn't look any better. Every inch of my body screamed with agony now that my adrenaline had crashed, and I was pretty sure I'd fractured a bone or two. However, while I'd taken a physical beating, the painful buzz in my head was gone. Our fight had expelled whatever had been festering inside me since I left Ohio, and that was worth every black eye and fracture.

Roman leaned his head back against the wall, his expression drained of anger. "Do you ever regret it?"

I didn't have to ask what he was referring to. "All the damn time."

Our breaths slowed to normal in the silence. It wasn't a comfortable quiet, but it wasn't destructive either. It just was.

"I tried looking for you," I said. "After college. Multiple times. You were a ghost."

"There's a reason for that." His reply carried hints of warning and tiredness.

A long-buried protective instinct flared to life. Despite our tumultuous history, he was still my younger brother. I didn't have the resources to protect either of us back then, but I did now. "What have you gotten yourself into, Rome?"

"Don't ask questions you don't want the answers to. It's better that way—for both of us."

"At least tell me you didn't have anything to do with Wellgrew's death."

Orion Bank had been in chaos since his untimely demise. The new head of the bank was an idiot who seemed like he was *trying* to run the institution into the ground, and Wellgrew's death had been ruled an accident despite people whispering otherwise.

"Don't worry about him." This time, Roman's warning came through loud and clear. "He's dead. That's it. It's over."

I wiped a hand over my face. My palm came away bloody.

I wasn't a boy struggling to survive in Ohio anymore, but maybe, beneath the money and power, I was still a coward. Because despite the alarm bells that rang with every word out of Roman's mouth, I chose to ignore them.

We'd reached a temporary truce, and though I'd never admit it, it felt good to be around family again—enough so that I didn't dare peel back the mask and see what my brother had become.

# CHAPTER 33

*Alessandra*

"THE RSVPS ARE ROLLING IN." SLOANE TAPPED HER phone screen with a satisfied smile. "Christian and Stella Harper, yes. Ayana, yes. Buffy Darlington, yes. It's going to be a great event."

"Of course it is. I organized it," Vivian joked.

It was the week after New Year's, and Sloane, Vivian, Isabella, and I were combining our weekly happy hour with party prep at the store. I had mocktails on hand for Vivian, who was entering her eleventh week of pregnancy. "On a serious note, this place looks amazing, Ále. The grand opening will be a hit."

"I hope so." Nerves fluttered in my stomach. "Thank you both for your help. Truly. I couldn't have done this without you."

There were perks to having a superstar publicist and event planner as my best friends. Sloane and Vivian were in charge of logistics while I scrambled to finish my collage in time for the event.

After an agonizing but much needed, realistic look at my timeline, I'd scrapped my original plan to recreate every project that'd been ruined in the flood and poured my energy into one big centerpiece instead. It would serve as the gallery's featured showcase, and I would round it out with a few smaller pieces from home. The new layout was a gamble, but it was the best I could do without pushing back the opening date. My contracts with the caterer and DJ were nonrefundable, so I couldn't postpone even if I wanted to.

I surveyed the store. Backroom construction was ongoing, but in just a few weeks, the main floor had been transformed into something photo-worthy. The front desk and delicate floral displays took up the right side while the left side was dominated by the cafe. I only had room for the marble coffee counter, a velvet booth, and two tables, but they added a touch of coziness to the space. The only thing missing was the pressed flowers centerpiece and a few finishing details.

I'd skipped my holiday trip to Brazil for the first time in my life and worked around the clock to put everything together. It'd been worth it.

"How was your date on Saturday?" Isabella asked. "Better than the Dalton fiasco, I hope."

"It's hard for any date to go *worse*." I hadn't heard a peep from Dalton since the Christmas gala. There were rumors he'd been kicked out of Valhalla but no confirmation yet. "To answer your question, it was fine, but there won't be a second date."

I hadn't given up on my foray into the dating world after my, er, tryst with Dominic in the library. The sex had been incredible, but I'd meant it when I said I wanted to see other people. Despite the holidays, I'd squeezed in a comedy show with a musician after Christmas and grabbed drinks with a nice high school teacher over the weekend.

I didn't care that the dates went nowhere. It was about meeting new people and experiencing what it was like to be with someone else. Luckily, neither the musician nor teacher had tried to lure me back to their apartments for a secret sex tape, so that was a plus.

"I can't believe you guys had sex in the library at the same time," Vivian said. "Or that there's a *secret room* and you didn't tell me."

Isabella and I flushed We'd told our friends what happened at the gala, which was a mistake in hindsight because Vivian and Sloane hadn't stopped teasing us about it. At least they hadn't brought it up around Marcelo.

Since I couldn't go to Brazil for Christmas, he'd flown up instead. We'd spent a long weekend attending Broadway shows and gorging on overpriced pastries. My mother FaceTimed us from St. Barts on Christmas Day, which was more thoughtful than we'd expected.

"It wasn't my place to tell," Isabella said defensively. "It's a Young family secret, and you guys *can't* tell anyone else."

Sloane let out a delicate snort. "Why would I tell anyone about your and Kai's sex lair? I'd have to disinfect it before I ever stepped foot inside."

Isabella tossed a crumpled piece of brown paper at her, and our prep session quickly devolved into a laughing, breathless paper fight.

"Stop!" I squealed when Vivian pelted me with paper balls. "When did you get so violent? You're supposed to be the nice one!"

"I'm constantly tired, my breasts are sore, and I have to convince Dante not to insulate me with bubble wrap every day," she said. "I need to release some tension."

Fair enough.

I was just glad my friends weren't grilling me about Dominic. They'd been shocked but not necessarily surprised by my sex confession—a fact I chose not to examine too closely—and they'd complied with my request not to talk about it. I wouldn't know what to say anyway; I was as confused about the status of my relationship as they were.

Dominic and I had left each other a few voice notes since the gala. They were generic greetings like *Merry Christmas* and

*Happy New Year,* but he'd also sent a handwritten note and a custom jewelry-making kit for the holidays. I was surprised and touched that he'd remembered the casual hobby I'd picked up in Buzios, but there was only so much we could say via text and gifts. We were overdue for a real conversation.

My phone buzzed with a new message while my friends wound down their play fight.

*Speak of the devil.*

My heart leapt in my throat. Dominic rarely texted, which was why it took a minute for me to wrap my head around his words.

**Dominic:** Meet me at the Saxon Gallery tonight. 8pm. I have something for you.

———

I was too curious not to show.

After my friends left and I closed up shop, I took the subway to the Saxon Gallery on the west side, where Dominic waited in the reception area.

The first thing I noticed were his bruises. Yellowish-purple splotches mottled his cheek and jaw, and a scabbed-over cut sliced over his right eye. He looked like he'd gotten into a fistfight with a wild animal.

"Oh my God," I gasped. "What happened?"

"My brother showed up again." His tone dried. "You could say we worked out our issues."

God. I thought *our* relationship was complicated, but his entanglement with his brother might be worse.

I reached for him out of instinct before hesitating. We weren't married anymore. I had no business fussing over him the way a wife would, but the sight of him hurt had my heart tangled in knots.

It shouldn't. He was fine, and the wounds would heal. And yet...

I brushed my fingers over the darkest bruise. His skin was soft beneath his stubble, and the knots tightened into a messy tangle.

I missed touching him outside of sex. I missed being able to wrap my arms around him for no reason or give him an absentminded kiss on the cheek when he was working. I missed all the little things that once made us us, but I was also too scared to fall back into my comfort zone.

A thousand knots were preferable to a second heartbreak.

Dominic watched me without moving. His chest rose and fell in a steady rhythm, but tension lined his jaw like he was afraid he would scare me off if he made one wrong gesture.

"Why do men always resort to violence?" I asked, attempting to lighten the static cloaking the air. "Therapy exists, you know."

"Our problems go beyond therapy. Besides, I'm not the only one who's bruised." Satisfaction filled Dominic's face, but his eyes softened when my fingers trailed over another bruise on his jaw.

I shook my head. *Men.* "I can't believe you didn't tell me."

"I didn't think you cared."

My movements stilled. Silence floated between us before I dropped my arm. "Well, I hope you're icing it regularly," I said, skirting his reply. "Purple-black doesn't look good with your suits."

The corner of his mouth tugged up. "Noted."

We walked deeper into the gallery, which featured a whimsical glass flower exhibition by Yumi Hayashi. Visiting one of her exhibits had been on my bucket list for years, but the dates never lined up with my schedule, and I'd been so distracted by the divorce and store opening I hadn't realized there was a new show this winter.

"I'm surprised you asked me to meet you here," I said. "You're not an art person."

I'd chosen all the art in the penthouse. Dominic was a genius with numbers, but if I'd left the décor up to him, the penthouse would've made a chessboard look colorful.

"I'm not, but I thought this particular exhibit would be good inspiration," Dominic said. "In case you need it for your projects."

Warmth curled in my stomach. He could be so damn sweet when he wanted. "Thank you."

"You're welcome." His soft, intimate murmur ghosted down my spine.

The earlier electricity returned, sending tiny zips through my chest until I dragged a much-needed breath into my lungs. "I guess it's not a popular exhibition," I said, trying desperately not to notice the way his body heat sank into my skin or the brush of his shirt against my arm. "There's no one else here."

"I hired out the gallery." Dominic pushed a hand into his pocket. "It's better without the crowds, and I wanted to be alone with you."

I couldn't summon an adequate reply to that.

The exhibition consisted of seven rooms, each themed around the flora of different regions. I didn't speak again until we reached the seventh and final exhibit featuring flowers native to Asia.

"About what happened at the gala." I stopped in front of a giant lotus lantern. It was the room's only source of light, but it was enough to illuminate the tension lining Dominic's shoulders. "I…" The right words fought to escape. "I can't promise anything more than sex."

He was the *only* man who could set me on fire with one touch. Denying our attraction was futile, and my pre-Christmas dry spell had been torturous. I hadn't realized how much I'd missed physical touch until I received it.

Was entering a sex-only relationship with my ex-husband a terrible idea? Absolutely. But we were already on this ride; I might as well enjoy it while it lasted.

Dominic's eyes flickered in the dim lights. "I can work with that."

*That's it?* I wasn't sure whether my next breath contained relief or disappointment. I'd expected him to push back, but he seemed willing to follow my guidelines.

However, surprise tripped my heartbeats when Dominic slowly moved behind me. Silence thrummed and held me captive as his warm breath trailed sensation down my spine and his fingers traced up my arms.

My back brushed his front, and the hairs on the nape of my neck rose in anticipation. It hurt to be this close to him, to feel the intimacy that we'd lost. Every rise and fall of his chest caused mine to clench; every beat of our hearts hammered home a reminder.

*He hurt you.*

*You left him.*

*He's still here.*

*You want him.*

*He hasn't given up.*

*What if, what if, what if.*

All true, even if one conflicted with another.

Goose bumps shivered across my skin when he kissed my neck. The memory of his lips against my skin was the sweetest torture, soft yet firm, gentle yet commanding.

"What do you want, *amor?*" he whispered.

Our breaths echoed as he waited. Dominic never waited. He was action and movement and command. I was the one who'd always waited. I waited for dinners that we never shared and evenings together that never came.

*What do I want?* I wanted agency, which I'd lacked so often in our marriage. I'd walked tthe tightrope of dutiful wife and desire for years, and I wanted a world where I made the rules for myself instead of merely following them.

*I can only promise sex.*

My first implicit rule. Perhaps tonight was the night to implement it on my terms.

My heartbeats fluttered as I ran my hands across his shoulders and slowly lowered his jacket off his chest. Surprise flared on his face, but he followed my cue and slid it down his arms, folding it to the side of him. He rolled his shirtsleeves up with careful, measured movements, never taking his eyes off mine. With every flick of his wrist, the wedding band on his left hand glinted in the dim lights.

He'd never taken it off, not even after we divorced. The sight inexplicably fanned the flames slowly burning their way through my stomach. Vulnerability coursed through me while heat pooled between my legs and pulsed in an empty ache.

Our movements stilled, and we were left staring at each other as electricity buzzed through the air.

"Don't stop now," Dominic said softly. "Show me what you want." It was a plea wrapped in a simple command, but nothing about this was simple. This was the moment that surpassed everything before. This was submission in a way I'd never been part of.

I laced my fingers through his and pulled him to the darkest corner, where only a sliver of light broke through the shadows. A soft press of my hands had him on his knees, and lust flickered in my veins as he followed my lead and propped one leg over his shoulder. The sight of my tan skin draped over his crisp white shirt made my head spin.

He pushed my skirt up and slid my underwear to the side. "Fuck, baby, you're so wet." His whisper sent goose bumps down my spine. "Do you see the way I need you? The way I'm desperate to feel you any way you'll let me."

My heart ached when I thought about every night he chose his empire while I was left cold in the shadows. Every night I wished he needed me and not a higher number in his bank account.

I ached for a man I wished I didn't love yet desperately wanted.

Dominic trailed slow, lingering kisses up my thigh before

running his mouth across my pussy. The coolness of the wall soaked through my back as his tongue speared into me, and right there, in the corner of the gallery, with my leg on his shoulder and his hands braced on hips, he ate me out like a man starved.

The flames ignited into a wildfire. Every probe of his tongue sent pleasure crashing through me; every expert lick of my clit weakened my knees until I grabbed fistfuls of his hair and held on for dear life.

The knife's edge of my control began to cut me in half the same way his wickedness did. I knew better than to believe sex was mending my broken heart, yet it felt like he was plucking the shattered edges of who we were out, one by one, with every lick and suck.

"More," I whimpered. "Please, don't stop. Don't—ah!" My cry keened through the room as he gripped my hips harder and tongue fucked me into a swollen, dripping mess on his face.

My fingers slipped and slid against reality. Everything blurred until there was only me, him, and the relentless march of pleasure through my body.

As much as my control over tonight had fueled me, it'd also pulled me deeper into his orbit. Each tremble and shiver of my body felt like both a win for my independence and a chip in my defenses.

Dominic grazed his teeth across my clit and thrust two fingers inside me. My squeal filled the empty gallery as I jerked against the sudden invasion. His other hand left me, and my breath vanished again when I looked down and saw with his hand fisted around his cock. He stroked himself with hard, rough strokes as he groaned into my pussy.

"Does tasting me get you off?" I gasped. I'd never seen him move with such intensity, and I'd always loved watching him touch himself and bring himself to completion just for me.

I was no longer an afterthought but an obsession. To be the object of Dominic's desires was the one thing I'd loved and mourned. I didn't trust him with my heart, but I trusted him with my body.

"Fuck, yes." His breath was hot against my skin. "I'll never get enough of you. I would fucking drown in you if you'd let me."

His words lit a match that slowly burned its way toward the inevitable. He must've felt it because he watched me with a rapt, ravenous expression as I trembled around his fingers.

"Do I give you what you need, *amor*?"

A lie fell from my lips. "No."

But being in control felt like a fantasy as he conquered me with his hands and mouth. I didn't want to give myself to him, but my resolve began to crumble at his feet. My juices dripped down my thighs as my heart beat in time with the way he penetrated me. The way he sucked and licked like he'd never been more determined to wring every bit of pleasure out of me.

The past crashed away in a wave, and the orgasm burned closer.

It was then that I felt him shudder and groan again into my pussy. He'd come on the ground at my feet, spilling his promises against the tile. The way it felt to have him kneeling in front of me, fucking me with his hand and fucking himself, sent me over the edge.

Pressure burst, and white light exploded behind my eyes as I gushed into his mouth.

I kept my control, but I'd lied to myself.

Dominic still owned me.

# CHAPTER 34

## *Dominic*

"OH GOD." THE SOUND OF RUSHING WATER NEARLY drowned out Alessandra's moan. "Oh god...*oh fuck. Dom!*"

She let out a strangled cry when I slammed into her, the sound of my name reducing my restraint to tatters. Her wet hair was wrapped around my fist, and her hands splayed against the tile as I fucked her mercilessly against the wall. Broken sobs poured out with each brutal thrust.

Sometimes she liked it sweet and slow; other times she liked it fast and rough. There was a certain headiness to knowing which she wanted, and my inkling that she craved the second type was echoed in the way her pussy gripped my cock.

Heat raced down my spine and drummed in my pulse. I wanted to tell her how good she was, how I wanted to bury myself inside her until I was tattooed across every inch of her heart and body and how she would always be mine.

But I didn't.

I bit the words that threatened to spill out of me into the slope of her shoulder. One hand tightened its grip and tugged her head back; the other curved its way up her waist and over a soft breast.

Her nipple strained against my palm as she bucked back against my thrusts.

"Spread your legs wider for me, sweetheart." My teeth scored her skin, turning my soft words into a hard command. "I want to see my cock stretching that pretty little cunt."

A full-body shudder wracked Alessandra's slim frame. She didn't hesitate to obey, and I almost wished she hadn't because the sight of her taking me was enough to drive me to my knees.

"Perfect," I groaned, so turned on it was a miracle I didn't blow right then and there.

We fit so damn perfectly. Her body molded to mine like it was made for me. Sliding into her was the closest I'd ever come to heaven, and fuck, I never wanted to leave.

In and out, faster and deeper. The steady drum of water pounded my back as I drove deeper, our wet skin slapping against each other in a dirty, erotic symphony no number of showers could cleanse.

Alessandra let out another whimper. She was close. I could feel the telltale stiffening of her muscles, and I spun her around right before she came.

Rivulets of water dripped down her face and onto her chest as she tossed her head back, her mouth parted to make way for a keening, breathless cry that rocked us both to the core.

I couldn't hold back anymore. The spasms from her orgasm were still rippling around me when I pulled out and painted her with my cum. The shower washed it off sooner than I would've liked, and then we held each other in the comedown, our heartbeats syncing, our ragged breaths drowning beneath the steady rush of water. I wanted to encase this moment in amber, but as always, it ended too soon.

Alessandra disentangled herself from my arms and stepped around me. Cold rushed over my body as I turned off the shower and watched her towel off, my chest already hollowing at her impending departure.

*I can't promise anything more than sex.*

So that was what we did for the past three weeks. She called me when she wanted to see me, and I showed up. She went on dates I never asked about, and I extended invitations she never accepted.

It wasn't much of a relationship, but if that was all she was willing to give, then that was what I'd take.

I wrapped a towel around my waist and followed her into the bedroom. We'd met at the penthouse today instead of her apartment or a hotel, which was unusual. She usually avoided our old home like the plague.

Did she walk through the front door and remember our champagne-fueled celebration after we closed on the house? When she picked up her dress from the bed, did she see the hundreds of nights we'd spent in each other's arms? Did this place remind her of us so much that simply breathing its air felt like a fucking stab in the heart?

Because that was what it felt like for me. The house was a torturous limbo of memories. It killed me to stay, and it killed me to leave.

"You don't have to leave yet," I said. "It's Friday night. We can order food, watch a movie. There's a new Nate Reynolds film out." Nate Reynolds's action blockbusters were our guilty pleasure.

Alessandra hesitated, her eyes skimming over our bed and the engagement photo on the nightstand. We'd taken it in front of the library at Thayer where we first met. We were half kissing, half laughing, and we looked so young and clueless about what our future would hold that I almost envied my past self for his brash confidence. Camila tried hiding the picture after Alessandra moved out, and I'd almost fired her on the spot.

No one touched that photo.

Alessandra's throat worked with a swallow. Indecision rippled across her face, and a dangerous seed of hope sprouted in my stomach. She wasn't brushing my suggestion off the way she usually did.

*Say yes. Please say yes.*

"I can't." She jerked her gaze away from our engagement photo and finished zipping up her dress. "I have…I have a date later."

Her admission blindsided me with a vicious blow. It shouldn't have. I knew she was dating other people; Dante and Kai had confirmed as much based on their significant others' gossip. But knowing something and hearing it were two different things.

"Oh." I forced a smile past the crushed husk of hope. "Next time then."

"Yeah," she said softly. "Next time."

The door closed with a gentle click, and she was gone. If it weren't for the faint scent of lilies, I would've doubted she'd ever been there at all.

I got dressed and turned on the TV, but I couldn't make it past the first five minutes of the Nate Reynolds movie. It reminded me too much of Alessandra. I tried to work, but I couldn't focus. Even a deliberately brutal session in the private gym couldn't clear my head.

Who was she on a date with? Where did he take her? Had they kissed yet? Did she sigh when he touched her, or did she count the minutes before she could go home?

My imagination tormented me with images of Alessandra and her faceless date until I couldn't take it anymore. I grabbed my phone and dialed the only person I knew with zero personal connection to her.

He picked up on the first ring.

"Meet me at The Garage in an hour," I said. "I need a drink."

---

The Garage was a shitty dive bar in the East Village, famous for its strong drinks and bartenders who didn't give a shit whether the customer was crying, vomiting, or passed out as long as they paid.

It was the perfect place for drowning one's sorrows, which was why an assembly line of miserable-looking men crowded the bar on a Friday night.

"Jesus Christ." Roman's lip curled as he surveyed the room. "I feel like I just walked into a Heartbroken Saps Anonymous meeting."

I knocked back my third shot of the night without answering.

"That bad?" He took the seat next to mine, his black sweater and pants blending seamlessly into the bar's seamy darkness.

We'd talked a few times, but this was our first in-person meeting since our knockdown, drag-out fight before Christmas. I still trusted Roman as far as I could throw him, but our bubbling antagonism had simmered down into wary caution over the past month. He also hadn't been tied to any more suspicious deaths, so there was that.

"Alessandra's on a date." The words tasted sour at the back of my tongue.

"Hasn't she been dating this whole time?" He motioned the bartender. "Bourbon. Neat."

"She's never told me she was going on a date right after we had sex."

"Ah." Roman grimaced as the pierced and tattooed server slammed the glass down. Dark liquid splashed over the sides onto the sticky counter. He took a sip and grimaced harder. The alcohol here tasted like nuclear waste; it was part of its questionable charm, or so those in the know said.

We drank in silence for a while. Neither of us were the

share-our-feelings and comfort-others type, which made him the perfect drinking partner. I didn't want to rehash my problems with Alessandra; I just wanted to feel less alone.

If someone had told me three months ago I'd be feeling sorry for myself over shitty whiskey in the East Village while my long-lost brother silently judged me, I would've asked what drugs they were on.

*How the mighty have fallen.* Thank fuck neither Dante nor Kai were here to witness my misery. They would never let me hear the end of it. Neither would Roman, but I didn't have to see him every week.

"If you ever see me this torn up over a woman, shoot me," he said after my fifth shot. "It's pathetic."

*Definitely* not the comfort-others type.

"You mean like the time you cried when Melody Kettler dumped you to date that exchange student from Sweden?" I wasn't above firing shots from old weapons.

Roman's jaw clenched. "I didn't cry, and she didn't dump me. We took a break."

"Whatever helps you sleep at night."

"Out of everything that's happened, my *break* with Melody Kettler is the least likely to keep me awake." He finished his drink. "Trust me."

My lighter clicked in time with my heartbeats. I'd taken it out when I sat down, but I hated seeing something so beautiful in a place so ugly.

*Out of everything that's happened.* It'd been fifteen years. I couldn't imagine the things Roman had seen and done. "How bad was juvie?"

"It could've been worse." He didn't look at me. "How much ass did you have to kiss on your way up the ladder?"

The tension split, and a rancorous laugh rustled my throat.

Maybe it was the shots. Maybe it was the give-no-shits air permeating the bar. Whatever it was, I answered truthfully about how I'd built Davenport Capital—the networking, the knocking on doors and, yes, the ass-kissing before I secured my first investors. He shared tidbits of his life over the years—the various jobs, the scrapes with the law, and the martial arts training, which he'd put to good use during our fight, the fucker.

We weren't who we used to be, and our relationship would never return to the way it was. But it felt good to talk to someone who knew me before everything changed, and I became someone I didn't recognize.

# CHAPTER 35

*Alessandra*

THE ELEVATOR DOORS SLID OPEN ON MY FLOOR.

I stepped out, my feet aching from my earlier walk to Midtown then downtown for dinner and drinks. I could've taken the subway or a car, but walking cleared my head. If I didn't have time for yoga, which I'd continued after Buzios, I went outside and wandered the streets until I felt better about whatever was on my mind. These days, there was only one person who featured regularly during my wanderings.

I rounded the corner. Someone sat slumped outside my apartment, his back against the wall and his legs outstretched. A rumpled jacket lay on the floor next to him.

"Dom?"

"Hey." He smiled up at me, his eyes glassy. "You're back."

"What are you doing?" I resumed my steps and stopped in front of him. I'd moved out of Sloane's apartment and into my own at the start of the year. Thank God for that or she would've raised hell about this.

"I missed you." He didn't get up. Pink glazed the high planes of his cheekbones, and he looked so sad and forlorn it wrenched at more than a few heartstrings.

"We saw each other just a few hours ago."

"I know."

My pulse slowed like it had been dropped in honey. *Don't fall for it, Ále.* But I couldn't help it.

I fell again, just a little bit.

"Come on." I reached down and pulled him up. "Let's get you inside before someone sees you and calls the cops." The nosy old lady in 6B would have a conniption if she spotted a drunk stranger in "her" hallway.

Dominic stumbled into my apartment. My brows pulled together as I locked the door behind us. "Did you fall into a vat of whiskey?" He *reeked* of alcohol. The scent oozed out of his pores, overpowering the fresh flowers I kept by the entryway.

"I had drinks with Roman." He pushed a hand through his already-disheveled hair. "I couldn't sleep."

"It's nine o'clock," I pointed out. "A little early for bed." I steered him to the couch, afraid he would collapse if he didn't sit soon. He swayed with each step.

I hadn't seen Dominic this drunk since, well, ever. He was usually fastidious about monitoring his alcohol intake. He said he'd seen too many people slide into alcoholism and addiction growing up, and he hated the loss of control that came with imbibing too much.

He slumped against the cushions and looked up at me again. His throat worked with a swallow. "How was your date?"

There'd been no date. Instead, I'd attended a jewelry-making class (I liked the one I took in Buzios so much I'd signed up for a similar workshop in the city) before parking myself at a bar in Soho, where I ordered one apple martini, read three chapters of a thriller Isabella recommended, and people watched. It wasn't the most exciting night, but it was what I'd needed after leaving Dominic.

"It was fine." Guilt pulled at me, fraying my thoughts. I hated lying, but I'd almost caved when he'd asked me to stay earlier that day. I never cuddled and I never slept over after we had sex, but being in that room and seeing the bed we'd shared, the engagement photo we'd taken…lying about a date was the only thing I could think of to remove myself in that moment.

"Good." Dominic swallowed again. "I hope he didn't take you out for tacos. You hate tacos."

I didn't hate them so much as I avoided them due to sheer trauma. I got food poisoning from a fish taco in college and hadn't touched one since.

"He didn't." Why did the backs of my eyes ache so much? I must be hormonal if I was tearing up over freaking tacos.

Silence took us hostage. The air turned humid, thick with nostalgia, and the seconds stretched with enough tension to warp my thoughts and emotions into a jumbled mess.

Dominic's gaze consumed mine. "Are you happy, Alessandra?"

A spark of clarity burned through his intoxication and into my soul.

I wish I had a concrete answer. In many ways, I *was* happy. I had a thriving business, wonderful friends, and a burgeoning social life. I'd discovered new hobbies and was living independently, *for myself*, for the first time in my life.

But there would always be an emptiness where we used to be. An absent piece only he could provide.

I didn't need him, but I missed him so desperately it felt like I did.

"Get some rest," I said, sidestepping his question. "We'll talk in the morning."

Dominic didn't argue. By the time I retrieved a blanket from the linen closet and returned to the living room, he'd already passed out.

A swath of silver illuminated his furrowed brow and mouth. Most people found peace in slumber, but not Dominic. Whatever plagued him during the day followed him into his dreams.

Later that night, I stared at the ceiling, my mind restless. Midnight had bled into the early hours of morning, and the air was redolent with the scent of flowers. A vase of golden roses sat next to the bed along with the note I'd found tucked in my bag that afternoon.

> *#18 out of a thousand.*
> *Love, Dom*

I closed my eyes against a familiar burn.

Dominic wasn't the only one who couldn't find peace tonight.

## CHAPTER 36

*Dominic*

I WOKE UP WITH A HANGOVER FROM HELL. Jackhammers smashed against the inside of my skull with bone-rattling force, and cotton filled my mouth. A slice of sunlight shone through the gap between the curtains and nearly fucking killed me.

I planted my forearm across my eyes with a groan. *No more alcohol for me.*

I liked a good Macallan, but at that moment, the thought of imbibing another drop of whiskey made my stomach lurch.

What the hell happened last night? I was usually good at controlling myself when it came to drinking. People did all sorts of dumb shit when they were intoxicated, and I made it a point to do as little dumb shit as possible.

It was hard to think through the raucous construction site splitting my head, but bits and pieces of the previous evening slowly filtered through the chaos.

*Alessandra. Date. Drinks. Roman. More drinks.*

My stomach lurched again, both at the reminder of Alessandra's date and the shitty dive bar I'd drank my weight in. No wonder I felt like ass. Nothing humbled a man more than cheap liquor and bad decisions.

"Here." A laughing voice roused me from my misery. "This will make you feel better."

I lifted my head, another jackhammer striking at the movement.

Alessandra stood at the end of the couch, fresh-faced and beautiful in a yellow sundress. Damp chestnut waves brushed her shoulders, and the heady scents of her perfume and shampoo filled my nostrils.

I looked like utter shit while she looked like she'd stepped out of a fairy tale.

*Fan-fucking-tastic*. This wasn't what I'd had in mind when I made the stupid, drunken decision to wait outside her apartment like a desperate creep last night. Screw Roman for not stopping me; he'd gotten a call from work (which he'd refused to elaborate on) and left me to my worst impulses.

"If you see me come within five feet of whiskey again, feel free to slap me." I forced myself to sit up so I could take the proffered water and *pastéis*. Alessandra had introduced me to the fried pastries during our first trip to Brazil, and I'd been a fan since. "Whoever invented shitty drinks deserves to be shot."

Her eyes glittered with mirth. "I've never seen you so hungover or disheveled. I should take a picture. Otherwise, no one will believe me."

"Funny. Rub it in, why don't you?" I brought the water to my lips, but I was so disoriented I spilled some of it over my shirt. I bit out a colorful curse.

Alessandra's entire body shook. "Priceless," she gasped through bouts of laughter. She lifted her phone and snapped a photo, her cheeks creased with a wide grin.

"I swear to God, Ále, if I see that photo online, I'll post the one of you sleeping with your mouth open on the train," I threatened, but a reluctant hint of amusement tugged at my mouth. It was hard to stay upset when she was smiling, even if it was at my expense.

"It might be worth it." She wiped the corners of her eyes, her giggles smoothing the last edges of my annoyance.

"You look happy," I said. "I don't remember the last time I made you this happy."

Maybe it was a temporary happiness, but it was happiness all the same. I'd made her cry enough that seeing her laugh was worth the bruises to my ego.

Alessandra's humor faded, disappearing into the tension that sparked, sudden and electric, around us.

"I guess that was part of the problem." Her sad smile seeped into the cracks of my heart. "There was no clear defining point between the *before* and *after* of our marriage. Somewhere along the way, the lines between happiness and resentment got blurred, and here we are."

A lump blocked my throat. "And here we are."

I wished we didn't have to take this road, but part of me was glad we did. As much as Alessandra leaving destroyed me, I would rather suffer through our separation than have her live in silent misery for the rest of our lives. Our divorce had been the shock I desperately needed to get my head out of my ass and realize what was truly important in my life.

I set my food aside and stood. Nerves slowed my pace, but soon I was in front of her, my chest tight and my mouth dry. The jackhammers in my head retreated beneath the ache sweeping through me. Forget the hangover; nothing hurt more than knowing I'd hurt her. It was knowledge I'd have to live with for the rest of my life, but I hoped our future could overpower the wrongs of our past.

"Do you remember the night we finished cleaning up after the burst pipe? We ordered takeout, and you asked where I was supposed to be instead of at the store."

Alessandra nodded, her expression wary.

"I told you there was nowhere else I'd rather be, and I meant it," I said. I wasn't a sharer by nature. I'd kept my problems to myself growing up because no one else gave much of a damn, and I locked my emotions in a box because every piece of vulnerability was a weakness other people could exploit. But the past few months had chipped away the lock, slowly but surely, until it lay in pieces at her feet.

No more hiding. No more running away. It was now or nothing.

"I could tell you didn't believe me because I've spent the better part of the decade living out of my office, but I wasn't there all the time because I loved it. I was there because I was terrified that if I left, it would all crumble down." The admission scraped past the thundering of my pulse. It was a truth I'd avoided facing for too long. I thought money and power could erase my insecurities, but while they'd solved my old problems, they also gave rise to new ones. "Everything I'd worked for, everything I'd achieved. I looked out the window at the city people say I conquered, and I only saw a million more ways I could fail. I thought that if I accumulated *enough*, I would finally be safe. But here's the thing." I swallowed the emotion scalding my throat. "I left my office for weeks when I went to Brazil and I hardly missed it. But when I came home and found you gone…that night, and every night since, has felt like an eternity. *Saudades de você.*" *I miss you. In the deepest, truest sense.*

Alessandra dropped her gaze as I continued. "Maybe I overstepped by waiting for you after your date, but I was drunk and miserable and…" The teeth of agony ate at me. "I needed to see you."

I'd braced myself for the possibility she'd be with her date. I'd convinced myself I could handle it when in reality I probably would've smashed the fucker's face in and ruined everything. Luck had been on my side in that regard, but I didn't feel particularly lucky as I stood there, heart in my hand, waiting for her to do with it as she pleased. After all, it belonged to her. It always had.

"I didn't have a date last night," Alessandra said in a small voice.

Twin arrows of surprise and jubilation fell somewhere north of confusion.

"Then why…"

She looked up again, her eyes glittering with emotion. "Because I was afraid of getting too attached again. At the penthouse, you asked me to stay, and I almost did. I didn't want…I don't…" She inhaled a shuddering breath. "I'm scared I'll go back and lose myself again. I'm scared you'll get comfortable and erase the progress we've made. I can't go through this a second time, Dom. *I can't.*" Her sentence broke into a sob, and just like that, my heart slid out of my palm and shattered all over again.

---

## Alessandra

Dominic's arms engulfed me. "You won't," he said fiercely. "We've come too far. I won't let us go back to that place."

He'd always been good at saying the right thing. *Doing* the right thing was a lot harder, and every time I took a step toward believing him, some unidentifiable creature inside me yanked me back into the shadows of fear.

"You can't promise that." I pulled back from him and swiped at my tears. God, how many times had I cried over the past few months? I was turning into one of those weepy, dramatic characters I hated in TV shows, but there was nothing I could do about it. If I could control my emotions, we wouldn't be where we were. "What's the difference between then and now, Dom? When we got married, you stood next to me and promised I'd never face the world alone." Shards of glass embedded in my chest. "But I did."

Emotion churned through the room like a summer storm, sudden and violent, sweeping away the pretty words and pulls of attraction to reveal the crux of it. The reason why, despite all the things Dominic had done and the true remorse he'd shown, I hadn't allowed myself to truly let go. He was sorry now because it was easy to be sorry. He had a team who could handle things while he took time off from the office, and he was lucky there'd been no emergencies while he was gone. But what happened the next time he had to choose between another billion dollars and me? When there was a conflict between a VIP client meeting and a regular Friday night date?

Pain ravaged his face, but his response was quiet and steady. "The difference is, back then, I thought I had nothing to lose. Now, I realize I have everything to lose." Sadness reflected in his smile. "You."

*You.* I never thought one word could hurt so much.

The war between believing him and retreating to safety raged through me. Another small sob shook my shoulders as Dominic pressed his forehead to me.

"Give us another chance," he begged. "One last chance. I swear I won't fuck it up. I know my word doesn't mean much to you anymore, but tell me what you want me to do, and I'll do it." His tears dripped into my own. "Anything. Please."

There was nothing he could do on his own that he hadn't already done. I could wait for a sign from the universe, some incontrovertible proof that Dominic had changed and wouldn't regress back to the uncaring workaholic I'd lived with for far too long, but signs were open to interpretation. They existed at the whim of an unseen force, and I was tired of letting others dictate my life.

At the end of the day, I had to do what was best for me and go with my gut, and my gut told me that no matter how many people I dated or how far I tried to run, I couldn't outrun my heart.

"One last chance." Dominic's body sagged with relief at my response. "Please don't break my heart," I whispered. That was the only request I had.

"I won't." His ragged breaths matched my own. He kissed me again, his embrace so sweet and desperate and searching it seeped into every molecule of my body. "I lost you once, and I never want to lose you again."

I had nothing except faith tethering me to his promises, but wasn't that the foundation of any relationship? Trust, communication, and faith that the other person loved us and that we could weather any storm together.

Dominic and I didn't work the first time, but sometimes, the strongest things were those that had been broken and healed.

## CHAPTER 37

*Dominic*

ALESSANDRA AND I SPENT THE ENTIRE WEEKEND AT HER apartment. Eating, talking, having sex. We came up for air once, when her crotchety neighbor banged on the door and yelled at us for being "too loud and vulgar," but other than that, the days passed in a blissful haze.

We were back together. We weren't married again, but we'd slept in the same bed and she'd invited me to her grand opening. It was a giant leap compared to our previous baby steps, and the high lasted well into Monday, when I arrived at the office an hour later than I usually did because I'd made us breakfast.

I whistled my way down the hall, ignoring my team's wide-eyed stares. Caroline intercepted me by the elevators and followed me to my office, where she crossed her arms and eyed me the way one would an escaped tiger. "Are you sick? Do you need me to call a doctor?"

"I'm fine." I turned on my computer and pulled up the latest numbers. "Why? Do I look sick?"

"No. You're just...smiling so much." She tapped her fingers against her arm. "Maybe I should call Dr. Stanley just in case. You have several important client meetings—"

"Caroline." I interrupted her. "I said I'm *fine*. Now, do you have work updates for me, or would you rather switch to a medical career?"

She instantly snapped back to chief of staff mode. "There are rumors something big is coming out this week re: a bank," she said. "I can't confirm anything yet, but people are nervous. Whatever it is...it's supposed to be seismic."

I'd heard the same rumors. Wall Street was rife with leaks and whispers. Half the time, they amounted to nothing, but I kept my ears to the ground anyway. "Keep digging," I said. "I don't want any surprises."

"Understood."

The rest of the workday passed uneventfully. I left the office precisely at five, which garnered me a fresh wave of jaw drops and bug eyes. No one in finance ever left work on time, but there was a first time for everything.

"Don't stay too late," I told one of the junior associates on my way out. "Meet your girlfriend for dinner. Enjoy your night."

I assumed he had a girlfriend. Otherwise, the desk photo of him with his arm around a smiling blonde was fucking weird.

He gaped at me with an odd mix of shock, terror, and reverence. "Y-yes, sir."

I stopped by my usual floral shop on the way to Floria Designs and picked up a golden rose. They didn't sell them normally, but I made it worth their while to fly in fresh blooms daily.

"Hey. How's everything going?" I greeted Alessandra with a kiss.

"Good." She looked a little frazzled, but she smiled when I handed her the rose and note. *#21 out of a thousand*. "I'm running around like a headless chicken, but other than that, I'm okay."

"Anything I can do to help?" Floria Designs' grand opening was this weekend. The shop looked great, but Alessandra wouldn't relax until it was over. She was a perfectionist when it came to events.

"Can you clone me or add more hours to the day?" She blew a strand of hair out of her eye.

"I can have my people look into it, but I can't guarantee you an answer you'll like before Saturday." I placed a hand on the small of her back and steered her toward the exit. "In the meantime, let's eat."

"I can't eat. I have to answer a thousand emails, I haven't picked out a dress for the party yet, and I—"

"Ále." We stopped by the door. "Breathe. It'll all get done. Tracy is arriving tomorrow, right?"

Tracy was one of her virtual assistants. She was flying in to help with prep and attend the opening. Alessandra's other assistant just gave birth, so she couldn't make it.

"Yes, but—"

"It'll all get done," I repeated. "When did you last eat? If it was before noon, dinner is nonnegotiable."

"Fine," she relented. A cab whooshed by when we stepped outside, blanketing us with car fumes as it nearly ran over a bike messenger. The bike messenger screamed something obscene; the cab driver rolled down his window and flipped him off. "It's ironic you're telling me to eat when you're the one who always skips lunch."

"Not always." I kept my hand on her lower back and gently moved her so I walked on the outside of the sidewalk. "I had a black coffee and half a sandwich today." A grin flashed at her half- amused, half-exasperated stare.

She still had work to do after dinner, so I took her to the gourmet burger shop down the street from Floria Designs. We'd just placed our orders when my phone lit up with a new message.

"Is that your brother?" Alessandra accurately read the pinch in my brow. There was only one person in the world who drew that kind of reaction from me.

"Yes. He wants to meet for drinks." I didn't want to blow him off after his first normal outreach (breaking and entering my apartment didn't count), but I sure as hell wasn't leaving Alessandra either.

"Tell him to meet us here. I'm serious," she said when I slid her a look laced with disbelief. "You talk about him so much, and we have to meet eventually."

"I'm not sure he's a burger-and-fries type of guy."

"Ask anyway." Alessandra reached for her soda. "It can't hurt."

———————

*Alessandra*

I regretted asking Dominic to invite his brother the minute he showed up.

Roman was both as handsome and unsettling as I remembered. He greeted me with a cool smile and was polite enough, but there was something about him that set off level-five alarms. Maybe it was the way he moved like a predator stalking the night, or maybe it was the ice anchoring that cold, green gaze. Dominic was ruthless but very much human; there was no humanity behind his brother's eyes.

"Dom says you're in town for work." I attempted to make conversation after our previous discussion about the latest Nate Reynolds film petered out. "What do you do?"

He cut his burger with surgical precision. "I'm in resolutions."

"What does that mean?"

"I fix problems other people can't solve." Roman offered nothing else.

I glanced at Dominic, who met my eyes with a small shake of his head. He was used to his brother's reticence, but part of the reason I'd asked him to invite Roman was so we could get to know each other better.

"I see." I filled the ensuing silence with another stab at drawing Roman out of his shell. There had to be *some* topic he could expand on. "I guess you travel a lot then. Where were you before you came to New York?"

"Here and there." Another clean slice of meat and bread. "I can't talk much about work. It's confidential. You understand."

"Let me guess. If you told me, you'd have to kill me?" I joked.

Roman's smile didn't reach his eyes. "Something like that."

A chill drew goose bumps out of hiding. Quiet mushroomed again, interrupted by the occasional clink of silverware and chatter from nearby tables.

"You've been watching too many action movies, Rome," Dominic said just as the silence was getting unbearable. "Come up with something more original next time."

Roman let out a small laugh. The tension dissipated, replaced by a debate over whether Keanu Reeves' John Wick or Nate Reynolds' Jason Rath was the better character.

I guess Roman didn't mind talking about movies if his brother was the one who brought it up.

Dominic's hand found mine under the table and squeezed. I squeezed back even as unease leaked into my blood. I loved that he was reconnecting with his brother, but I worried that his lingering guilt over what happened in Ohio was clouding his judgment.

How much did he really know about Roman's life since they were teens?

"What about you, Alessandra?" Roman's gaze settled on my face again. "John or Jason?"

"Neither, unfortunately. I'm not big on assassin movies."

Another laugh, this one containing a hint of something I couldn't quite pinpoint. "Too bad. You're missing out."

"I doubt it," I said lightly. I wasn't big on blood and violence. Explosions and car chases, yes. Torture, no.

Mocking amusement flashed in Roman's eyes, and another rash of goose bumps pebbled my skin. There was something about him…

I tried not to judge people by their cover, but gut instinct told me he was someone that would eliminate any obstacles that stood in his way by *any* means necessary.

And my gut was rarely wrong.

# CHAPTER 38

*Dominic*

I WALKED DOWN THE LENGTH OF MY OFFICE AND stopped in front of the second to last rack. "This one." I picked out a shimmering gold dress.

"Excellent choice." Lilah Amiri smiled. "It'll look wonderful on her. Shall I have it shipped directly to her apartment?"

"Yes. Charge it to my account."

Since Alessandra didn't have time to find an outfit for her grand opening, I'd asked one of her favorite designers to bring over a selection of dresses she might like. I thought the gold one suited her best. She'd always looked good in the color, and the cut was simple, feminine, and elegant.

I'd already marked the opening in my calendar, set an alarm, *and* tasked Caroline and Martha with reminding me should I somehow forget about it come Saturday. I'd learned from my mistakes. I wasn't missing so much as a coffee date again, much less something so important to Alessandra.

Our renewed relationship was still on tentative ground, but we were quickly settling into a new, better normal. Casual date nights, lazy weekends, frequent calls and texts…they reminded me of when we first started dating in college. The difference was, I had a better appreciation for what we had—and what I'd almost lost. I also didn't have to scrape together cents and dollars for a nice meal anymore, which was a nice bonus.

I settled behind my desk as Martha ushered Lilah and her assistant out of my office. My staff was adjusting to my more relaxed schedule. Hell, *I* was adjusting to my schedule. After years of working myself to the bone at the expense of everything else, it felt strange to put my phone down for extended periods of time and not watch the moon rise from my office every night. Relaxing in Brazil was one thing; relaxing in New York was another.

I didn't hate it. The fear of losing everything I'd built was still there, but the voices had subsided from screams to whispers.

I'd just pulled up the numbers for my latest acquisition when my phone rang. *Kai.*

The sight of his name packed a rush of adrenaline. He never called in the middle of the workday unless there was major news, and as CEO of the world's largest media conglomerate, he had his finger on the pulse more than anyone I knew.

"Check your email." No greeting, no goodbye before he hung up. The news must be fucking huge.

Gut instinct told me it had to do with the rumors roiling Wall Street this past week, and a quick click of the mouse proved me right.

The stock market closed in one minute. It was prime time for anyone who wanted to drop a bombshell that would upend the next morning's trading session, which was exactly what an anonymous whistleblower had done.

Kai had sent me a dyslexic-friendly version of a white paper alleging major fraud at DBG, a massive regional bank. Bogus transactions, solvency issues, cover-ups at the highest level of management. If the allegations were true, it'd be one of the largest bank fraud cases in U.S. history.

The markets were going to be a bloodbath. I'd be surprised if DBG retained a fraction of its value by the end of the week.

Implications and possibilities flooded my mind with a crackling, swirling buzz. Adrenaline pumped harder through my veins and kicked my heart into overdrive.

This was it. The crisis I'd been waiting for.

"Sir." Caroline appeared in the doorway, her face pale. The cacophony behind her told me we weren't the only ones who'd read the white paper. Shouts and curses layered over the shrill ring of phones; an associate rushed past and nearly knocked Caroline over. She didn't ask if I'd heard the news; she knew better. "What do you want to do?"

I'd waited my entire career to make my mark and I had, in many ways, but my previous accomplishments weren't enough. What I had in mind though? It would be more than enough. It would make me a legend.

"Call in everyone, including legal, finance, and the board." I stood, my blood electric with possibility. "We're buying a bank."

---

The chaos started the second I woke up on Friday and continued well into the night.

As predicted, DBG's stocks plunged to record lows, and the media frenzy incited a run on deposits that brought one of the biggest regional banks in the eastern United States to the brink of ruin in less than twenty-four hours.

My plan was simple. In order for DBG to remain solvent, it needed capital, quick, and I had plenty of capital—enough to buy it out over the weekend before it fully collapsed.

The tight turnaround meant my team was working around the clock to get everything in order. DBG was fully onboard, and we kept in constant communication with them throughout the day.

We were still in the hastily set up war room next to my office at midnight when my phone rang.

*Unknown caller.*

It was either the person who'd been messing with me in the fall—Roman said it wasn't him, but I was still skeptical—or it was another journalist. News of my impending buyout had leaked from DBG's side, and I'd been fielding calls all fucking day.

"What?" I barked. I motioned for my general counsel. He rushed over and took the stack of papers I shoved in his arms.

"Don't buy the bank." The distorted voice sliced through my work fog like a dagger. I stilled, a cold sensation crawling down my throat and into my lungs. "If you do, you'll die."

# CHAPTER 39

*Dominic*

I DIDN'T GO HOME FRIDAY NIGHT. I GRABBED A FEW
hours of shut-eye in the room I'd set up right after Alessandra
left, when I couldn't stand to sleep in our bed alone, and woke up
before sunrise to finish the paperwork. Most of my team crashed
in the office as well.

Buying a bank was a huge deal not only for me but for the
entire company, and the air teemed with a whirling cocktail of
nerves, excitement, and tension. Anything could go wrong before
Monday; it was our job to make sure nothing did.

By the time Saturday evening rolled around, I'd already pushed
last night's call to the back of my mind. There were plenty of people
who were against the buyout, including the heads of the other
regional banks. DBG's collapse would benefit them in the long run,
and none of them were above intimidation. However, I doubted
any of them would follow through on the threat of murder.

"We're almost done." Dark circles ringed Caroline's eyes.
Behind her, takeout boxes, coffee cups, and stacks of documents
littered the conference table. "Contracts will be ready by morning
at the latest."

"Good." I checked my watch. I had to leave soon to make it to Alessandra's grand opening on time. "Call me only if it's an emergency. I don't want a single text unless someone died or the building is burning down."

The DBG crisis had bulldozed us during the worst weekend possible, but I would make it work. Like Caroline said, we were in the home stretch, and I trusted my team to hold the fort down until morning. The rest of the night was about Alessandra.

Caroline took my order in stride. "Understood."

I quickly showered and changed in my office's en suite bathroom. Two minutes to get downstairs. Thirty minutes to get to the grand opening, depending on how bad traffic was. Timing was tight—I'd stayed longer than I should've to nail down an essential clause in the contract—but it was doable.

I rushed into the elevator and jabbed at the button for the lobby.

*Forty. Thirty-nine. Thirty-eight.* The elevator passed each floor with excruciating slowness. For the first time, I regretted situating my office on the highest floor of Davenport Capital's headquarters.

It stopped on the thirtieth floor. The doors opened, but there was no one waiting on the other side. Twenty-fifth floor, same thing.

I checked my watch again. My window for arriving on time narrowed by the second. I hoped like hell the traffic gods were on my side, or I was fucked.

I stopped again at the seventeenth floor.

"For fuck's sake!" I needed to talk to building management about these damn elevators. I reached out to press the close button, but a soft *click* pulled my attention up.

Black metal glinted inches from my face, its barrel as steady and unwavering as the hand that held it.

Shock waves rippled through my body. *No.* Perhaps I was

delirious from lack of sleep because this made no fucking sense. Except, in a perverse way, it did.

*I should've known.* The coppery taste of betrayal welled in my throat when Roman's gaze met mine.

"I'm sorry."

Sincere regret laced his voice as he looked me in the eyes and pulled the trigger.

# CHAPTER 40

## *Alessandra*

THE TURNOUT FOR THE GRAND OPENING EXCEEDED my expectations. If Dominic and I were still married, it would be a no-brainer because everyone wanted proximity to the Davenport name. But the fact we'd divorced and every VIP I'd invited was present and accounted for? It was astonishing.

A quick scan around the room showed Buffy Darlington holding court with the socialites from the old guard while Tilly Denman reigned over the new wave of It girls. Ayana looked resplendent in emerald, Sebastian Laurent made his first society appearance since the Le Boudoir fiasco, and Xavier Castillo lounged on the velvet booth, his tousled dark hair and lazy grin attracting a plethora of admiring glances, though his eyes remained on Sloane. I even spotted the notoriously reclusive Vuk Markovic, whose massive body dwarfed his chair with laughable ease.

It should've been the best night of my life. And yet...

I glanced at the clock. The party started half an hour ago, and Dominic wasn't here yet.

Unease whispered through my gut. *He'll be here.* He was

probably stuck in traffic. Saturday nights in Manhattan were hellish for drivers.

I took a fortifying sip of champagne and took great care not to spill it on my dress. Lilah Amiri had sent it to my apartment Thursday night, courtesy of Dominic, who'd done an incredible job of choosing the perfect color and style. He knew me well, and he clearly remembered the event was tonight if he'd gone to the trouble of dress shopping for me.

*He'll be here*, I repeated to myself.

"Congrats, babe!" Isabella popped up with a drink in hand and Kai in tow. She engulfed me in a huge, perfumed hug. "Look at all this. It's *amazing*."

"Thank you." I smiled and tried to set my worries aside. She was right. The night *was* amazing, and that wasn't me getting a big head.

I'd opened a physical store in less than four months. Granted, I'd had luck, connections, and a steady cash flow on my side, but it was an accomplishment worth celebrating regardless of how many people showed up tonight.

I'd set a goal for *myself,* no one else, and I'd achieved it. Pride dampened my earlier misgivings, and I chatted with Kai and Isabella for a bit before mingling with other guests I didn't see as often.

"We should sit," I heard Dante say as I passed by him and Vivian, who was showing the tiniest hint of a baby bump. Anxiety laced his tone. "I read an article that said you should stay off your feet when you're pregnant, and you've been standing for hours."

"It's been forty minutes," Vivian said. She patted her worried-looking husband on the arm. "I'm *fine*. I'm pregnant, not incapacitated."

"What if—"

"What if we get another one of those delicious canapés?

Excellent idea. Come on." She steered him toward the food table. "I'm craving pickles, and you need a drink."

I held back a laugh. Dante was always protective of Vivian, but his concern had kicked into overdrive since her pregnancy. I was surprised he didn't bubble wrap her and glue her to his side until she gave birth.

"Hi, Sebastian. Thanks so much for coming." I made a point to say hi to Dominic's friend, who'd been dealing with a media firestorm since Martin Wellgrew's death at his event. Sebastian had always been lovely and genuine, which was a rarity in Manhattan high society, and he didn't deserve the unfair treatment from the press.

"I wouldn't miss it." A trace of exhaustion tinged his smile. "Congratulations on the store. It looks great."

"Thank you." Sympathy softened my voice. "How are you doing?"

"I could be worse." He offered a shrug. "*C'est la vie.* The media does what the media does. Look at Dominic and DBG."

My heart ricocheted at the sudden and unexpected mention of Dominic's name. The DBG fiasco had dominated headlines since Thursday, but we hadn't had a chance to talk in person because I'd been slammed with party prep, and he'd been busy with the buyout.

"What do you mean?"

"Just that they're running wild with the buyout news depending on which side they fall." Sebastian shook his head. "It's a huge deal, but this weekend must be nuts for Dom and his team. I heard no one's left the office since yesterday morning. I bet they have to work through tonight as well."

"Right." I swallowed the growing lump in my throat. "Make sense. Well, thank you again for coming out. Don't forget to grab a gift bag before you leave."

*I bet they have to work through tonight as well.*

Sebastian's words echoed through my head as I made my way around the room. I tried to focus, but I couldn't shake the mental image of Dominic poring over his documents, so lost in his work he forgot about everything else.

*No.* He said he would be here. He'd texted a few hours ago promising he would be on his way soon. He wouldn't go back on his word again. Right?

However, the more time passed, the tighter the rope of dread wound around my chest. Old me would've rationalized his absence. The DBG buyout was a record-breaking deal that needed to be completed within a tiny window of time; *of course* Dominic should prioritize it over a small store opening. It made practical sense.

But that was the problem. Our marriage fell apart because we'd focused too much on practicality and not enough on our feelings, including how I felt about always coming in second place to work.

He knew how I felt now, and he'd promised time and again he would change. But this was his first big test since we got back together and he wasn't here.

A fist closed around my heart. I would be okay with a quick drop-in. Even if he showed his face for two minutes before he rushed back to work, I would understand because at least that meant he'd remembered and taken the time to see me.

But as the minutes ticked by, and the party wound down, it was clear that Dominic wasn't coming at all.

# CHAPTER 41

## I REACTED ON INSTINCT.

I grabbed Roman's arm a split second before he pulled the trigger; the shot went wide, the bullet pinging against steel as we fell back into the elevator and the doors slid closed.

His gun clattered to the floor. We lunged for it at the same time, but Roman drove his elbow into my ribcage right as my fingers brushed the metal.

Thuds and grunts, fists against flesh. The air evacuated from my lungs, replaced with a desperate, primal need for survival.

I didn't allow myself to think. If I did, I'd have to confront who the gun belonged to. Whose number I'd called when I needed someone to talk to. Whose reemergence in my life I'd accepted despite misgivings because I'd slipped up once and allowed sentimentality to get the best of me.

Unlike our fight at the penthouse, this one didn't shed blood, but it bruised harder than any of our previous blows.

Roman finally got the upper hand when my phone rang and split my attention for a fraction of a second. A twist of his arm, and I was pinned against the wall with a gun pressed under my chin.

We stared at each other, our breaths heavy with exertion and something deeper than physical struggle.

My phone stopped ringing. The ensuing silence was so vast and charged it warped the tenor of my voice.

"Nice seeing you too, Rome," I rasped. Somewhere, in the dim recesses of my mind, I realized the elevator had stopped moving. We must've hit the emergency switch. "Now can you tell me, exactly, what the *fuck* is this?"

The fog of shock had gradually dissipated, giving way to a thousand unanswered questions. For example, why the hell my brother was trying to kill me and why, if he wanted me dead, he hadn't attempted to finish the job earlier. He'd had plenty of opportunities over the past month when my guard was down.

Why now? Why here? And why the look of regret in his eyes when he'd pulled the trigger?

Roman's jaw ticked. "I can't let you go through with the deal."

What—realization threaded through the sense of betrayal simmering in my gut. "DBG? This is about a goddamn *bank*?"

"I tried to warn you."

*Don't buy the bank. If you do, you'll die.* Last night's strange call resurfaced with razor-sharp clarity.

"You said you weren't behind the unknown calls." I recognized the absurdity of my accusation. If he wasn't above murder, he certainly wasn't above lying.

"Not the ones from the fall." Roman's eyes flickered beneath the lights. "That was them. They were…displeased about me making contact with you. The calls were a warning to me more than you."

My blood drummed in my ears. *Them.* "Who do you work for?" I had my suspicions, but I wanted him to say it.

"I can't tell you." His grip tightened around his gun. "Let's say I fell in with the wrong crowd."

"Classic Roman."

He didn't smile. "I wish I didn't have to do this."

"So don't." My eyes stayed on his. "Whoever they are, they're not here. It's you and me. That's it."

I was painfully aware of the cold metal against my skin and the seconds ticking by. There was a strong chance I wouldn't walk out of this elevator alive, and the only thing I could think of was Alessandra.

The grand opening was in full swing. Did she think I'd forgotten about her? That I wasn't going to show because I was too busy with the buyout? It was her big night, and I might ruin it the way I had so many other things in the past.

I didn't fear dying as much as I feared never seeing her again.

Regret hardened into determination. *Fuck that.* We'd just gotten back together, and we had our entire lives in front of us. I wasn't letting that go without a fight.

"Why do you care so much about the bank?" I stalled. If I could distract Roman for just one second... "What difference does my buyout make?"

"None to me. A hell of a lot to my client."

"It's funny." An acrid taste welled on my tongue. "You talked so much about loyalty, yet here you are, choosing a client over your brother. So much for family."

His jaw ticked again. "Don't pin this on me. If you'd listened—"

"To an anonymous caller using a voice distorter? I can't imagine why I wouldn't take business advice from someone like that." I could barely hear my voice over the thudding of my heart. "At least be honest. There's a part of you that's always wanted to do this. You wanted to make me pay for my betrayal, and this is your chance. So do it. Right now, face to face. You've waited fifteen years for this." I grabbed his wrist and forced the gun tighter against my skin. "*Do it.*"

*Click.*

My heart outpaced my breaths. Oxygen thickened into sludge, and acrimony raked across my skin like razor blades.

My brother's eyes blazed, and for a second, just a second, I thought that was it.

But then Roman hissed out a curse, and the sensation of metal disappeared from my skin. He stepped back, his gun still trained on me.

"If I don't kill you," he said, "they'll kill both of us. Unless…"

I waited, suspended between relief and dread.

"You give up the deal. Walk away from DBG, Dom, and I might be able to convince them to let us live."

"Done."

"Don't lie to me." Roman knew me too well to take me at my word. "If I let you leave and you complete the buyout anyway, no amount of security could save you or me. It won't be about the client anymore. It'll be about their reputation, and they would go to *any* lengths to protect their reputation. Trust me." Shadows crept through his eyes, the echoes of horrors better left buried.

The hammer of my pulse caused my veins to hurt.

I'd planned to do exactly what he suspected. I would walk out, sign the deal, and hunt down whoever was behind tonight. I wouldn't rest until *they* were dead, every single one of them.

"It's a bank." Roman kept his gaze on mine. "One bank. Is it worth what you might lose?"

The hammering intensified.

It should've been a no-brainer. Give up the deal and live without looking over my shoulder every day. But the DBG buyout wasn't about *one bank*. It was about the culmination of everything I'd tried to do since I was old enough to realize I didn't have to stay in my shithole town.

No one had ever bought a bank this size before the age of

thirty-five. I'd be the first. It would be a *fuck you* to every naysayer I'd encountered and every teacher who said I would amount to nothing. No matter what happened after, it'd ensure I go down in the history books.

Immortalized. Unerasable.

It would be security and my legacy.

I wasn't afraid of Roman's mysterious backer; I had my own connections and enough money to bury them alive. But winning wasn't guaranteed, and I wasn't the only one at risk.

How much was I willing to gamble to achieve everything I'd ever wanted?

"The ball's in your court, Dom," Roman said, his voice low. "What will you choose? Your legacy or our lives?"

# CHAPTER 42

## Alessandra

HE NEVER SHOWED.

The party wrapped up early because of an impending thunderstorm that drove people home before they got caught in the flash flood, but I didn't mind. The grand opening was already a smashing success, and I'd exhausted my social battery for the night.

Plus, it was hard to smile and pretend nothing was wrong when my heart was breaking before it fully healed.

"Maybe he got in an accident," Isabella said. "He could be in the hospital right now, trying to tear off his IV so he can run out and see you. I'm sure he didn't forget."

"*Isa.*" Vivian glared at her. "Don't joke about something like that."

"What? Stranger things have happened." Isabella drew her bottom lip between her teeth. "I don't buy that Dominic forgot or chose not to come. Not after everything he did to win Alessandra back."

"You two." Sloane pointed at Dante and Kai, who froze in unison. No one wanted to be the target of her ire. "Where's your friend?"

297

"He hasn't answered our calls." Kai recovered first and gave me a reassuring smile. "I'm sure he's on his way. He probably got held up."

"Or mugged," Dante said. He shrugged when Vivian redirected her death stare at him. "I'm sorry, *mia cara*, but it's a possibility."

"Guys, it's okay." Exhaustion drained my vocabulary to the bare necessities. "It's not your problem. Go home. I'll clean up."

"I'll help." Sloane grabbed a trash bag.

"No," I said firmly. "You've done enough."

"But—"

"You can't—"

Despite their protests, I forced my friends out the door minutes later. I appreciated their concern, but I wanted to be alone.

I went through the motions of throwing out trash and storing leftovers in the fridge. It was like watching someone cosplay me; she looked like me and moved like me, but she didn't *feel* like me. She was a stranger cosplaying my dream life.

I paused in front of the collage I'd spent weeks painstakingly creating. It took up the entire right wall. Bright, vibrant petals gradually faded to muted browns that dominated the center of the piece before a hint of color crept back into the canvas.

Life, death, rebirth. It wasn't subtle, but I didn't want it to be. I wanted it as a reminder of what I'd left and what I never wanted to fall back into again.

"Ále."

My spine stiffened at the voice behind me. I should've locked the door, but I'd been too distracted by Dominic's presence. My self-preservation instincts went right out the window the instant he entered the picture.

"You're late." I didn't turn, afraid that if I did, I would start crying and never stop.

"Sweetheart—"

"No, wait. That's wrong." Disillusionment splintered the rhythm of my words. "You're not late; you never showed. The party is over, Dominic. You don't need to be here."

"Yes, I do." His presence brushed my back, heavy with regret, and I closed my eyes against a fall of tears as his hand gently touched my arm. "Because you're here."

"Then where were you before? Were you at work?"

Silence.

"Yes or no, Dominic."

Another, deeper silence chipped at the pieces of my heart. Then, so quietly I almost didn't hear him, "Yes."

A tear dripped off my chin, and the browns in the centerpiece blurred into one amorphous monster that colored every shade of my world.

When would I learn?

"But it's not what you think."

His hands grasped my shoulders, and he turned me around, meeting my anguished eyes with his own. Desperation sculpted his face. "I wanted to be here, *amor*. I swear. I was on my way when... God, you wouldn't believe me if I told you."

"Try me." I shouldn't indulge him. I'd heard every excuse imaginable over the years—*it was an emergency, five hundred million was at stake, the prime minister invited me to dinner and I couldn't say no*—and I didn't need another one. But I did need closure, and if I didn't ask, I would always wonder.

"It was Roman."

Surprise rippled through me. That, I hadn't expected.

"I admit, I stayed later than I should've working on the contract," Dominic said. "I was rushing to get to your party on time when I...ran into my brother."

I listened, caught between perilous hope and skeptical disbelief, as he explained what happened from the elevator to the gun to his brother's ultimatum.

"I know it sounds completely unbelievable, but it's what happened," he said when he finished. "I swear."

I didn't know what to think. On one hand, what he said was so ridiculous I was almost insulted he thought I would fall for it. On the other, that was exactly why it was believable. Dominic wasn't prone to hyperbole. His excuses had always been grounded in reality, not in stories that could be the plot of a Nate Reynolds film.

"If you don't believe me, look online. I put out a press statement about the deal that should've been published…" He glanced at the clock. "Ten minutes ago. Roman wouldn't let me go unless I confirmed with the press."

Palpable waves of tension rolled off him as I pulled out my phone, my heart in my throat.

I didn't dare hope, but when I saw the headline, something inside me caved.

*In a shocking late-night statement, Davenport Capital has announced it is no longer acquiring DBG Bank. The embattled bank has been under immense pressure since Thursday…*

"Obviously, I didn't tell them about Roman, but it proves what I said about scrapping the deal is true," Dominic said. His throat bobbed, his expression carved with nerves. "I wouldn't do that unless I was forced. You know I…fuck." Nerves gave way to alarm as a tiny sob escaped my throat. "Please don't cry, *amor*. I can't stand it." He rubbed a tear away with his thumb, his voice cracking ever so slightly.

I tried to stop them, but my tears poured out faster than I could manage. They welled from somewhere deep inside me, a secret pool where a monster forged from my darkest fears and insecurities lurked. It kept Dominic at arm's length in case he backslid into old habits, and it hurtled me toward the worst-case scenario at the first sign of trouble. But the more I cried, the more the pool drained until said monster was a weakened shadow of itself.

I buried my face in Dominic's chest, my shoulders heaving with sobs.

"I thought you forgot." I hiccupped, mortified by my cries but too overcome to care.

"I know." He tucked me closer to his body and pressed his mouth to the top of my head. "I'm so sorry for not putting you first before. For treating you in a way that made you think I'd forget you. It was inexcusable, but I'll never do it again." Sincerity softened painful regret. "I promise."

The last dam holding me together collapsed.

Thunder boomed as he held me, unflinching beneath the force of my sobs. The storm had broken, and the ferocious lash of rain against the windows served as an oddly soothing soundtrack while nature and I both released our emotions in torrential downpours.

Dominic had left work in the middle of a historic, multibillion-dollar deal. He'd had less than seventy-two hours to close the deal and he took time off for me. For some, it was the bare minimum, but for him—for us—it was everything. It didn't matter that the deal hadn't gone through or that he'd missed the actual party; what mattered was the effort and care.

I didn't know how long we stayed there, my face against his chest and his arms around my waist, but by the time my tears subsided, the rain had slowed to a faint drizzle.

I lifted my head and wiped my face. "For the record," I said. "Your only acceptable excuse for missing important events going forward is if you're held at gunpoint."

Dominic's shoulders loosened, and relief poured through his

raspy chuckle. "Noted," he said, giving me a tender kiss. "Though I'm hoping to keep such incidents to a minimum."

"Me too." I kissed him back, warmth spreading from my chest in cautious, winding tendrils.

I doubted we'd seen the last of his brother and whoever hired him to kill the DBG buyout, but we'd deal with that later. For now, I chose to soak in our triumph over the first real, concrete obstacle of our new relationship.

Whatever was coming, we'd handle it. Together.

# CHAPTER 43

IF FRIDAY HAD BEEN CHAOS, MONDAY WAS MAYHEM.

Without a federal bailout or the capital from my scrapped deal, DBG collapsed, sending shock waves through the financial world. Market turmoil reached dizzying heights, and the FDIC (Federal Deposit Insurance Corporation) swooped in to manage the aftermath.

The mood in the office was somber. The far-reaching implications of a major bank failure aside, my team had worked their asses off on the buyout, and I'd killed it with no explanation or warning. I couldn't tell them the truth behind my decision, so I made up an excuse about risk management that only half of them bought.

It didn't make me the most popular person in the office that day, but I didn't care. I didn't mind being the villain if it meant protecting the people I loved.

"Will that be all, sir?" Caroline asked after our daily briefing. She was professional enough not to display her rancor, but a trickle of it leaked through in her ramrod-straight posture and tight mouth.

I nodded, distracted by an incoming call from Kai. I waited until she left before I answered. "Don't tell me there's another bank failure on the horizon."

"Not exactly," he said. He sounded so stunned I instinctively straightened. "Check Twitter. It's...fuck, I've never seen anything like it. It makes DBG's collapse look like child's play."

Kai's uncharacteristic drop of the f-bomb sent every hair on the back of my neck on end. Even if Roman hadn't killed me, I might die from adrenaline overdose before the week was over.

I didn't have to search hard to find what Kai was talking about. It was all over Twitter—and Facebook, and Reddit, and Instagram, and TikTok, and every other information-sharing platform I could think of.

It wasn't a white paper. It was a signed contract between two parties for services rendered that laid out, in painstaking detail, how the new CEO of Sunfolk Bank hired a private mercenary company to take down their competition by any means necessary.

Martin Wellgrew, Orion Bank.

The white paper, DBG.

*Holy fuck.*

And just like that, the wildest Monday in decades got even wilder.

---

It took experts only a few days to verify the authenticity of the contract. The mercenary company's name and details were redacted, but it didn't matter. Tug on one loose thread and the whole scheme unraveled.

Jack Becker, the CEO of Sunfolk Bank, recently took over after his father died. The bank was already struggling compared to its competitors, and Jack's reckless, impulsive management style had dug its grave deeper. Facing immense pressure from the board either to resign or turn the company around, he'd opted for a third choice—take down his competitors until Sunfolk was the last one left standing.

It was an implausible, mind-boggling plan that was straight out of the movies. It was hard to believe anyone in real life would be bold enough or stupid enough to try and pull something like that off, but idiots were born every day.

"Anything?" Alessandra wrapped her arms around me from behind. We'd returned from a dinner date earlier and I'd checked the news while she showered.

I shook my head. It'd been a week since the contract leaked, and Roman was gone in the wind again.

I didn't know what made him turn on his company. He'd been home free after convincing me to scrap DBG's buyout, but whatever it was, it'd made him target number one. People like his former employer wouldn't stop until they'd hunted him down, and I lived in dread of the day his body washed up or, worse, wasn't found at all.

"I'm sure he's okay," Alessandra said softly. "He knows how to handle himself."

"I hope so." I turned my head and gave her a soft kiss. I didn't know where Roman was, but at least she was safe, sound, and by my side.

I'd fired my old security company and hired Christian Harper's team instead. The switch had been a long time coming, and within twenty-four hours, his men had completely revamped my home, office, and personal security. Alessandra was still living in her apartment, so we'd accounted for her and Floria Designs as well.

If Roman's old employer targeted me because of my relationship to him, I was ready, though I hoped that day never came. If Alessandra got hurt because of me, I would never forgive myself.

Later that night, when she was sound asleep, I stole out of the bedroom to check the news again. It was a compulsion I couldn't shake. Some people were addicted to social media or video games; I was addicted to scanning the headlines for mentions of anyone who could be Roman.

*Nothing.*

Relief didn't get a chance to fully form before a familiar ring cut through the slice.

*Unknown caller.* A surge of unease leaked into my bloodstream.

"Hello?" Caution shrouded my voice. The caller could be one of two parties, and when I heard the soft breath on the other end, a tingle of relief loosened the fist around my heart.

Somehow, I knew. We weren't brothers by blood, but some things transcended blood.

"If you need me, I'm here," I said quietly. The longer he stayed on the phone, the greater his risk of exposure. "Take care of yourself."

A catch in his breath, then…nothing. He'd hung up.

"Everything okay?" Alessandra asked drowsily when I returned to the bedroom. She was a light sleeper, and the sound of the door closing must've awakened her.

"Yes." I climbed into bed and brushed my mouth over her forehead. Roman had risked his life by reaching out, but he made sure I knew he was okay. Perhaps I was doing him a disservice by underestimating him. He was a survivor; we both were. "Everything's perfect."

# CHAPTER 44

## Alessandra

*Three months later*

"ARE YOU SURE YOU'LL BE ALL RIGHT?"

"Yes. *Go.*" Jenny waved me off. "It's your birthday. Have fun! I promise I won't burn the store down."

"That's not funny after the iron mishap."

Guilt suffused her face. "That was one mistake, okay? I learned my lesson. Now go spend the day with your hot boyfriend or the next iron incident won't be a 'mishap.'"

"Fine. Twist my arm. Leave it to me to hire someone who threatens their own boss," I muttered good-naturedly on my way out.

Jenny had been one of my virtual assistants before she moved to the city to be closer to her family. Hiring her to help me run the shop had been a no-brainer.

Despite my reluctance to leave her on her own at the start of graduation season—pressed flowers were a surprisingly popular graduation gift—my misgivings melted at the sight of Dominic waiting for me on the curb.

He leaned with his back against his car, looking like he'd stepped off the cover of *GQ* in jeans and a slate gray button-down with the sleeves rolled up. Sunglasses hid his eyes, but his slow smile warmed every inch of my body.

"Look at you. Feeling fancy now that you're a bank owner, huh?" I teased. He rarely drove his Porsche in the city, but seeing him in front of, next to, or behind the wheel did unholy things to my libido.

"As a matter of fact, I do." His rough drawl sent a breathless shiver from my head down to my toes.

As of yesterday, Dominic—or rather, Dominic's company—was officially the new owner of Sunfolk Bank. The institution that'd been responsible for so much of its competitors' turmoil had landed in hot water itself the past three months. The leaked contract had only been the tip of the iceberg; after his arrest and detention, the CEO had been found dead in his cell due to an "undisclosed incident." Everyone suspected foul play, but no one could confirm anything.

Since then, Sunfolk had burned through *two* CEOs and multiple board resignations before Dominic stepped in. He gave them an offer they couldn't refuse, they accepted, and he cemented himself in corporate history.

He was still worried about his brother and paranoid about Roman's former employer coming after us, but we hadn't run into any trouble yet. I think Dominic realized he couldn't spend his life looking over his shoulder, so he'd calmed down on the constant check-ins and insisting we visit secure locations only.

I followed him around to the passenger side and slid into the seat after he opened the door. "So, Mr. Davenport, what do you have planned?" I arched a playful brow. "I expect nothing but the best after the way you hyped today up."

My birthday fell on a Wednesday this year, and Dominic had

insisted on us taking the day off work so we could "celebrate big."

He grinned. "It wouldn't be a surprise if I told you, would it?"

He slipped his hand over mine and held it on the center console as we wound our way through the city. I glanced at his profile, my heart embarrassingly full.

I didn't care where we went. I was just happy spending the day with him.

Dominic and I were officially dating, which felt strange to say when we'd once been married, but neither of us wanted to rush back into marriage without ironing out our issues. And truth be told, dating was *fun*. No complications, no pressure, just simple enjoyment of each other's company.

I suppose it was easier when you knew the other person was the love of your life, but regardless, I wanted to savor every step of relationship 2.0.

Half an hour later, we arrived at Teterboro Airport, where his jet waited for us on the tarmac.

Curiosity sparked. "Are we going to Brazil again?" My brother would be thrilled. We'd visited him last month to celebrate his promotion at the restaurant, and I thought he'd been happier about our rekindled relationship than his own career advancement.

A mischievous glint passed through his eyes. "No. It's a little closer to home."

---

He took us to DC, the city where we met, dated, and fell in love. The city where we got married and planned to celebrate our ten-year anniversary. It'd encapsulated so much of our relationship that stepping onto its streets was like stepping back in time.

The nostalgia intensified when our driver dropped us off at our first stop of the day. Black exterior. Crooked red sign. Windows advertising the "best burgers in the city." Some things changed, but this place hadn't.

My throat closed with emotion. "Frankie's." The site of so many late nights and stolen touches all those years ago.

I hadn't expected the impact it would have on me. Dominic and I hadn't visited DC in years, which was why I'd insisted on coming for our anniversary. It was so close to New York that weekend trips should've been common, but he always wanted to go somewhere farther, more glamorous.

St. Moritz. St. Tropez. St. Barts. Despite what it meant to us, DC had never made his list except for work—until now.

"Exactly as we left it," Dominic said. "With a few improvements."

"I hope so." A watery laugh rustled in my chest. "Eleven and a half years is a long time to go without any changes."

"Yes, it is."

Soft, silent understanding melded our glances together before we looked away. Our fingers interlaced as we walked into the diner, familiar enough to set me at ease but new enough to send butterflies fluttering through my stomach.

Frankie's, Thayer, Crumble & Bake for my favorite lemon cupcakes followed by a stroll along the Georgetown waterfront and aimless wandering through the new neighborhoods and shops that'd popped up since we left…it was the ideal mix of comfort and novelty. Dominic couldn't have planned a more perfect birthday.

"God, I've missed this city." I wouldn't live here again. I'd outgrown what DC could offer, personally and professionally, but being back was like slipping into a beloved, worn pair of jeans.

Dominic drew me closer to his side and kissed the top of my head. "We can visit any time you like."

This close to sunset, the waterfront was filled with people. Students, couples, and families thronged the benches, but one particular family drew my eye. The couple was young, likely in their mid-twenties, and they looked blissfully happy as they cooed at the baby sitting in the mother's lap.

Longing gripped me so fiercely and suddenly it brought me to a standstill.

Dominic and I hadn't talked about children since we agreed we both wanted them one day. That'd been at the start of our marriage. So much had changed since then, but I still wanted a family—with him. Only him.

Dominic followed my gaze. "Cute kid," he said softly.

"Yeah." I swallowed past a sharp ache. He hadn't pushed me to take things further or faster than I was comfortable with. We were exclusive now, but I suspected he wasn't sure if I *wanted* to get married again one day. "Ours will be cuter."

His gaze snapped to mine. I could see the moment the implication behind my words sank in because his mouth blossomed with the tenderest, most beautiful smile I'd ever seen.

"Yes, *amor*," he said. "They will."

*Four months later*

THAT SUMMER, ALESSANDRA AND I MOVED IN TOGETHER. She broke her lease early and I sold the penthouse in favor of a brownstone nestled in the heart of the West Village. It was massive, boasting four stories, a rooftop deck, and a medium-sized backyard (which was a luxury and a half in Manhattan), but it still had a cozier vibe than our old home.

We brought Camila and the rest of our household staff with us. Camila had been skeptical of the move, but once she saw the kitchen, which was even bigger than the one in the penthouse, she was all in. Despite her initial grumblings, I suspected she was so happy we were back together that she would've moved with us to a shack in the woods if we'd asked her to. She treated Alessandra like a surrogate daughter, and her patience with my divorce-induced mood swings had run thin.

After we closed on the house, Alessandra and I hired an interior design consultant but decorated most of it ourselves.

For once, I worried less about buying the most expensive items and more about what fit with our lives.

Our foyer boasted fresh flowers and graceful trinkets instead of the priceless but somewhat terrifying marble bust I'd successfully bid on in a Sotheby's auction, and Alessandra talked me out of building a miniature golf course in the backyard simply because I could. Neither of us even *liked* mini golf.

Fortunately, she'd acquiesced to a rooftop hot tub and the construction of a private elevator. There was only so much I was willing to give up when it came to luxuries.

I did, however, also donate a vast sum of money for the establishment and maintenance of the Ehrlich Scholarship Fund at Thayer University. The need-based scholarships would offer full rides to a dozen incoming students every year starting this fall. Professor Ehrlich had been an avid fan of mini golf, but I suspected that if he were alive, he would've liked the scholarships even more.

Sometimes, I missed the penthouse and what it represented—the first big sign that I'd made it, whatever *it* was—but that house had been for me. This house was for us, and it was time I made it official.

"Dom?" Alessandra's voice floated from deep within the entrance. "Are you home?"

"In the garden!" I called out. Sweat slicked my palm, which was ridiculous. I'd done this before, but when it came to Alessandra, every time felt like the first time for everything.

I would never look at her and not marvel at the fact she was mine. I would never think about how close I'd come to losing her and not thank God she came back to me. I would never kiss her and take the opportunity for granted again.

She appeared at the back door, her hair shining beneath a dapple of sunlight. She'd had brunch with her friends that morning, and her cheeks glowed with a wash of pink.

"No offense, babe, but I hope you're not trying to garden

again." Alessandra slid the glass door closed behind her and eyed her beloved flowers with suspicion. "Remember when you almost killed my New England aster?"

Floria Designs was thriving both online and in its physical store, which meant it needed more inventory. She sourced most of the blooms for her business from suppliers, but she'd also started growing her own in the garden we'd installed in lieu of the mini golf course.

The café and gallery/flower shop concept was a huge hit, and though I hated Aiden's continued presence in her life—no New York landlord checked on their tenants *that* often without hidden motives—I loved seeing her happy. It was the only reason I hadn't bought his company out from under him. For some reason, Alessandra considered him a friend, and she would *not* be happy if I pulled that stunt.

"New England aster...was that the purple or pink one? I'm *kidding*." I laughed at her glare. "I know better than to touch your asters again. In my defense, the shears slipped. It was an accident."

"Sure. Ask the poor flowers if they care," she said with a playful huff.

My grin softened into something easier, simpler. Smiles came more readily to me these days, born out of a warmth that had been missing for the majority of my life. It was the type of feeling that soothed the edges of my frustration when something went wrong at work, that lightened my steps on my way home and painted the world in vivid shades.

I'd been lying in bed one lazy Saturday morning, watching Alessandra yawn and snuggle into my chest, when I finally put a name on the feeling.

Contentment.

No matter how much money I lost or made in a single day, I was, at my core, happy because I had everything I needed in front of me.

Thoughts of Aiden, Floria Designs, and the rest of the world faded away as the moment hit me like a freight train.

This was it. *She* was it. Some part of me had known that since the minute I laid eyes on her all those years ago, but that didn't make what I was about to do any easier.

It didn't matter that I'd spent months planning for this or that we'd gone through hell and made it to the other side. I wanted this to be perfect. It was what she deserved.

"Speaking of flowers, I have something for you." My nerves felt like barbs in my stomach as I handed her the golden rose. A tiny white note was tied to the stem.

Alessandra's face lit up even though I gifted her the bloom daily. "I was wondering when I'd get my daily countdown," she teased. "What happens when we reach one thousand?"

I didn't have to think; the answer had been there all along.

"Then I'll start the countdown again, and again, for the rest of our lives. Because that's how long I want to spend with you."

Her expression gradually morphed into stunned belief as I dropped to my knee and retrieved a small velvet box from my pocket.

My heart was a pounding mess as my fingers shook around the box. I would lay myself bare to her a million times for one more chance with the girl who never gave up on me. It didn't matter if I was trying to pass a college class or build an empire in her honor, she would always be my driving force.

"Alessandra, you are the most important thing to me. Being your husband will always be my greatest honor and accomplishment. No victory will ever taste as sweet as the press of your lips against mine. I lost you, and I don't deserve you." I swallowed hard against the memories of what we'd overcome.

"But I vow to always hear you over the sound of my ambition. I will always be curious about you. You've shown me the value of always learning, growing, and caring, and I've never loved you more than in this moment. Watching you choose yourself when I didn't will always prove as a reminder to me of your incredible strength and what a privilege it is to call you mine. I want to spend the rest of my nights with you. I want to spend the next decade working to be the man you always deserved. I want my greed to be for your love, your laughter, and our life together. I can't bear to be parted from you. Please, Ále, will you be my wife?"

A soft cry broke free from her throat. Alessandra's eyes shimmered as she uttered the one word worth more than any of the billions in my bank account.

"Yes," she sobbed. "Yes, I'll be your wife."

Slipping the ring on her finger felt like sliding a lock into place, but this lock wasn't a prison; it was a promise.

Her mouth met mine with the taste of salt. We were both crying, and I knew with rock-solid certainty that no meeting or dinner would ever matter as much as the way her joy felt surrounding me. Every sacrifice would exist as a balance of love with my ambition.

I would spend forever becoming the man she always believed me to be.

---

## Alessandra

Our second wedding took place on a rooftop overlooking the city. We'd visited dozens of venues before we settled on this one. It was the perfect blend of whimsy and luxury, and it felt indescribably more *us* than the traditional church wedding that'd kicked off our original marriage.

The first time, we did what we were supposed to. This time, we did what was right for us.

Almost all of our friends and family were in attendance, including my mother, who shockingly showed up with the same husband as the last time I saw her. Bernard must've been doing something right; maybe the fourth time was the charm.

Even Aiden was in attendance with the beautiful paralegal he'd started dating two months ago. Our relationship was strictly platonic, and despite Dominic's suspicions over the other man's friendliness—apparently, he found it hard to believe landlords could be, well, helpful—Aiden was clearly besotted with his new girlfriend. He'd barely taken his eyes off her all night.

The only person missing was Roman. Dominic hadn't heard from him since his abrupt disappearance after the contract leak that took down Sunfolk's old CEO. He could either be dead, dying, or sunning himself on a remote island in the Pacific. No one knew, and even Dominic's money and connections couldn't track down his brother's whereabouts.

I could tell Roman's uncertain fate worried him, but whenever I asked him about it, he simply said Roman could take care of himself.

I didn't press Dominic about the issue further. Maybe one day, Roman would make a reappearance. Until then, life went on.

"You've had quite the year, haven't you, darling?" My mother clucked her tongue, pulling me out of my wayward thoughts. "Marriage, divorce, marriage *again*. Why, you're giving me a run for my money!"

Marcelo snorted out a laugh, which he quickly turned into a cough when she glared at him. Bernard was busy taking advantage of the buffet, so it was only the three of us.

"I don't think anyone can give you a run for your money in that department, Mom," I said dryly.

"*Shhh*." She blanched. "What did I tell you about calling me that in public? *Mom* sounds so old. Address me as Fabiana. That way, we sound like best friends, which we are." She patted my arm. "Mothers and daughters are always best—oh! I see Ayana. I wonder if she booked the *Vogue* cover?" She flitted off, our conversation forgotten.

I suppose me marrying a billionaire wasn't quite as exciting when said billionaire had already been her son-in-law. Otherwise, my mother would be screaming from the rooftop—literally—about how her daughter landed Dominic Davenport.

"Hey, at least she showed up," Marcelo said after she left. "That's a win." He stepped closer and kissed me on the cheek. "I know I said this already, but congratulations. It's nice to have a brother-in-law again. The same one. *Again.*" He laughed when I swatted him lightly in the stomach. "Seriously, I'm happy for you and Dom. You guys were always meant for each other. You just had to...take a detour first."

My brother could be an idiot, but occasionally, he dropped a pearl of truth.

Dominic and I spent the first half of the reception greeting and mingling with guests. I'd forgotten how much time brides and grooms spent with other people during their own weddings.

Half the Valhalla Club was in attendance, including the ever terrifying but oddly intriguing Vuk Markovic, whom I had yet to hear speak a single world. He shook our hands in the receiving line and promptly disappeared. Xavier Castillo was also here, looking devastating in a black suit. He was currently lounging in a chair with a drink in hand and his other arm draped over the shoulders of a pretty brunette. No tie, jacket off, collar open, and gaze amused as Sloane stalked past him without sparing him a glance. He was woefully against dress code, but he was so charming no one called him out on it.

Meanwhile, Dante and Vivian came with their adorable newborn daughter, Josephine, or Josie for short, who was the subject of many guests' *oohs* and *aahs*. Vivian was my bridesmaid alongside Isabella and Sloane, so Dante took care of the baby most of the night. Seeing the big, gruff CEO melt over his daughter made *me* melt because I couldn't stop picturing Dominic in his place.

*Speaking of which…*

"Tell me why we invited so many people again," he said when we finally caught a moment alone. "I don't even know who half of them are."

"Dom, you vetted the entire list."

"I must've blacked out during that part because"—he narrowed his eyes at a distinguished silver-haired gentleman by the bar—"who the hell is *that*?"

I camouflaged an irrepressible laugh. "He's the vice president of Sunfolk Bank."

Dominic stared. Hard. "Christ. I need a drink." He shook his head, his exasperation melting into a rueful smile. "I'm sorry, *amor*, but if I have to make small talk with one more person instead of dancing with you…"

"It's okay. I feel the same way." My stomach fluttered when he whisked two glasses of champagne off a passing server's tray and handed one to me. *This was it.* "No, thanks."

His eyebrows popped up. "Are you sure? You haven't had a drink all night."

"I'm sure." The flutters turned into full-on kicks. "In fact, I won't be drinking alcohol for the next eight months."

Dominic's glass froze halfway to his lips. He slowly lowered it, his expression gradually shifting from confusion to stunned belief. "Are you…"

I nodded, unable to contain my smile *or* nerves. "I'm pregnant."

I'd totally stolen Vivian's method of breaking the news but screw it. If it worked, it worked.

The sound of glass shattering drew startled glances from the guests, but we didn't care.

A half laugh, half sob bled out as Dominic stepped around the champagne glasses and swept me up in his arms. Then he was kissing me, and we were laughing and crying together.

I hadn't planned on telling him about my pregnancy during our wedding. It was already a big enough day, but it felt right.

Happiness had found me again. I'd found myself, and Dominic had found joy in things outside his relentless ambition. Never in our life together did I think I would see him without the lines of worry that everything would disappear but rather with lines around his eyes from laughter.

When his gaze met mine on that rooftop, I knew I would always be his. Most importantly, I knew he would always be mine. He would miss a dinner here and there, but he would always come home with a desire for our marriage. He would never again be the man who didn't show care and curiosity. I would never again be the wife who pretended.

We were honest and open, and we truly loved each other more today than the day we'd married for the first time.

Our hearts had scars that would never go away, but they also glowed and grew with every new day that came to us.

Thank you for reading *King of Greed!* If you enjoyed this book, I would be grateful if you could leave a review on the platform(s) of your choice.

Reviews are like tips for author, and every one helps!

Much love,
Ana

———————

Can't get enough of Dominic & Alessandra?

Download their bonus scene at
anahuang.com/bonus-scenes

———————

*Keep in Touch with*
*Ana Huang*

**Reader Group:** facebook.com/groups/anastwistedsquad
**Website:** anahuang.com
**BookBub:** bookbub.com/profile/ana-huang
**Instagram:** instagram.com/authoranahuang
**TikTok:** tiktok.com/@authoranahuang
**Goodreads:** goodreads.com/authoranahuang

*Acknowledgments*

To Becca—This story truly wouldn't have been possible without you, and I'm so proud to call you not just my editor but also my friend. Thank you for calming my late-night anxiety attacks, keeping me hydrated, and stocking my kitchen with seaweed snacks on top of, you know, creating a book. One day, we'll get matching "Stop it!" sweatshirts to celebrate.

To Vinay—You've probably heard way more about this book than you wanted to, but thank you for answering our endless questions about the high-stakes world of finance and indulging our requests for something "wild but feasible." You nailed it.

To Brittney, Salma, and Rebecca—Thank you as always for providing feedback on how to do the characters and story justice. You help make them shine, and your story reactions to never fail to make me smile.

To Ana—Thank you for your detailed notes on Brazilian culture and language. They really helped elevate the story and highlight Alessandra's background. P.S. Your notes about the food made me want to visit Brazil (again). I'm starting to think I have to go back every year...

To Tessa—Thank you for your honesty and feedback on the dyslexia component of this book. I appreciate you taking a chance on such an early draft, and I'm so happy you reached out when you did. It was fate!

To Amy and Britt—Thank you for working with such grace and pressure under tight deadlines. You are the best.

To Christa, Madison, and the rest of the team at Bloom Books—Thank you for making this such a special release for me. It's our first hybrid release, and I'm blown away by everything we've achieved together. Here's to many more celebrations in the future.

To Ellie and the team at Piatkus—Thank you for taking my stories global. It was such a pleasure meeting you in London, and seeing my stores in bookshops across the world will never stop being a pinch-me moment.

To Kimberly, Joy, and the team at Brower Literary—Thank you for your incredible patience, support, and commitment to helping my books find new readers. You are my rock in this wild publishing world.

To Nina, Kim, and the team at Valentine PR—This is our fourth release together, and each one gets better and better. Thank you for all your hard work and for making my release weeks such a breeze!

To Cat—I'm obsessed with both your covers and you. The end.

To my readers and Ana's Twisted Squad—Your excitement for Dominic and Alessandra was palpable. Thank you for loving my characters, for the edits and annotations, and for sharing my work. I love you all.

xo, Ana

# Discover the world of Ana Huang's bestselling Kings of Sins series.

## Available now from Piatkus.

*King of Wrath*
Dante & Vivian's story

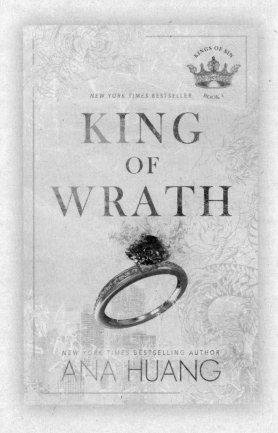

*King of Pride*
Kai & Isabella's story

# Don't miss Ana's bestselling Twisted series

Available now from

**Keep reading to discover the addictive love story of Alex and Ava in *Twisted Love* . . .**

THERE WERE WORSE THINGS THAN BEING STRANDED IN the middle of nowhere during a rainstorm.

For example, I could be running from a rabid bear intent on mauling me into the next century. Or I could be tied to a chair in a dark basement and forced to listen to Aqua's "Barbie Girl" on repeat until I'd rather gnaw off my arm than hear the song's eponymous phrase again.

But just because things could be worse didn't mean they didn't suck.

*Stop. Think positive thoughts.*

"A car will show up...*now*." I stared at my phone, biting back my frustration when the app reassured me it was "finding my ride", the way it had been for the past half hour.

Normally, I'd be less stressed about the situation because hey, at least I had a working phone and a bus shelter to keep me mostly dry from the pounding rain. But Josh's farewell party was starting in an hour, I had yet to pick up his surprise cake from the bakery, and it would be dark soon. I may be a glass half full kinda gal, but I wasn't an idiot. No one—especially not a college girl with zero fighting skills to speak of—wants to find herself alone in the middle of nowhere after dark.

I should've taken those self-defense classes with Jules like she wanted.

I mentally scrolled through my limited options. The bus that stopped at this location didn't run on the weekends, and most of my friends didn't own a car. Bridget had car service, but she was at an embassy event until seven. My rideshare app wasn't working, and I hadn't seen a single car pass by since the rain started. Not that I would hitchhike, anyway—I've watched horror movies, thank you very much.

I only had one option left—one I *really* didn't want to take—but beggars couldn't be choosers.

I pulled up the contact in my phone, said a silent prayer, and pressed the call button.

One ring. Two rings. Three.

*Come on, pick up. Or not.* I wasn't sure which would be worse—getting murdered or dealing with my brother. Of course, there was always the chance said brother would murder me himself for putting myself in such a situation, but I'd deal with that later.

"What's wrong?"

I scrunched my nose at his greeting. "Hello to you too, brother dearest. What makes you think something is wrong?"

Josh snorted. "Uh, you *called* me. You never call unless you're in trouble."

True. We preferred texting, and we lived next door to each other—not my idea, by the way—so we rarely had to message at all.

"I wouldn't say I'm in *trouble*," I hedged. "More like... stranded. I'm not near public transport, and I can't find a rideshare."

"Christ, Ava. Where are you?"

I told him.

"What the hell are you doing there? That's an hour from campus!"

"Don't be dramatic. I had an engagement shoot, and it's a thirty-minute drive. Forty-five if there's traffic." Thunder boomed, shaking the branches of nearby trees. I winced and shrank farther back into the shelter, not that it did me much good. The rain slanted sideways, splattering me with water droplets so heavy and hard they stung when they hit my skin.

A rustling noise came from Josh's end, followed by a soft moan.

I paused, sure I'd heard wrong, but nope, there it was again. Another moan.

My eyes widened in horror. "Are you having *sex* right now?" I whisper-shouted, even though no one else was around.

The sandwich I'd scarfed down before I left for my shoot threatened to make a reappearance. There was nothing—I repeat nothing—grosser than listening to a relative while they're mid-coitus. Just the thought made me gag.

"Technically, no." Josh sounded unrepentant.

The word "technically" did a lot of heavy lifting there.

It didn't take a genius to decipher Josh's vague reply. He may not be having intercourse, but *something* was going on, and I had zero desire to find out what that "something" was.

"Josh Chen."

"Hey, you're the one who called me." He must've covered his phone with his hand, because his next words came through muffled. I heard a soft, feminine laugh followed by a squeal, and I wanted to bleach my ears, my eyes, my *mind*. "One of the guys took my car to buy more ice," Josh said, his voice clear again. "But don't worry, I got you. Drop a pin on your exact location and keep your phone close. Do you still have the pepper spray I bought for your birthday last year?"

"Yes. Thanks for that, by the way." I'd wanted a new camera bag, but Josh had bought me an eight-pack of pepper spray instead. I'd never used any of it, which meant all eight bottles—minus the one tucked in my purse—were sitting snug in the back of my closet.

My sarcasm went over my brother's head. For a straight-A pre-med student, he could be quite dense. "You're welcome. Stay put, and he'll be there soon. We'll talk about your complete lack of self-preservation later."

"I'm self-preserved," I protested. *Was that the right word?* "It's not my fault there are no—wait, what do you mean 'he'? Josh!"

Too late. He'd already hung up.

Figured the one time I wanted him to elaborate, he'd ditch me for one of his bed buddies. I was surprised he hadn't freaked out more, considering Josh put the "over" in overprotective. Ever since "The Incident," he'd taken it upon himself to look after me like he was my brother and bodyguard rolled into one. I didn't blame him—our childhood had been a hundred shades of messed up, or so I'd been told—and I loved him to pieces, but his constant worrying could be a bit much.

I sat sideways on the bench and hugged my bag to my side, letting the cracked leather warm my skin while I waited for the mysterious "he" to show up. It could be anyone. Josh had no shortage of friends. He'd always been Mr. Popular—basketball player, student body president, and homecoming king in high school; Sigma fraternity brother and Big Man on Campus in college.

I was his opposite. Not *un*popular per se, but I shied away from the limelight and would rather have a small group of close friends than a large group of friendly acquaintances. Where Josh was the life of the party, I sat in the corner and daydreamed about all the places I would love to visit but would probably never get to. Not if my phobia had anything to do with it.

*My damn phobia.* I knew it was all mental, but it *felt* physical. The nausea, the racing heart, the paralyzing fear that turned my limbs into useless, frozen *things*...

On the bright side, at least I wasn't afraid of rain. Oceans and lakes and pools, I could avoid, but rain...yeah, that would've been bad.

I wasn't sure how long I huddled in the tiny bus shelter, cursing my lack of foresight when I turned down the Graysons' offer to drive me back to town after our shoot. I hadn't wanted to inconvenience them and thought I could call a car and be back at Thayer's campus in half an hour, but the skies opened up right after the couple left and, well, here I was.

It was getting dark. Muted grays mingled with the cool blues of twilight, and part of me worried the mysterious "he" wouldn't show up, but Josh had never let me down. If one of his friends failed to pick me up like he'd asked, they wouldn't have working legs tomorrow. Josh was a med student, but he had zero compunction about using violence when the situation called for it—especially when the situation involved me.

The bright beam of headlights slashed through the rain. I squinted, my heart tripping in both anticipation and wariness as I weighed the odds of whether the car belonged to my ride or a potential psycho. This part of Maryland was pretty safe, but you never knew.

When my eyes adjusted to the light, I slumped with relief, only to stiffen again two seconds later.

Good news? I recognized the sleek, black Aston Martin pulling up toward me. It belonged to one of Josh's friends, which meant I wouldn't end up a local news item tonight.

Bad news? The person driving said Aston Martin was the *last* person I wanted—or expected—to pick me up. He wasn't an *I'll do my buddy a favor and rescue his stranded little sister* kinda guy. He was a *look at me wrong and I'll destroy you and everyone you care about* kinda guy, and he'd do it looking so calm and gorgeous you wouldn't notice your world burning down around you until you were already a heap of ashes at his Tom Ford-clad feet.

I swiped the tip of my tongue over my dry lips as the car stopped in front of me and the passenger window rolled down.

"Get in."

He didn't raise his voice—he never raised his voice—but I still heard him loud and clear over the rain.

Alex Volkov was a force of nature unto himself, and I imagined even the weather bowed to him.

"I hope you're not waiting for me to open the door for you," he said when I didn't move. He sounded as happy as I was about the situation.

*What a gentleman.*

I pressed my lips together and bit back a sarcastic reply as I roused myself from the bench and ducked into the car. It smelled cool and expensive, like spicy cologne and fine Italian leather. I didn't have a towel or anything to place on the seat beneath me, so all I could do was pray I didn't damage the expensive interior.

"Thanks for picking me up. I appreciate it," I said in an attempt to break the icy silence.

I failed. Miserably.

Alex didn't respond or even look at me as he navigated the twists and curves of the slick roads leading back to campus. He drove the same way he walked, talked, and breathed—steady and controlled, with an undercurrent of danger warning those foolish enough to contemplate crossing him that doing so would be their death sentence.

He was the exact opposite of Josh, and I still marveled at

the fact that they were best friends. Personally, I thought Alex was an asshole. I was sure he had his reasons, some kind of psychological trauma which shaped him into the unfeeling robot he was today. Based on the snippets I'd gleaned from Josh, Alex's childhood had been even worse than ours, though I'd never managed to pull the details out of my brother. All I knew was, Alex's parents had died when he was young and left him a pile of money he'd quadrupled the value of when he came into his inheritance at age eighteen. Not that he'd needed it because he'd invented a new financial modeling software in high school that made him a multimillionaire before he could vote.

With an IQ of 160, Alex Volkov was a genius, or close to it. He was the only person in Thayer's history to complete its five-year joint undergrad/MBA program in three years, and at age twenty-six, he was the COO of one of the most successful real estate development companies in the country. He was a legend, and he knew it.

Meanwhile, I thought I was doing well if I remembered to eat while juggling my classes, extracurriculars, and two jobs—front desk duty at the McCann Gallery, and my side hustle as a photographer for anyone who would hire me. Graduations, engagements, dogs' birthday parties, I did them all.

"Are you going to Josh's party?" I tried again to make small talk. The silence was killing me.

Alex and Josh had been best friends since they roomed together at Thayer eight years ago, and Alex had joined my family for Thanksgiving and assorted holidays every year since, but I still didn't *know* him. Alex and I didn't talk unless it had to do with Josh or passing the potatoes at dinner or something.

"Yes."

*Okay, then.* Guess small talk was out.

My mind wandered toward the million things I had to do

that weekend. Edit the photos from the Graysons' shoot and, work on my application for the World Youth Photography fellowship, help Josh finish packing after—

*Crap!* I'd forgotten all about Josh's cake.

I'd ordered it two weeks ago because that was the max lead time for something from Crumble & Bake. It was Josh's favorite dessert, a three-layer dark chocolate frosted with fudge and filled with chocolate pudding. He only indulged on his birthday, but since he was leaving the country for a year, I figured he could break his once-a-year rule.

"So..." I pasted the biggest, brightest smile on my face. "Don't kill me, but we need to make a detour to Crumble & Bake."

"No. We're already late." Alex stopped at a red light. We'd made it back to civilization, and I spotted the blurred outlines of a Starbucks and a Panera through the rain-splattered glass.

My smile didn't budge. "It's a *small* detour. It'll take fifteen minutes, max. I just need to run in and pick up Josh's cake. You know, the Death by Chocolate he likes so much? He'll be in Central America for a year, they don't have C&B down there, and he leaves in two days so—"

"Stop." Alex's fingers curled around the steering wheel, and my crazy, hormonal mind latched onto how beautiful they were. That might sound crazy because who has beautiful *fingers?* But he did. Physically, *everything* about him was beautiful. The jade-green eyes that glared out from beneath dark brows like chips hewn from a glacier; the sharp jawline and elegant, sculpted cheekbones; the lean frame and thick, light brown hair that somehow looked both tousled and perfectly coiffed. He resembled a statue in an Italian museum come to life.

The insane urge to ruffle his hair like I would a kid's gripped me, just so he'd stop looking so perfect—which was quite irritating to the rest of us mere mortals—but I didn't have a death wish, so I kept my hands planted in my lap.

"If I take you to Crumble & Bake, will you stop talking?"

No doubt he regretted picking me up.

My smile grew. "If you want."

His lips thinned. "Fine."

*Yes!*

*Ava Chen: One.*

*Alex Volkov: Zero.*

When we arrived at the bakery, I unbuckled my seatbelt and was halfway out the door when Alex grabbed my arm and pulled me back into my seat. Contrary to what I'd expected, his touch wasn't cold—it was scorching, and it burned through my skin and muscles until I felt its warmth in the pit of my stomach.

I swallowed hard. *Stupid hormones.* "What? We're already late, and they're closing soon."

"You can't go out like that." The tiniest hint of disapproval etched into the corners of his mouth.

"Like what?" I asked, confused. I wore jeans and a T-shirt, nothing scandalous.

Alex inclined his head toward my chest. I glanced down and let out a horrified yelp. Because my shirt? White. Wet. *Transparent.* Not even a little transparent, like you could *kind of* see my bra outline if you looked hard enough. This was full-on see-through. Red lace bra, hard nipples—thanks, air-conditioning—the whole shebang.

I crossed my arms over my chest, my face flaming the same color as my bra. "Was it like this the entire time?"

"Yes."

"You could've told me."

"I did tell you. Just now."

Sometimes, I wanted to strangle him. I really did. And I

wasn't even a violent person. I was the same girl who didn't eat gingerbread man cookies for years after watching *Shrek* because I felt like I was eating Gingy's family members or, worse, Gingy himself, but something about Alex provoked my dark side.

I exhaled a sharp breath and dropped my arms by instinct, forgetting about my see-through shirt until Alex's gaze flicked down to my chest again.

The flaming cheeks returned, but I was sick of sitting here arguing with him. Crumble & Bake closed in ten minutes, and the clock was ticking.

Maybe it was the man, the weather, or the hour and a half I'd spent stuck under a bus shelter, but my frustration spilled out before I could stop it. "Instead of being an asshole and staring at my breasts, can you lend me your jacket? Because I really want to get this cake and send my brother, your best friend, off in style before he leaves the country."

My words hung in the air while I clapped a hand over my mouth, horrified. Did I just utter the word "breasts" to Alex Volkov and accuse him of ogling me? *And* call him an asshole?

*Dear God, if you smite me with lightning right now, I won't be mad. Promise.*

Alex's eyes narrowed a fraction of an inch. It ranked in the top five most emotional responses I'd pulled out of him in eight years, so that was something.

"Trust me, I was not staring at your breasts," he said, his voice frigid enough to transform the lingering drops of moisture on my skin into icicles. "You're not my type, even if you weren't Josh's sister."

*Ouch.* I wasn't interested in Alex either, but no girl enjoys being dismissed so easily by a member of the opposite sex.

"Whatever. There's no need to be a jerk about it," I muttered. "Look, C&B closes in two minutes. Just let me borrow your jacket, and we can get out of here."

I'd pre-paid online, so all I needed was to grab the cake.

A muscle ticked in his jaw. "I'll get it. You're not leaving the car dressed like that, even wearing my jacket."

Alex yanked an umbrella out from beneath his seat and exited the car in one fluid motion. He moved like a panther, all coiled grace and laser intensity. If he wanted, he could make a killing as a runway model, though I doubted he'd ever do anything so "gauche."

He returned less than five minutes later with Crumble & Bake's signature pink-and-mint-green cake box tucked beneath one arm. He dumped it in my lap, snapped his umbrella closed, and reversed out of the parking spot without so much as blinking.

"Do you ever smile?" I asked, peeking inside the box to make sure they hadn't messed up the order. Nope. One Death by Chocolate, coming right up. "It might help with your condition."

"What condition?" Alex sounded bored.

"Stickuptheassitis." I'd already called the man an asshole, so what was one more insult?

I might've imagined it, but I thought I saw his mouth twitch before he responded with a bland, "No. The condition is chronic."

My hands froze while my jaw unhinged. "D-did you make a joke?"

"Explain why you were out there in the first place." Alex evaded my question and changed subjects so quick I had whiplash.

*He made a joke.* I wouldn't have believed it had I not seen it with my own eyes. "I had a photoshoot with clients. There's a nice lake in—"

"Spare me the details. I don't care."

A low growl slipped from my throat. "Why are *you* here? Didn't figure you for the chauffeur type."

"I was in the area, and you're Josh's little sister. If you died, he'd be a bore to hang out with." Alex pulled up in front of my house. Next door, AKA at Josh's house, the lights blazed, and I could see people dancing and laughing through the windows.

"Josh has the worst taste in friends," I bit out. "I don't know what he sees in you. I hope that stick in your ass punctures a vital organ." Then, because I'd been raised with manners, I added, "Thank you for the ride."

I huffed out of the car. The rain had slowed to a drizzle, and I smelled damp earth and the hydrangeas clustered in a pot by the front door. I'd shower, change, then catch the last half of Josh's party. Hopefully, he wouldn't give me shit for getting stranded or being late because I wasn't in the mood.

I never stay angry for long, but right then, my blood simmered and I wanted to punch Alex Volkov in the face.

He was so cold and arrogant and...and...*him*. It was infuriating.

At least I didn't have to deal with him often. Josh usually hung out with him in the city, and Alex didn't visit Thayer even though he was an alumnus.

*Thank God.* If I had to see Alex more than a few times a year, I'd go crazy.